DELILAH DEVLIN

# Into The Darkness



red
AVON
*An Imprint of* HarperCollins*Publishers*

This book was originally published in trade paperback by Avon Red in April 2007.



AVON RED
*An Imprint of* HarperCollins*Publishers*
10 East 53rd Street
New York, New York 10022-5299


ISBN: 978-0-06-136343-6
ISBN-10: 0-06-136343-X
**www.avonred.com**



First Avon Red mass market printing: July 2007
First Avon Red trade paperback printing: April 2007



Printed in the U.S.A.

10 9 8 7 6 5 4 3 2 1

*This book is for my sister and best friend,*
*Myla Jackson,*
*who began this journey with me*
*and constantly inspires and challenges me*
*to be a better person and writer.*

# ACKNOWLEDGMENTS

This book was a labor of love—and not just mine. I have so many to thank I know I'll forget to mention someone!

Thanks to my critique partners for putting the polish on this project: Jo-Ann Power, Layla Chase, Myla Jackson, Megan Kerans, and Mary Fechter.

More thanks to "Team Delilah," my friends and readers who kept the story "real" and encouraged me all along the way: Heather, Di, Icia, Patti, Joy, Erin, Sharon, Jenn, and Serena.

A shout-out to my biggest fan: I love you, Mom!

And last, to my editor: Thanks, May, for believing in this story!

# CHAPTER

# I

"Rene, you dirty bastard, put your tongue back in your mouth."

Rene Broussard lowered his binoculars to watch the enticing twitch of their subject's ass beneath a pink sundress as she walked, carrying coffee and a sugar-coated beignet, toward a bench in front of Saint Louis Cathedral. That dress should have been outlawed—in the muggy New Orleans heat it stuck to her skin in all the right places. His body tightened with the purely involuntary reaction of a healthy male. He pressed the talk switch on the radio clipped to his jacket lapel. "You're just jealous, *chère*, 'cause you have no ass."

The radio squawked. "Do, too," his partner, Chessa Tomas, replied. "You just haven't taken a good look 'cause you know you can't have it."

"There is that." He shifted his gaze upward to the woman's face.

Even watching through the iron spokes of the fence surrounding Jackson Square, Rene knew this was their girl—only the Tennessee DMV photo hadn't done her justice. The other stats he'd pulled—Caucasian female, 25 yrs. old, 5'6", blonde hair, green eyes, 135 lbs.—also hadn't hinted at the cuteness of her saucy behind, the length of her softly rounded legs, or the shape of her breasts, high and uptilted. Just like he liked them. "Mmmm-mmm."

"Yoo hoo!" Chessa's voice broke in. "Are you gonna ogle her all afternoon, or are we pulling her in for questioning?"

Rene looked up to the balcony over Muriel's restaurant.

Chessa gave him a little wave and tilted her head toward her radio. "It's gonna rain, and I'd just as soon not get soaked."

Rene slid his small binoculars into a jacket pocket, and then glanced up at the sky. Gray clouds, heavy with rain, hovered just above the street lamps. The wind began to whip the colorful beach umbrellas above the street vendors' carts. Mother Nature was giving a preview of the tropical storm the weathermen predicted might hit during the weekend. Time to bring in Natalie Lambert.

Just as he rounded the corner of the fence, a devil wind picked up dirt from the street and swirled toward the row of benches, carrying with it an odd sulfurous odor. "*Merde*, I wonder if I remembered to latch my balcony doors?"

"That must be one helluva doughnut," Chessa murmured. "The lady seems pretty popular with the pigeons."

Weaving in and out of the psychics' fabric-draped tables and the street artists' booths, Rene kept an eye on his target as she tossed crumbs at the birds gathering around her feet. The little black whirlwind whipped through the crowding pigeons, ruffling their feathers and lifting a few off the ground. "Don't she know we have ordinances against feedin' those birds?"

"Breaking that particular law's the least of her worries."

He paused in front of an artist's stand, pretending to admire the watercolors. "My gut says she's the target, not the perp."

"Sure you're thinking with your brain?" Chessa asked, in her usual smart-ass tone. "Just 'cause she looks pretty in pink doesn't mean she's not a murderer. Why else would she run?"

The lady in question glanced toward the darkening sky and pitched the rest of her meal to the birds.

"Wouldn't you, if everyone around you was droppin' like flies?" Rene nodded to the seller and continued on his way toward the woman who looked like a tasty sherbet.

"I don't know—and right now, I don't care. Let's just pull her in before all hell breaks loose."

"All right," Rene said, injecting false irritation into his voice. "You're just bein' a bitch 'cause I woke you early."

"I don't want the sun peeking out from behind any clouds before we're done."

"Oh, I wouldn't want you to melt, sugar. Get your ass down here now. Let's do it."

"What the hell?"

Rene saw what caught his partner's attention at the same time. More birds arrived with an audible flutter of wings, settling onto the pavement and closing in on the woman who now yelled and kicked at the pigeons crowding around her ankles.

Frowning, he realized what had started as a small flock of birds, now numbered hundreds. Some hopped onto the bench beside the woman, while others surrounded her feet. They all appeared to be pecking at bare skin.

People nearby scattered, vendors abandoned their carts and tables and ran while the pavement quickly filled like an undulating gray sea.

Rene cursed and ran toward her, kicking away pigeons as more arrived in a dark, fluttering cloud to surround the woman who shielded her face and head with her arms, whimpering, while rivulets of blood streaked her ankles and hands.

He plucked her from the bench into his arms.

She swatted blindly, landing glancing blows on his nose and chin, her body arching in his arms, but he clamped her body tight to his and sped toward the unmarked sedan parked along Chartres Street. The beating of hundreds of flapping wings and the birds' harsh, screaming caws pursued them to the vehicle.

Chessa rushed from the entrance of the restaurant and matched his stride.

"The doors, Cheech!" he shouted.

She sprinted past him and flung open the back door.

Rene dove into the backseat, the woman clutched close to his chest, and yanked the door closed. Wings flapped in his face.

The woman on his lap whimpered and pressed her face into his chest.

Rene swung his fist at the kamikaze bird until he smashed it against the rear windshield. Panting, he didn't relax until Chessa slid into the driver's seat and started the engine.

"Du Monde's beignets aren't that good," Chessa said, tearing off her sunglasses. Her green gaze met his in the rearview mirror as she put the car into gear and careened away from the curb. Tires crunched the bones of birds. Two, three, four more slammed into the windshield. Others thudded dully against the metal exterior of the car, until at last they left the menacing flock behind.

Rene dragged air into his lungs, adrenaline still pumping through his body. He squeezed the woman too tight, but he couldn't let go. Not yet. "Goddamn!"

"Where to?" Chessa asked, one eyebrow quirked upward in the mirror.

Rene shook his head. *Not the station.* He took another deep breath and looked down at the woman who shivered in his arms, her head tucked against his chest like a child. Her scent, reminiscent of lemons and sweet apples, and the soft curves pressing on his thighs affected him more than he cared to admit. He cleared his throat, fighting for objectivity. A first for him. "Miss, can we take you home?"

Her bloodied hands clutched at his shirt, and she raised a clear blue gaze to meet his. "I'm not stupid enough to think your being here is a coincidence. Why don't you just take me to the station?"

Rene blinked. Her words were gutsy, even defiant, but he heard the underlying quaver in her voice. "Yeah, so we know who you are, Natalie. Maybe we're just keepin' an eye out to make sure you're safe."

"No one can keep me safe." Her lips twisted in a parody of a smile. "Even the birds know I'm toxic."

*   *   *

Natalie sat on a metal chair while Detective Broussard daubed sterile gauze at the small punctures marring her arms and hands. She glanced at his partner, who flipped closed the blinds, plunging the interrogation room further into gloom. The dense gray light seemed to match the woman's mood. Detective Tomas had paced the room since they'd first entered.

Natalie guessed she was pretty annoyed with her partner, intercepting more than one pointed glare, and wondered if there might be something between the pair. Detective Tomas was surely his match physically. Black hair, green eyes, and with a slim, wiry build Natalie could only envy.

"So, you wanna tell us what brought you back to N'Awlins?" Detective Broussard pulled a fresh square of gauze from the first aid kit and scooted back his chair. "Gimme one of your legs."

Natalie couldn't help but shiver at his command and lifted her left leg. Aware his steady stare fell to a broad expanse of exposed skin, she barely resisted the urge to tug the hem of her skirt lower. She almost wished his interest wasn't due to the crusty streaks of blood feathering her ankles.

Until recently, she'd never considered herself a very sexual creature, had never felt the compulsion to dabble in flirtation. But something about this man's Cajun drawl, husky build, and liquid brown eyes tugged a dormant femininity, newly discovered and yearning, into full flower.

Was this lust at first sight?

He pulled her leg across his thigh, and then dampened the gauze with antiseptic and wiped at the blood staining her skin. "Natalie?" His glance came back up to hers.

"Why am I in New Orleans?" she repeated his question,

feeling flustered. Good Lord, her whole world had shattered, and here she was falling into this cop's brown eyes. Even the sting of the antiseptic didn't stop her body from reacting to his proximity.

She shrugged, pretending nonchalance. "I don't know. I used to live here." Her words were unconvincing even to her own ears. Besides foiling a killer, she had her birth mother to find—something that had no bearing on the murders of her adopted family. Somehow, keeping that secret gave her a small measure of power.

His attention returned to her leg.

How easily he distracted her. She imagined what his hand would feel like caressing the back of her ankle as opposed to the impersonal grip he used to turn her leg. Her mouth went dry as he methodically cleaned her small wounds. Despite this unexpected and heady attraction, she reminded herself he was a cop—something she hadn't much use for lately.

"We've read through the reports from the Memphis PD, right after your parents were killed," he said, his voice uninflected with suspicion or emotion. "They didn't consider you a suspect." He rolled her leg outward and swabbed upward. The scratchy gauze grazed the inside of her knee.

Growing more uncomfortable by the moment beneath his tender care, Natalie felt her cheeks warm. The oddest urge to reach out and touch the dark brown hair that curved around his ears washed over her. She forced her attention back to the conversation. "And now they do . . . believe I killed them?"

He gently cleaned another puncture and reached for ointment, which he applied with one finger to the wound. "First your parents, then your roommate . . . it's not looking good to them." His glance came up, pinning her—almost as if he were trying to see inside her soul.

He probably just wanted to see whether she'd squirm. "Tough. I didn't do it. I would never hurt them," she said, her voice growing thick, her gaze never wavering beneath his.

"We should have taken her to the emergency room," the woman detective said, flopping down into the seat across the metal table from Natalie. She leaned forward. "Although, you seem to heal pretty fast."

Natalie heard a note of suspicion in the other woman's voice and looked down at the dozen or so little punctures, already covered with scabs, and the blue bruises where the birds' beaks hadn't broken the skin. "I've always been a quick healer."

The two officers shared a charged glance.

"We might have jumped to the same conclusions the Memphis PD did," Detective Broussard said, releasing her leg, "but the murders bear a striking resemblance to a string of unsolved crimes we've been investigating for a while here."

"It just seemed a little too coincidental that your parents and Ms. Masters were killed in Memphis," the female cop said, "and now, you've shown up on our killer's home ground."

Natalie slipped her foot into her pink slide, glad to be free of the big detective's disturbing touch. "I don't know anything about other murders. I came to New Orleans because I know the city. I'm comfortable here." That was only part of the truth. She hated feeling defensive and lifted her chin. "But you already know that."

"Yeah, we do," Detective Broussard said. "You went to Tulane. But moving back into your old neighborhood probably wasn't too smart. If you wanted to disappear—"

"Who said I wanted to disappear?"

Neither police officer blinked or moved.

Natalie felt a strange satisfaction . . . she'd surprised them. "Do you really think I'd take a walk around Jackson Square if I were hiding?"

A frown darkened his handsome face. "Are you telling us you deliberately stayed in the open with a killer on the loose? One who might be targeting you?"

Natalie didn't reply. If they were so smart, they could figure it out for themselves.

"Why?" the female cop asked, the single word coming fast and blunt as a bullet.

Natalie kept her expression shuttered for a long moment, but the two appeared ready to out wait her little show of defiance. She blew out a breath in irritation. "Maybe I'm just tired of looking over my shoulder all the time. It's not like I expected him to follow me."

"Him?" Again, Miss Quick Draw fired the question.

Natalie shrugged. "Him, it, them. Does it matter?"

"You think you were followed?" Detective Broussard asked, his voice soft and disarmingly low.

How'd he guess? She shrugged, unwilling to open her mouth and give them any more clues to pounce on.

"Why do you think you were followed?"

He wasn't going to leave it alone. Why was she resisting him? He wasn't the bad guy. "My next door neighbor said a plumber tried to get into my apartment last night while I was out getting a bite. But I don't have a leak or a backed up toilet."

He picked up more clean gauze and indicated with a curl of his fingers that she should give him her other leg.

Natalie didn't know if she could bear his touch again. The temperature in the room escalated each time she gave herself into his care. She held out her hand for the gauze. "I can do it."

He lifted a brow in challenge, a small smile curving his lips, drawing her attention to his mouth.

God, she wished she hadn't looked! Her body tightened, the skin across her chest flushing with heat.

His hand curled again.

Sighing, Natalie slid her right leg over his thighs and resigned herself to more sensual torture.

"Your super didn't order the work?" His tone remained casual as once again he scraped dried blood from her leg.

"At ten o'clock at night?" She regretted the sarcasm bleeding into her voice. The two of them didn't really deserve the brunt of her frustration and fear. "It's him . . . I just know. I'm not paranoid," she said, hating the hint of hysteria entering her voice. She drew a calming breath and continued. "It's happening again. I can feel it."

"What do you mean you can feel it?" Detective Tomas's eyes narrowed.

Damn! Would she get off her back? "It's just a feeling I get . . ." she ground out, ". . . when something's not quite right. A smell. Something not in its place."

"Your intuition didn't give you a warning before your parents were killed?"

A stab of guilt left Natalie breathless. Her angry defiance crumpled. "I had only just started having these prickling sensations . . . like someone was watching me. But I wasn't home when it happened . . . when they were murdered. I'd gone to the store to pick up groceries for my mom. I took her keys . . ." For a moment, she was standing in the doorway of her home, looking at the carnage that had been her parents, their throats laid bare. Her gut twisted at the remembered horror.

Detective Broussard's fingers tightened on her calf. "So, someone was tryin' to get into your apartment last night?"

His deep voice calmed jangled nerves, while his thumb smoothed up and down the back of her ankle in an oddly comforting caress. "Why not run again?"

Natalie shook herself, grateful he'd changed the subject and drawn her back from that doorway. "I didn't run before. There just wasn't anything left to stay for."

"You were trying to lure him today, weren't you?" the female cop asked, not letting her partner deflect the original line of questioning. "What would you have done if he'd come near you?"

Natalie tossed back her hair and narrowed her glance. "I bought a gun. It's in my apartment."

"And if he'd caught you in the open today? What the hell good would it have done you?" The other woman snorted. "Do you even know how to fire a gun?"

"He doesn't work like that, during the day, and yes, I can hit what I'm aiming at," Natalie said, lifting her chin.

Detective Tomas shrugged. "So you know enough to flip the safety off. How come you're so sure he wouldn't go for you in the daytime?"

"I just know he prefers to strike in the dark," she said, feeling like a butterfly tacked to a mounting board beneath the other woman's hard stare.

"You know this based on . . . ?"

"Three deaths—my parents and my best friend." Natalie resented the woman's look of disbelief and gritted out, "I just know he waited for the dark to take them."

"Let me guess. You took a walk today, just in case he was watching. Were you taunting him?"

Natalie flushed.

Detective Tomas lifted one eyebrow. "If he only strikes at night, why lure him during the day?"

Put that way, her actions didn't make much sense. Maybe, she didn't have it right. Natalie shrugged again, feigning indifference while her faulty strategies deflated like a slow-leaking tire. *Damn, I'm so tired of being scared.* "Maybe I am getting a little paranoid," she admitted, lifting her gaze to Detective Broussard and wanting him to understand. "But I feel like someone's watching me all the time."

The female detective leaned across the table, her eyes alert for any misstep. "You dressed special for him—made sure you looked sweet as candy—all sugar and spice."

Angry at the accuracy of the woman's guess, tears of frustration clouded her vision. "I'm tired of waiting for it to happen!" She halted. She hadn't meant to shout. That wasn't her—wasn't who she'd been before. Under their relentless stares, she added, "But then, the birds attacked . . ." She glanced away and discovered she'd bunched the fabric of her skirt in her hands. Frowning, she smoothed out the wrinkles.

Detective Broussard patted a scabbing puncture with antiseptic, and then tossed the gauze toward a metal trashcan. "All done," he said, aiming a glare at his partner.

Was he ticked on her behalf? Was she pathetic for hoping he felt a little drawn to her?

"Yeah, what was up with the birds?" Detective Tomas asked.

Suddenly, the last bit of tension drained from Natalie, leaving her tired and confused. "I don't know. I was just giving them my beignet when that tiny whirlwind whipped through them." She turned to the man, relieved to see compassion softening his eyes. She paused before blurting, "Did you see their eyes?"

He shook his head. "What about their eyes?"

Natalie didn't want to say it, knowing how weird it would sound, but decided to forge ahead anyway. It seemed important to mention it—and she always followed her instincts. "Their eyes were red. I've never seen pigeons with red eyes, and they seemed to glow."

His expression remained neutral, but he leaned forward. "Could it have been a trick of the light?"

With him so close, his broad shoulders filling her hungry gaze, the room seemed smaller, warmer. The moment paused like water dripping slowly from a faucet.

"Maybe you were scared," he said softly.

She hadn't imagined what she saw, but the truth made her sound foolish. So she nodded. "Probably."

"You know," he said, his tone intimate, "you need our protection."

She closed her eyes for a moment before returning his penetrating stare. "I don't want anyone else hurt . . ."

"Do you think your parents and friend were killed because of you?"

She shrugged.

"Let me guess," the female cop said, heavy sarcasm in her tone. "You just know."

Detective Broussard threw his partner a quick irritated frown before returning his gaze. "We can take care of ourselves, Natalie."

The faint French inflection in his pronunciation of her name made her shiver.

"We're going to keep watch over you 'til we catch this killer."

"You?" she asked, and then wished she'd bitten her tongue rather than reveal her eagerness.

"Sure," he said, a small smile lifting the corners of his lips. "But we'll swap off. I'll get a daytime team to stake out your place. Cheech and I will take the night shift."

Not him *personally*. "Cheech?" she asked, glad he'd misinterpreted her previous question.

He nodded to Detective Tomas. "My partner, Chessa is her given name. I'm Rene—since it looks like we'll be getting to know each other."

For the first time in weeks, Natalie felt a glimmer of hope the nightmare might end. Like maybe, for once, she didn't have to face her fears alone. She wished she could believe they'd keep her safe.

"I'm not through with my questions, *Rene*," Chessa Tomas gritted out.

Rene Broussard's back stiffened, but he nodded to his partner.

Feeling abandoned, and a bit like she was watching a "good cop-bad cop" inquisition, Natalie straightened in her chair and turned her head to face the other woman. "What else would you like to know?" she asked, keeping her tone even.

Chessa blew out a breath, and then folded her arms over her chest. "Are you sexually active?"

Only the incessant buzz from the fluorescent lamp hanging above the metal table broke the long silence.

Natalie's face heated in mortification.

"Cheech, is this necessary?" Rene asked, his expression dark and guarded.

At Chessa Tomas's curt nod, he sat back in his chair.

Natalie's glance cut to his partner. Her emotions, brittle as thin glass, spiked toward anger once more. "Why is that any of your business?"

"Just answer the question."

Chessa's unrelenting stare and the naked nature of the question itself cracked the barrier of Natalie's self-control. Her eyes watered, and she shook her head. "No." *Such a stupid question. What did she know?*

"When was your first period?"

Sweet Jesus! What the hell did that have to do with any of this madness? Nevertheless, Natalie cleared her throat and whispered, "Two weeks ago."

She heard Rene's indrawn breath, but didn't dare face him. So she was a freak of nature! Only her mother hadn't thought it odd. She'd assured her that her time would come.

Chessa Tomas stood and walked around the table to kneel beside Natalie's chair. The first hint of an emotion other than impatience softened the tense angles of her face. "Are you feeling sexual hunger for the first time, *now*?"

Natalie clamped her lips closed and glared at the woman.

"Natalie, I really do need to know." Chessa's steady gaze, now free of any derision, held hers for a tense moment.

Tears spilled from her eyes unexpectedly. She crossed her arms in front of her and nodded.

Chessa looked away. "Well, fuck!"

"What the hell's this all about, Cheech?" Rene asked, his voice strained.

Chessa drew in a deep breath and stood. "I hate to burst your bubble, partner, but I think we've got bigger problems here than catching a serial killer."

# CHAPTER 2

Rene raked a hand through his hair. "What the fuck was that all about?"

"You tell me!" Chessa crossed her arms over her chest, a scowl darkening her face.

Rene avoided her gaze and instead looked through the two-way mirror into the interrogation room where Natalie sat alone, staring into the mirror like she could see them. "What are you talkin' about? I wasn't the one grillin' her like she was the killer. We both know that's not true."

"As far as Memphis is concerned, she's still a suspect. And *you* were playing footsie."

Rene's cheeks burned. "I was just cleanin' her up."

"Dammit! I've never seen you touch a female suspect except to cuff 'em."

Rene shot back a glance at Chessa. "She was injured. Bleeding. I did what anybody would."

She leaned in close, staring into his face. Although shorter by a head, she still managed to look pretty intimidating.

Knowing what he did about her capabilities, he knew that look wasn't a bluff. He stiffened.

"Tell me, Rene." Her voice was soft, but held steely intent. "Don't you think your reaction was just a little odd? You were all over her."

His shoulders bunched tight with frustration as he clutched the frame around the mirror. He hated how she'd read his interest that easily. She might be his partner, but she didn't have any business getting inside his head. Nobody did. He glared. "What? You jealous, Cheech?"

Rather than reacting with a sarcastic jab, which was her favorite defensive weapon, Chessa laid her hand on his forearm. Her always caffeine-intense expression was now taut and worried. "Think, Rene! She's putting out 'fuck-me pheromones'! You're drawn to her, but it's happening too fast to be natural."

He shook his head, narrowing his eyes. "She's an attractive girl. My reactions were entirely normal." He bit out his words. "I didn't cross any lines."

One eyebrow crooked upward. "Then why didn't you let me tend her wounds?" she asked softly.

Uncomfortable beneath her searching stare, he shifted on his feet. He didn't have a real answer. "Maybe, I didn't want you tempted by all that blood."

"Fuck that!" she muttered beneath her breath, closing her eyes briefly. She let go of his arm and faced the mirror. "Her attraction isn't natural. But I may know what this is." She closed her eyes, her mouth twisting. "No wonder I was so pissed off."

"Chessa," he growled, "You're not makin' any damn sense. Those questions you asked her—"

Chessa avoided his glance and stared at Natalie. "Believe me, you don't wanna know the truth. In fact, it's better you forget what you heard."

"She's not a suspect." He tensed, expecting Chessa to disagree.

Instead, she nodded. "I know. By the age of our cold case files, we both know she can't be the killer."

"All right, I'm confused. If we're sure these crimes are related and she's not a suspect, then why grill 'er?"

Chessa glanced back into the interrogation room. "Look, I can't say much right now. Just trust me when I say this is outside the department's jurisdiction."

Something about the urgency in her voice raised the hairs on the back of his neck. He held back the questions teeming inside his head.

Chessa began pacing like a nervous cat. "I have to act fast—and you have to trust me. She's a goddamn disaster magnet, and we have a full moon rising soon. I need you to keep her out of trouble—out of sight."

"Me? Where the hell are you gonna be? And what does any of this have to do with the moon?" At her impatient glare, he waved her off. "You know? I don't wanna know."

"We'll drop by her place, check it out," she said, as if he hadn't spoken. "Have her pack a few things. Then I'm leaving you."

"Dammit, Cheech, what's goin' on here?"

"Trust me. Take her to your place. Make sure you're not followed. I'll contact you later."

"This is *family business*, isn't it?" Of course it was. The prickling that bit the base of his spine during Chessa's heated interrogation should have warned him. "Your people aren't gonna harm her, are they?"

"I promise that's the last thing we want to happen. But you'll be alone with her." She grabbed the lapels of his jacket and pushed him back against the glass, getting in his face. "Whatever you do, partner, *don't fuck her*."

Rene's head snapped back. "I don't fuck on the job!" he seethed.

"Well, you've never faced her brand of temptation before." She pressed him harder, her expression dead earnest. "Don't let her get a bite."

He sucked in a deep breath, disappointed. "She's a vampire then?"

Chessa shook her head. "I'm not a hundred percent sure what she is. But we don't have time for this conversation."

"Probably better to keep me clueless, huh?" he asked, a bitter taste at the back of his throat. Natalie Lambert wasn't for him.

That's all he really needed to know.

"Yeah. Buy me some time, partner. I have a lot to do, and the night's slipping away." She released him. "Let's roll."

Natalie unlocked her apartment door, for once not bothering to peer up and down the hallway. Tonight, she had two armed cops at her back.

She opened the door and breezed through, glancing around her one-room apartment to make sure she hadn't left anything embarrassing in plain sight. The room was a mess, but she hadn't been planning on bringing guests home when she'd left earlier that day. Natalie turned to allow the officers to pass inside.

"Pack what you need for a couple of nights," Chessa said, her glance flitting around the apartment.

Natalie wondered if the woman was always this intense. Her rudeness was beginning to wear on every last one of her nerves.

Rene's gaze was on the puddle of rumpled clothing next to the sofa bed. Her nightgown, a sheer blue scrap of silk, lay on top. When his glance met hers, Natalie wasn't imagining the heat banked in his expression. No, indeed. She could feel it like a blast from a furnace.

She thrilled at knowing the feeling was mutual. She'd stopped fighting her attraction. Having never felt such a strong sensual pull at just the sight of a man, she considered this anomaly a gift. One she'd just enjoy for what it was, because she didn't have the luxury of time to explore these new feelings.

Natalie opened her closet and pulled out a small suitcase. Under his watchful stare, she grabbed underwear, T-shirts, and a couple pairs of shorts and jeans and shoved them into the case. Then she hurried to the bathroom, packed her toiletries, and grabbed another nightgown from the hook at the back of the door.

When she returned to the main room, she dug under the bed for her sneakers. She tried to ignore the fabric of her sundress riding up her thighs as she reached, and the fact Rene's gaze burned over every inch of exposed skin.

She stilled. Funny, how she could feel that—as if he'd touched her.

"What's going on here, Nat?"

Natalie jerked back, sneakers in hand and looked toward the door of her apartment.

Her next-door neighbor hovered in the doorway, suspicion evident in the scowl furrowing his forehead as he eyed her two bodyguards. Simon looked as though he'd just risen from bed. His sun-streaked blond hair stood in spikes around his head. He wore a rumpled brown T-shirt bearing his video store logo and blue jeans. His feet were bare.

"Hi, Simon." She darted a glance at the two cops whose hands already rested on their holstered weapons. "It's okay, he's a friend."

Simon's glance flickered over Rene, then caught sight of the female detective. His back stiffened. "You've never had guests, Natalie. I was a little worried when I heard the commotion." When he looked back, his frown was darker than before. "You were gone a long time."

Natalie gave him a half-hearted smile. Explanations would have to wait. "I had a little problem. These two police officers rescued me."

He raised an eyebrow—a silent question mark.

Her lips twisted. "They know everything. And I'm not busted—yet."

His lips clamped shut, but his frown reflected worry.

Warmed by his concern, Natalie gave him a half smile.

When her whole world had been ripped apart, Simon had been there for her, welcoming her back.

"Who's this guy?" Rene asked, a dark glower hooding his eyes, his shoulders taut like he still expected he'd have to defend her.

His caution on her behalf excited her, even while she reminded herself he was just doing his job. But his alarm was misplaced—Simon with his lean build posed no physical threat to Rene Broussard. "This is Simon Jameson, and like I said, he's a friend. I worked in his video store while I was in college. This is his apartment I'm subletting. He lives next door."

"Does he live alone?" Chessa bit out, asking Natalie even though her gaze drilled Simon.

"Yes. Unless you count Kestrel."

Chessa's expression grew impossibly darker.

"Kestrel's a bird, although I don't think she knows it," Natalie added, wondering at the suspicion clouding Chessa's face and the answering enmity she read in Simon's straight posture.

Chessa stalked toward Simon. "You're aware of the problems following your *friend*, yet you didn't call for help?"

Simon's eyes narrowed, but he didn't back away from the woman's intimidating stance. "I'm here to support Nat. I watch over her, but it's not my place to interfere with how she handles her problems."

"Even if she's not aware of possible solutions?"

"Her destiny will unfold as it is meant to be revealed," he replied, his words clipped.

*What the hell did that mean?* Natalie shook her head. The two seemed to know each other, and Simon obviously didn't like the frosty detective very much—a sentiment Natalie could match. "I don't understand. Do you two know each other?"

"No!" Chessa whirled on her heels. "You've got everything?" At Natalie's nod, she turned to Rene. "You know what happens now. Remember what I told you."

Rene nodded and shot a glare at Simon, then grasped Natalie's elbow to guide her toward the door.

As she passed Simon, his hazel glance grew distant. "I'll see you soon," he murmured.

Feeling like flotsam swept along on a roiling tide, Natalie resisted Rene's hold for a moment and stared back into her apartment. Chessa and Simon stood toe-to-toe, their words hushed but heated by the looks of their rapid-fire conversation.

"Don't stop, now," Rene said, pulling her down the hallway. "I'm takin' you somewhere safe."

"I don't understand. Everyone else seems to know what's happening, but I feel like Alice falling down the rabbit hole."

"*Chère*, you've just had a taste of my life working with Chessa Tomas," he said, his lips quirking into a small smile. "She may seem like a ravin' bitch at the moment, but she has her reasons. She'll fill us in later."

"You trust her that much?"

"With my life."

They exited the apartment building onto the sidewalk, which was illuminated by a single streetlamp, the light dulled to a pale halo by the heavy, moist air. Shadows encircled them.

To Natalie's already fried nerves, every darkened corner hid menace—all directed toward her.

Natalie grew still. A sound, like rushing wind carrying dozens of whispers, pricked her ears. "Someone's here."

Rene stiffened, and his gaze searched the darkness. "I don't see anythin', but I'll trust your instinct." His hand moved down her arm to grasp hers. "Ready to run for it?" he whispered.

She grabbed his hand and nodded.

"Now!"

They ran, Rene taking the lead, pulling her along. Natalie's slides hampered her, so she kicked them off and ran barefoot for his car, parked along the curb further down the street.

The wind whipped closer, bringing the smell of rotten eggs—the same smell she'd detected when the birds attacked. "Rene!"

"I know!" he shouted over his shoulder. "Run faster!"

The whispers grew louder, accompanied by a buzzing that sounded like a million angry bees.

As they neared the car, Rene dropped her hand and aimed his remote to unlock the vehicle. They dove inside and slammed shut the doors.

Natalie screamed as a cloud of large winged bugs smacked against the car.

Rene fired the ignition and pulled away, his wiper blades smearing green carcasses from the windshield. After a few moments, they left behind the angry cloud of bugs. Rene blew out a deep breath and cast a quick glance her way. "That don't happen every day. You okay?"

Shaken, Natalie felt a little giddy after the wild run. She

gulped air into her burning lungs and reached for her seat belt. "I don't know. How am I supposed to feel? Right now, I'd love a big can of insect repellant."

He snorted and glanced into his rearview mirror. "Pigeons, locusts? What's next? Your life's a helluva lot more excitin' than mine."

The odd attacks and the murders of her parents—on the surface they might not seem related, but her gut told her they were. She hadn't the knowledge to draw the necessary connections. But who would?

Natalie leaned back against the seat and shut her eyes, weary now the danger had passed. The smell of leather, mixed with a hint of Rene's spicy aftershave, permeated the black sporty sedan. The seats were buttery soft. The engine growled, low and controlled. The man liked his comforts and power at his fingertips.

The car was like him, muscled and sexy, yet understated—and comfortable. He made her feel safe. She almost wished she could find something about him she didn't like so their inevitable parting wouldn't be so hard. Although they'd only met a couple of hours ago, she felt a connection—and an exhilarating attraction.

The car slowed to turn a corner, and she opened her eyes.

Rene's face was taut, his glance constantly darting to his mirrors.

She straightened in her seat. "Do you think we're being followed?"

"No. I'm sure we're not." He aimed a tight smile her way. "I didn't take a direct route home, and I haven't spotted a tail."

"We're going to your place? Not some safe house?" Pleasure filled her, leaving her a little breathless.

"My house is safe."

He was taking her to his home. They'd be alone.

Those unexpected sensual feelings returned. Her nipples beaded. Desire curled inside her belly.

Rene's hands tightened on the steering wheel, a muscle flexed at the side of his jaw. His gaze didn't stray her way again.

The tension in the vehicle was thick—fragrant with unspoken yearnings. Or so, Natalie hoped.

They drove back into the French Quarter and turned into a narrow alley that ran behind a row of tall narrow houses with iron gates, postage stamp-size backyards and single-car garages. He hit a button in the roof of the car, and one door slid up.

After he pulled inside and the garage door lowered, he reached into the back seat for her bag. "Home sweet home," he muttered, still not meeting her eyes.

Natalie followed him through a door that led into a mudroom, halting behind him as he paused to punch in the code to reactivate the security system. Then she trailed him through the kitchen and into a living room.

Her gaze took in the large fan suspended from a high ceiling and tall windows with forest green curtains. The walls were pale beige, the furniture dark and heavy. Finally, she turned to find him staring.

A muscle in his square jaw flexed, and his back stiffened. "I'll put your things in my bedroom. I converted the other bedroom to an office, so I'm taking the couch. Try to get some sleep."

He wanted to put some space between them.

Feeling a little deflated, Natalie nodded. "I'd like to shower."

Rene led the way up a narrow staircase and down a hallway that ended in a door that opened to a balcony. His bedroom was to the right and sparsely furnished. The bed loomed large with a navy duvet and lots of pillows in the same dark blue and wine.

He set the case on the mattress and pointed to a closed door. "Bathroom's through there." He turned to leave and then shook his head. "Damn. I'm sorry. I never asked if you were hungry or wanted somethin' to drink."

Her stomach was in knots. She was hungry all right, but not for food. She shook her head in denial.

"Anyway, if you're hungry afterward, I'll scare up somethin' from the kitchen."

She found it unflattering how quickly he fled the room.

Sighing, Natalie walked to the French doors and pulled aside the curtain. The doors opened onto a long balcony that overlooked a small courtyard paved with a pale stone which reflected the lamplight from the empty street beyond.

Although the exterior echoed the shabby gentility of a bygone era, she knew the old antebellum-era house had to be a stretch on a detective's salary. There was more to Rene Broussard than met the eye.

She let the curtain fall back and padded across the beige carpet to the bed and opened her case. The mystery surrounding the man was one she wasn't destined to discover. And the quest that had brought her back to New Orleans had to go on hold for now.

Pulling out her nightgown and toiletries, she focused on mysteries more imperative than her late-blooming libido and the search for her birth mother—like why she'd suddenly become bug and bird bait, how Rene's partner had known about the changes occurring to her body, and why Chessa and Simon had been arguing.

Rene closed his cell phone with a snap. Chessa hadn't picked up. Whatever "arrangements" she was busy making were ones she didn't want to communicate, and that was just fine with him. The strange occurrences of the past few hours fit squarely in Chessa's dark realm. They simply underscored the fact he was better off keeping the hell away from Natalie Lambert.

Lying on the sofa in the living room, he listened to the creaks of the house settling after the heat of the day. The overhead fan stirred the air, but did little to cool his agitation.

Although he'd stripped off his jacket and shirt and removed his shoes, he still couldn't get comfortable enough to let his mind wander away from the blonde in his bedroom. Chessa had been right about those "fuck-me pheromones" the woman oozed. Why else would he be hard as a rock hours after he'd touched her soft skin?

Distance. Miles of it. That's what he needed. As long as he was down here and she was up there, he'd be fine.

Just a few more hours and he could hand her over to Chessa. However much the woman in his bedroom intrigued him, he'd seen enough in his time to know she was trouble—the kind he was better off leaving to his partner and her kind to handle.

Chessa had known straightaway something was up, and her instincts were always dead-on.

Although they'd been partners for over four years, Rene wouldn't say he knew her. While he didn't have a bead on *who* the real Chessa Tomas was because of her spiny public demeanor and secretive private life, he knew *what* she was.

If the fact they were the only detectives assigned permanent night shift hadn't clued him in, the first time he'd seen her take down a perp the size of a Saint's linebacker clinched it.

Having a vampire for a partner did have its perks. Street punks tended to squeal like piglets as soon as Chessa flashed her fangs. And they had a certain autonomy within the department to take on "special" cases—like Natalie Lambert's.

Only Chessa wasn't usually so uncommunicative concerning the nature of an investigation.

When the call had come from the Memphis PD that Natalie had left the area, and they suspected she would return to familiar territory, the details of the case hadn't rung any bells with Rene. However, Chessa had immediately noted the similarities with this crime and several in the "cold case" files. Crimes dating back over forty years. Young women, twenty-two to twenty-five years old, and everyone living with them—all savaged and drained of blood.

So the murderer was either pulling Social Security or not human.

Since he'd worked "otherkin" cases with Chessa before, her current reticence bothered him. Something bigger and probably closer to the real Chessa was at stake.

She'd said she wasn't certain what Natalie was—but he'd

sensed hesitation in her answer. Certainly, all signs indicated something *extra*-natural was going on here.

Chessa had nailed it when she'd said the girl was a temptation he'd find hard to resist—because he'd thought of little else other than sinking inside her moist depths since the moment he'd swept her off the bench in the park. He'd been in a constant state of arousal since he'd felt the first brush of her skin and breathed in her fresh lemon and apple scent. And that wasn't like him—he wasn't a pimple-faced kid. He could find plenty of sexual partners to take care of any urges he found too compelling.

He preferred to keep his personal life and his work separate. Never had he been tempted to break that rule. Not until today. Now, he felt like a silken tether bound him to the woman standing naked in his shower at this very moment.

So for tonight, he'd take Chessa's advice to heart and hunker down—keep his distance from the temptation just up the stairs.

Intending only to adjust himself for comfort, his hand smoothed down his naked belly to grasp his rigid cock through his blue jeans. Instead, he squeezed and imagined what it would feel like to rut against the soft juncture of her thighs. He remembered the gentle grind of her ass as she'd shifted within his arms in the back of the squad car.

"*Merde!*" He jackknifed to a sitting position, wincing at the pinch of rough cloth against his sex.

The welcome sting reminded him to trust Chessa had Natalie's best interests at heart—as well as his own. When his partner arrived, he was backing far away, because he'd be a goner if he came within ten feet of the sexy blonde upstairs.

# CHAPTER 3

Natalie couldn't sleep.

Not because she was afraid. For the first time in weeks, her stalker was the least of her worries.

Instead, her present danger lay in her own body's betrayal.

Heat simmered beneath the surface of her skin—a flush of warmth that spread across her chest and belly. The air around her felt close and heavy despite the fan circling above the bed.

Her heart beat too quickly. Her breasts grew heavy. Her nipples peaked against the thin silk of her nightgown. Then blood rushed to the juncture of her thighs, plumping her slick folds.

She might be inexperienced, but Natalie recognized the signs of desire.

The cause of her misery paced restlessly around the house. The creaking hinges of the doors he checked and rechecked gave away his unrest. The muffled thud of footsteps as he walked around the living room below, and the slap of his bare feet on the wooden steps when he came up to patrol the hall pinpointed his location.

He passed outside her bedroom now, his shadow darkening the space beneath the door. Natalie ached to call out to him. Was Rene exercising extreme caution or suffering like she was?

Reaching beyond the moment, Natalie wondered, why him? Why now?

An instinct—some kernel of inborn knowledge—told her this new *hunger* was related to the current moon cycle. Just as the changes to her body began with the first sliver of pale light from the new moon, her need unfurled like a heron's wings with the coming full moon.

This past month, she'd been steadily shedding the baby fat that plagued her adolescence, although her appetite, especially for blood-enriched meats, had increased. Her first period *ever* had come and gone. Then sensual awareness dominated her waking and sleeping thoughts.

For days, she'd dreamed of an anonymous lover in her bed. The things he'd done to her had left her breathless and blushing. If she managed to sleep tonight, she knew she'd find Rene's face, his jaw taut with desire, his shoulders bunched as he hovered above her, supplanting the hazy man of her dreams.

Why him? Although handsome, he wasn't the first good-looking man she'd ever encountered. But from the moment he'd pulled her from the park bench into his arms, her body recognized his claim. He'd held her close, his thickly muscled torso sheltering her from further harm. His strength and distinctive scent, a spicy heated musk, imprinted on her mind. If she closed her eyes, she was there once more, draped across his lap in the back seat of the sedan, awakening to desire for the first time.

Everything else—the horror of the attacks, the pain of her many little wounds—faded. She felt only his hard, muscled thighs beneath her bottom and the steely embrace that crushed the air from her lungs while he struggled for control.

She wanted to know those sensations again—and so much more.

Frustration humming inside her, she tossed back the bedcovers and padded to the French doors, flinging them open. She stepped into a wind that whipped her hair away from her face and the nightgown tight against her body. Infrequent drops of rain pelted her uplifted cheeks, cooling her skin.

A click sounded from the door further down the balcony. Clad only in jeans, Rene stepped out.

He was pure temptation, from brawny chest to bare toes.

"You shouldn't be out here," he said, his voice a grumpy, sexy rumble. "You set off the silent alarm."

With her heart thudding in her chest, she turned away. "I couldn't sleep."

"Well, how 'bout not sleepin' *inside*?"

His growling irritation made her smile. She felt the same way—bitchy, edgy, *wonderfully* horny.

She noted the tight set of his jaw, the rapid rise and fall of his chest, and felt an overwhelming urge to seduce him. And why shouldn't she?

The way she figured it, her days were numbered. The menace dogging her steps would eventually catch up. Why not grab for all the joy she could find in what was left of her life?

She leaned back against the balustrade on her elbows, making sure the silky gown pulled tight across her breasts.

His gaze lowered, lingering for a moment on her beaded nipples. "Cold?" he asked, his voice a rumbling, silky slide.

"Not really." She decided to make sure he didn't misinterpret the invitation. She sauntered toward him, stopping inches away from his rigid body. This close, she breathed in his musky male scent. The breadth of his solid chest and his height overwhelmed her, made her feel small, vulnerable—and intensely feminine.

He sucked in a deep breath. "Look, *chère*, whatever you're thinkin'—it's not gonna happen."

She cast him a challenging stare. "Because I'm not what you want?"

He shook his head. "Damn, you've got to know that's not it," he said, his voice raw. "This just isn't the right time."

She met his gaze, hoping she didn't look too needy, but wanting him to know she could be his—if he'd just reach out. "What if there never is a right time?"

His hands fisted at his sides. "I'm not lettin' anything happen to you."

She lifted her chin. "You can guarantee that?"

He glanced beyond her to the midnight sky, and he stayed silent.

Stubborn man. He thought he could withstand this chemistry of hormones and a waxing moon by sheer will. "Tell you what," she said. "How about a kiss? And I'll let it drop. It'll be enough, I swear." At his suspicious glare, she added, "Just a kiss."

He blew out a deep breath and rubbed the back of his neck. "Will you come inside then?"

"Yes," she said quickly. She'd promise anything just to draw him nearer. If he felt even a fraction of her need, he wouldn't be able to resist for long.

The muscles in his throat rippled, and he nodded. "All right. A kiss."

Shivering with excitement, she forced herself to keep her expression impassive.

When she stepped closer, he wagged his finger in front of her face. "Inside."

*Even better.* She turned to head toward her bedroom.

"Uh, uh." A crooked smile curved one corner of his mouth, and he snagged her wrist. "I guess that's not a good idea."

"Then here?" she asked, breathless at his first touch.

The heavens opened, and the rain fell harder.

He dropped her hand, shaking his head. "This is nuts."

As rain flattened her hair against her head, Natalie wanted to scream her frustration at his hesitation. Knowing her nightgown was soaked to transparency and hugged her curves, she leaned back against the iron balustrade on her elbows and stared, hoping he would make the first move to save her from making a worse fool of herself.

He muttered a soft curse and brought up his hand to cup her cheek. His thumb wiped at the moisture gathering there. His palm was warm and a little rough.

She shivered at the delicious thought of that hand smoothing the soft, cooling rain down her naked skin.

"Maybe this isn't the smartest thing for us to do," he whispered.

Natalie tilted her head to press her cheek against his palm. "Who wants smart? I'm only asking for a kiss."

His eyes narrowed, then his gaze dropped to her lips. When he leaned down, she guessed his intent—a quick peck and then he'd disappear downstairs again.

As he closed the distance between them, she grasped the back of his head, winding her fingers into his dampening, thick hair, and tugged him closer.

Rene groaned a moment before their lips met. Then he held himself still, not moving his mouth over hers.

Natalie sighed and opened her mouth to lick at his closed lips. The rain pelted their heads, the moisture on their bodies acted like a conductor for the electric, arcing charge that leapt between them.

Already, her body flowered. Her nipples tightened. Dew gathered at the juncture of her thighs. She leaned forward and rubbed her silk-covered breasts against his broad, wet chest, reveling in the spark of sensual heat that shot from her breasts to coil around her womb.

His breath hitched and his hands gripped the iron behind her, but he leaned into her, his chest pressing closer.

*Not close enough. More!* She tugged his hair hard and licked at the seam of his mouth, following her instinctive need to taste and tempt.

He gasped, his mouth opening—but not pressing deeper.

She surged inside, stroking his tongue with hers, slanting her mouth to softly encourage him to increase the pressure. Then she smoothed her hands down his neck to cup his shoulders, and down again, to scrape her fingernails along his spine.

His body trembled and a growl erupted from his mouth, filling hers with his sweet breath, while his tongue crowded past her lips to lap along her tongue, darting inside, then withdrawing and stroking back.

She hooked one leg over his hip, ignoring his initial, rigid resistance, to pull his lower body against hers, close enough now to rub the part of her that ached and swelled against the hard knot burgeoning at the front of his jeans. The hem of her nightgown bunched between their bodies, rising to bare her bottom and her moist sex as she rubbed harder against him.

Natalie lost herself in the kiss, writhing against him—her whole world narrowing as his kiss changed subtly, until he sucked on her tongue and the ridge of his cock ground against her swollen folds. She dug her fingers into the hard muscle of his back and strained closer, needing more, aching for him to fill the empty place inside her body and her heart.

Suddenly, he thrust himself away, stepping back.

Dismayed, Natalie opened her eyes and stared.

His hands were clenched at his sides. Ruddy color stained his cheeks. His lips thinned into a snarl. "This isn't gonna happen, *chère*."

"Why not?" she asked, surprised her voice didn't crack beneath the strain of her need and disappointment. "You can't say you don't want me. I felt how much you do."

He shook his head. "You're a pretty *fille*, sweetheart, but I don't mix business and pleasure. And I can't keep watch when you distract me."

Her legs trembled, and she sank back against the balustrade. Her body ached with unfulfilled desire. Tears filled her eyes as she sensed him withdrawing, steeling himself against their powerful attraction. "I've never felt this way before, Rene," she whispered. "And I'm afraid I'll never feel this way again. I ache—inside." Her voice broke and she turned her head, ashamed at the naked emotion she'd let him see.

"Don't do this. Let me walk away," he said, his voice hoarse. "I'm not the man for you. Not now."

Her next breath was more a ragged sob, but she held herself rigid to keep from letting him see how much she needed him. She whirled and grasped the door latch to escape inside the room.

She'd almost made it, almost gotten past him without crumbling, but a shiver racked her body as her hand closed around the knob. The soft sob caught her by surprise.

His hands settled on her shoulders, and he drew her back against his chest. "It's not that I don't want you," he whispered into her ear.

She tore from his hold and pushed open the French door. "Just leave me alone."

"Natalie—"

Grasping the edge of the door, she faced him, letting him see the tears falling on her cheeks to mingle with raindrops. "I've never made love with a man—hardly ever kissed before." She drew a jagged breath and the words spilled from her. "Now, I'm being hunted by someone who wants me dead. *And you can't protect me.* Not really. He can reach me anywhere.

I just wanted something beautiful . . . just once. Something just for me."

Blinded by tears, she started to shut the door, but he pushed back and entered the room. Then his arms closed around her.

She sagged against him, hating her tears, and the weakness that made her grateful for the warmth beneath her cheek and the strength of the arms supporting her trembling body. She clung to him, pressing her wet face against his skin.

"It's all right. Don't cry."

Silence closed around them, a watchful, pregnant quiet that grew while he stroked her hair and back.

His fingers lifted her chin. Their gazes met for a long moment. Natalie noted a pulse throbbing at his temple and felt the tightening of his arms around her. Her breath caught.

"These jeans stay on," he said, his whisper harsh.

She nodded as hope and excitement stirred again. She'd promise anything to prolong his embrace.

His hand slid along her hip and gathered her nightgown in his fist, drawing it up.

She leaned away from him and raised her arms. The silk caressed her skin, teased over her belly, dragged across her nipples, then was gone—and she was naked beneath his heated stare.

His eyelids lowered as his glance lingered on her breasts and dropped to the ruff of hair between her legs.

Shyness fled at the sight of his chest rising and falling faster. His face hardened, the skin drawing taut over the sharp blades of his cheekbones, his lips tightening.

His arousal was apparent to even her unschooled eyes.

The outline of his hard cock pressed against the front of his jeans.

She stood still as a statue, waiting for him to make the next move.

"Climb onto the bed," he bit out.

She turned, aware of his gaze on her back and ass, and crawled across the satiny coverlet. Her heart sped up as his feet padded across the carpet behind her. The bed dipped beneath his weight, and she lay down and rolled onto her back.

With only a golden shard of light from a distant street lamp beyond the balcony door, she watched him edge closer on his knees. His shadow blocked out the light, looming over her, large and dark as the sensual thrill building in her womb. Then he winced and straightened, and reached down to unbutton the snap at the top of his jeans. "This is gonna be hell."

She almost told him she had no objection to him shucking his pants, but she held her tongue, not wanting him to hesitate again. She couldn't bear it if he left her now.

He climbed over her, his denim-clad legs bracketing the tops of her thighs.

Lying beneath him, Natalie catalogued every sensation so that she'd never forget what being with him felt like. The moment felt . . . important. Beyond the fact this was her first time.

He leaned down, settling over her, his palms cupping her cheeks. His lips dragged over her forehead, her eyes, her nose, before sliding over her mouth.

The caress drugged her senses, setting her heart thumping loudly. Her hands cupped his rain-slick shoulders, urging him closer, but he slid down her body, nuzzling her neck, slanting over the tops of her breasts, until at last, he took a turgid nipple into his mouth and suckled her.

Natalie arched her back, pressing harder against his mouth, her fingers threading through his hair to grasp him tight to her breast and urge him closer.

As he sucked, warm cream seeped between her thighs, and she wriggled against his restraint, undulating her lower body to seek relief from the tension building inside.

Rene groaned and released the taut tip of her breast, then fluttered his tongue against it, soft and fast as a butterfly's wing.

She urged him toward her other breast and mewled like a kitten when his tongue curled around the straining nipple. Fire leapt beneath her skin, racing lower, and her head thrashed on the coverlet. Her body was no longer hers to control.

Like a puppet master, he tweaked one nipple with his fingers and sucked the other, pulling heat to the tips, until they stood rigid and engorged. When he bit her gently, she gasped and bucked beneath him. "Rene . . ."

"That's right. Let go," he murmured, and nudged a knee between her legs. "Let me hear your pleasure, *chère*."

Eager to feel his touch on the place that burned hottest, she spread her legs to let him slip between and rubbed her inner thighs against him. Cool air licked at her moist folds.

He scooted lower, his hands smoothing around her waist and down to cup her buttocks. He trailed kisses along her abdomen, sending shivers across her skin. When his tongue lapped at her navel, her belly jumped.

Overwhelmed by his lovemaking, Natalie trembled and gasped for breath. Her fingers tightened on his hair, and she tugged him lower.

Soft, strained laughter gusted on her belly, but he complied with her unspoken request and his lips glided down.

Then he was there, poised above her pussy. He blew a stream of hot breath over her. His hands encouraged her to raise her knees, and he pushed them open to splay wide.

Exposed, his for the taking, tremors racked her whole body. "Please, Rene," she whispered, and pulled his hair again, digging her fingertips into his scalp.

"Relax, sweetheart. Shhh," he crooned, more breaths washing over her. His hands smoothed up her inner thighs, pausing an inch on either side from her outer lips.

Then his fingers touched her, rubbing her plump outer folds, massaging her gently until her sex pulsed and emitted soft sucking sounds.

When his tongue slipped between to flutter the edges of thin inner lips, Natalie's shoulders rose off the bed, and she cried out. "*OhGodOhGodOhGod . . .*"

Fingers circled, rimming her opening, dipping just inside and slipping away, then returned to tease more moisture from her body. He groaned—a rumble that vibrated against her flesh.

"Christ, you're wet!" His tongue stroked inside and lapped twice more and retreated.

"No . . . more!" Natalie lifted her hips, seeking more of his intimate caresses.

"So sweet . . . you're killin' me, baby." His mouth closed around her inner folds, and he sucked, drawing, tugging them into his mouth to nibble gently.

Her hips pulsed and she followed his lead, finding a rhythm he encouraged with gentle squeezes of her ass that eased the ache building between her legs. She shuddered and moaned, her breaths becoming jagged and rasping.

"Come for me. Come for me, now," he whispered, and then the pad of his thumb slid up her cleft, glancing on the knot of bundled nerves at the top.

Natalie keened, long and loud, halting all movement to savor her escalating passion.

Rene rubbed her clitoris, circling lightly as the coil of excitement tightened inside her. He paused to dip fingers inside her and draw more moisture, then circled again, harder now, until the first burst of rapture rippled through her channel.

Suddenly, she cried out as an explosion, like a thousand splinters of light, catapulted her over the peak. She arched her body, thrusting into Rene's touch.

His fingers circled, his tongue stabbed inward—over and over, until at last the pulses tightening her pussy waned.

Slowly, her shudders weakened, and she dragged air into her starved lungs.

Rene shifted, climbing from between her legs and stretching to slide the length of his body alongside hers. He pulled her into his arms and tucked her head into the crook of his shoulder.

Natalie nuzzled his neck, sighing. "I think I'll sleep like the dead."

His lips grazed her forehead. "We're a full-service department, ma'am."

She heard the smile in his voice and quipped, "Well, not quite." Sliding her hand around his back, she hugged him. "But it was beautiful."

"My pleasure." His hand glided from her shoulder to her hip. "Go to sleep. I'll stay until you start snorin'."

"I don't snore," she grumbled.

"That's 'cause you don't sleep, do you?"

The tenderness in his voice almost undid her. Skin-to-skin, it was hard to remember she had secrets she couldn't share—and she would never have met him if he hadn't brought her in for questioning. "Sleep?" She struggled to remember his question. "Not much, lately," she murmured.

"I'll keep watch, sweetheart."

Natalie would have liked to stay awake a little longer and explore his body as thoroughly as he had hers, but he'd already gifted her with more than she'd dreamed.

She nuzzled his neck, enjoying the heat of his skin and the pulse that throbbed at the side of his neck. "Mmmmm . . . this is nice," she said sleepily.

His fingers combed her hair, and again, he kissed her forehead. "Sleep," he whispered next to her ear.

Her gums itched and tingled, and she ran her tongue lazily across the roof of her mouth but found no ease. She snuggled closer and breathed in his spicy scent.

Then just as her mind eased into dreams . . . she opened her mouth and bit him.

# CHAPTER 4

A shocked gasp and muffled "*Sonuvabitch!*" jarred her fully awake in an instant.

Natalie's eyes opened wide as blood, thick and rich, poured down her throat, spurting in rhythmic pulses that she gulped down as though dying of thirst.

Instinct guided her, quelling the urge to gag against the flavor and thickness. More viscous than water, less so than oil, it felt like cream on her tongue, tasting faintly metallic, yet delicious.

When the flow slowed to a trickle, she drew, sucking with her lips like a baby on a nipple.

Heat filled her mouth, spilling down her throat to her belly, then spreading outward and lower. Her appetite was ravenous. So was the lust building in her loins, plumping her labia and releasing a wash of desire that once again coated her lips and smeared her inner thighs. But this time, her arousal was so much stronger than before.

Delicious, wicked . . . sensual. She drank his blood like she wanted to take his cock—in lapping waves of heat.

Even his resistance excited her.

His hands clamped hard around her throat, short of actual strangulation—more a warning. "Natalie, for fucksake, let me go!" he said, his voice tight, anger radiating in the tension gripping his neck and shoulders.

Despite the pressure, she chided him with a murmur and ground her jaws to stab deeper until his fingers released her, her incisors lengthening in a final, sensual thrill that felt very like the hardening of her clit when he'd rubbed on it.

"Goddamn bitch!" he rasped. "Chessa warned . . . *oh God!*"

Part of her knew what she did was sick and twisted. She was hurting him, maybe even killing him. But the fierce hunger overrode her conscience.

*And she wanted more.*

Her arms slid around his torso and tugged to urge his heavy body over hers.

He offered pale resistance, his hands bracing against her shoulders. "*Sweet Jesus!*" he said, his tone anything but anguished.

Again, she murmured as she drank, urging him closer with her hands and rubbing her naked body against him.

Reluctance stiffened his spine, but he eventually acquiesced, easing over her, his breaths coming harsh and jagged, his body trembling. "Natalie, let go of my neck."

This time his plea lacked conviction. While intellectually

he knew he should resist, his body was succumbing to the desire, just as she was. His hips rolled, and he rubbed his rigid cock, still clothed in rough denim, against her delicate skin.

She opened wide her legs and reached for the top of his jeans. Her fingers curved like talons around the waistband, and she jerked them to open his zipper and shoved them down his hips, past his hard, round buttocks. His cock emerged from the parting zipper to fall against her belly.

Engorged, this thick shaft felt heavy and hard. Although she hadn't had any experience with sex, her body instinctively sought connection. Her belly curved, rubbing and caressing his shaft, and her knees rose on either side of his hips.

"No!" he gasped, and tried to hold himself away, but his action only aided her intent, giving her room to reach between their bodies and grasp his cock and push it between her legs.

When the blunt, rounded head of his sex brushed between her slick folds, he stilled. "Not gonna happen, *dammit*!" he seethed.

She sucked harder on his neck, punishing him, drawing on him until he trembled again and lowered his hips which forced him between her folds.

Natalie took him the rest of the way. Bracing her feet on the bed to lift her bottom, she circled on his cock, screwing him deeper inside, working his thick cock past her virgin walls.

She gasped at the pressure, gloried in the fullness. She pulsed her hips, reveling in the deepening pressure and the friction building between his shaft and her passage.

When his round, blunt head butted against the obstruction deep inside her vagina, he groaned.

Pain pierced through the sensual haze that had gripped her to that point. Tempted to force him deeper, one last shred of conscience caused her to hesitate.

Rene had been nothing but kind. Twice he'd risked his life to rescue her. How could she take away his choice in this most intimate act?

Although her body protested, growing rigid with denial, she withdrew her teeth from his neck and lapped to stem the flow of blood from the tiny wounds, finding that they closed quickly under the glide of her tongue. Skimming her tongue across the tips of her teeth, she felt them retract, like a cat's claws within their sheathes.

Rene pushed up on his arms and glared down. The fury banked in his eyes made her shiver with the first frissons of fear.

"I'm sorry," she whispered, not knowing how to explain what she'd done. "I didn't mean to—"

"Shut up." His jaws clenched tight, and his body trembled.

Tears filled her eyes, blurring the features of his face. "It was too strong—the need—I couldn't help it."

"Just shut up!" he ground out. He didn't press inside her any further, just held himself perfectly still, grinding his teeth with the effort.

But he didn't withdraw his cock.

That little fact took a couple of seconds to register. She kept silent, not wanting to anger him further, letting him take the time to decide for himself which way this would end.

"What the fuck did you do to me? I can't stop." His forehead fell against hers. "I'm so damn hard for you. I'm gonna hurt you, *chère*."

She shook her head, but bit her lip afraid to speak, and removed her hands from his shoulders, lowering them to the pillow beside her head. This was his decision—his alone. If he found the strength to fight the same overpowering urge to mate that she felt, she'd lose her chance to be with him.

His gaze dropped from her face to sweep over her breasts and lower to where their bodies joined. His nostrils flared and his jaw tensed. His whole body shuddered. "Damn you."

Then he withdrew—a slow slide that had her clenching inner muscles around him to hold him inside—all the way until only the head of his cock remained between her swollen lips.

Natalie held her breath, waiting, hoping—dying as every second ticked by. Her body quivered, anticipating, aching to be filled.

Rene closed his eyes, his jaws grinding closed, again. Another shudder rippled through him, vibrating the blunt crown poised at her entrance.

Her sex relaxed then clasped around him, emitting a succulent sound that embarrassed her.

"Ah, God," he groaned and adjusted his hands, one at a time on the mattress. "I can't stop. I can't—" He slid back inside with a firm flex of his buttocks—this time a smooth, easy glide.

"Yes! Oh, yes!" she cried out. She was soaking wet, oozing a creamy invitation.

His cock lapped and twisted in it, tunneling side to side, stretching her to take his girth.

Natalie's bottom quivered as she held herself high to take his strokes.

Rene twisted gently, rotating his hips, holding back, but unable to withdraw. His tight, rigid features reflected the helpless urge gripping her own body to finish the act.

When next he butted against the proof of her innocence, he opened his eyes. Searing heat and regret intermingled in the hard glare he leveled on her. He lowered his chest and bracing on one arm, reached beneath her to cup one buttock, pressing down with his hips to wordlessly urge her to the mattress.

Then tucking his face in the corner of her neck, he rocked against her, going only so deep. "Put your legs around my waist," he rasped.

Natalie awkwardly clasped his slim waist with her legs, hooking her ankles behind him. She found the movement angled her hips to ease his sliding movements, and she sighed.

Her arms closed around his shoulders, and she hugged him tight, resting her cheek against his sweat-slick skin.

Once, twice, he stroked inward, tapping her hymen. "Ready?"

"Please," she whimpered.

*"Fuck me,"* he groaned and rammed forward, pushing hard against it.

The stubborn membrane guarding her womb relented, tearing away, allowing him to slide deeper until his cock filled her to bursting.

Natalie gasped. The pain wasn't great, just a stinging sensation that subsided as he continued to glide inside her. However, the girth of his cock stretched her tight channel as he pushed himself deeper and deeper, his strokes coming faster now and sharper.

His breath gusted against her neck, and the muscles along

his back and shoulders bunched. The tension building in her core matched the strength of the thrusts he levered his hips to deliver. He lifted his head above hers, staring into her face. His expression was angry and strained at the same time. As he worked, stoking a fiery friction between them, his cheeks reddened, and sweat broke on his forehead and upper lip.

Faster, harder—both their chests jerked as their breaths hitched and gasped. Then the coil of desire, the one he'd taught her to recognize, curled inside her belly, tighter and tighter.

She sobbed and ground her hips against him to take him deeper still. "Jesus, harder, Rene! Please," she keened.

With his hands planted on the mattress, he lifted his upper body to give himself greater leverage and powered into her pussy, the force of his strokes driving breath from her lungs.

Hips braced high, she welcomed the slap of balls against the crease of her ass and the friction burning her pussy as he hammered faster and harder.

At last, Natalie shattered, crying out as a dark wave crested over her.

Rene spilled liquid fire into her womb, pumping to bathe her inner channel with his release. "*Merde!*" he muttered, pounding a fist into the bed even as his hips continued to rock. His forehead fell to the pillow beside her.

Natalie panted like a cat, the ripples gripping her channel slowing as the trembling in her thighs increased. She eased her legs to the mattress.

"Shit. That wasn't supposed to happen."

Not what she'd wanted to hear, but then again she hadn't exactly expected a profession of love, either. She'd pretty much forced him to have sex with her.

But he'd taken her virginity—a rather traumatic event for her, and part of her resented the fact that all he could think about was protocol and his partner's warning glances.

She sighed—the sense of connection broken—and pushed against his chest. "Get off."

"Get out" was what she meant. She needed privacy to regroup and pretend she wasn't different somehow. She'd forced him to fuck her. Damn near raped him.

And what about the bite? What the hell had that been about? Even now, her gums itched and her teeth ached.

Rene's body stiffened and he reared back. His face hardened and his eyebrows drew together in a fierce frown. "What the fuck did you do to me? I couldn't have stopped if a hurricane took the roof off mid stroke!"

She shook her head, unable to explain. What had felt powerful and natural moments before felt tarnished by the naked fury in his glare. "I'm sorry, Rene," she whispered.

He closed his eyes for a moment and drew a deep breath that flared his nostrils. "Shit!" His hips lunged again, delivering a last shallow thrust.

"I couldn't help it. I swear, I didn't mean to push you so far." *Liar!* She'd wanted it all. Even now her pussy clenched around him.

A deep shudder shook his shoulders and belly. "I knew better." When he looked at her again, his hard gaze softened a little. "I'm sorry Natalie. I'm not handlin' this like a gentleman." He breathed deeply, settling on top of her, and brushed her hair off her damp forehead. His gaze searched hers. "You don't even know, do you?"

She didn't like the regret twisting his lips. Guilt rose inside her, and with it, an acidic anger—all aimed at herself. "What? That you're a jerk?" she lashed back while trying to keep at bay the tears burning the backs of her eyes.

"That you're a vampire."

"A what?" She almost laughed—except what he said felt right at a very elemental level.

"That bite. You drank blood. I'm no expert, but I'm pretty sure that means you're a vampire. Chessa would know." He sucked in another deep breath and sighed. "It's why she warned me."

"All these changes I've been going through—they meant something? Like I'm becoming some kind of monster?"

"I don't see Cheech as a monster," he said softly. "She's pretty human. Bad tempered, grumpy—a helluva good partner." He sighed. "She's gonna have my ass when she gets here. I wasn't supposed to touch you. I'm thinkin' I should have kept my distance so I didn't tempt you."

She snorted, trying to keep things light when she was shaking inside. "You think you're so irresistible?"

"To you . . . yeah. I'm a walking blood bank. I'm sorry. I didn't mean to take it out on you. You're the innocent one in all this."

His eagerness to accept all the blame angered her. For a few moments there, she'd been the one in control—she wasn't about to let him take that from her. "I bit you. Made you . . . come inside me. How innocent does that make me?"

"I'm a grown man. I know better. I fucked your virginity all to hell."

She couldn't help the pout that pushed out her lower lip. "That's a lovely way of putting it."

The smile lifting the corners of his lips was self-deriding but tender, and warmed her to her toes. "You were amazin'."

She'd wanted praise, she realized. Her body flowered again—shocking her with the intensity of her renewed need. "Since we've already passed the point of no return . . ."

He shook his head, regret pursing his lips. "I won't compound the damage. I'm sure there's some sort of consequence I'm already gonna pay."

Still, he hadn't pulled away. His cock was stuffed deep inside her.

Her pussy tightened around him, and she bit her lip to hold back a moan. She smoothed her hands from his shoulders to his hard buttocks, pressing to bring him closer. "You make it sound like . . . being with me is wrong."

His cock pulsed inside her. "Neither of us has the full scoop." He drew in a ragged breath. "We should wait for someone to answer our questions."

"I don't have any, right now. Can't think, actually." She tightened her legs around him and squeezed inner muscles she hadn't known she had. "You feel incredible," she gasped.

"Jesus, don't do that." His cock stirred deep inside her. "So do you—feel incredible, that is. Hot, wet." He sucked in a deep breath as she gave him another squeeze. "*God.* We have to stop."

She offered him a small smile. "I think someone's got other ideas."

A smile lifted one side of his mouth. "Yeah, he's calling me all kinds of fool. But it's not happenin'."

"You said that before and look where we are," she drawled, feeling more confident by the second.

"Yeah, I did." His chest expanded around another deep

breath, and he looked away. Finally, he withdrew and rolled onto his back, placing his forearm over his eyes. "I should check the messages. See if Chessa's on her way."

Natalie didn't like his tone—all back to business. *Does he really think he can shut me out that easily?* She leaned over him, braced on one elbow to rake his body with her gaze. His cock lay against his thigh, glistening still from their combined juices. It didn't look so intimidating now his passion was spent, but it was still fascinating.

She trailed her fingers along his length, causing him to twitch.

"Don't even think it," he growled.

"You got to explore. Isn't it my turn?"

His cock twitched again, evidently agreeable to the idea.

"He doesn't follow orders well, does he?" she said, this time stroking his length with her palm.

"A mind of his own." His hand reached down to nudge hers away and cover himself. "Play with something else. God, I'm tired."

"Liar," she murmured. "But there's so much territory to cover." His broad, hairy chest seemed a great second choice. She combed her fingers through the hairs, tugging occasionally to make sure he wasn't really falling asleep. Although curling, his hair was surprisingly soft.

The hard muscle stretching beneath his warm skin was every bit as fascinating. Curved, steely strength. She'd felt the power he leashed when he'd picked her off the bench and held her close as he ran to the squad car.

All that strength belonged to her now. She just had to convince him of what she knew instinctively.

His breasts were so different from hers—his nipples not so. The texture of the disks was soft like suede beneath her fingertips, the centers tipped by tiny erect points.

She wondered if his were as sensitive and responsive to the flicker of a tongue. Leaning over him, she stuck out her tongue and touched it.

Breath hissed between his teeth, but he didn't protest.

Encouragement enough.

Remembering how good it had felt, she closed her mouth around his little nipple and sucked delicately, all the while smoothing the flat of her tongue on the tip.

"Natalie," he breathed. His fingers threaded through her hair. "You have to stop."

"Make me."

Rene pulled her hair, but the stubborn woman bit his nipple. Not hard enough to puncture, but she definitely got his attention.

His cock stirred against his thigh, and he realized with an almost overwhelming sense of doom that it was recovering faster than he'd ever known it capable of doing.

With each lazy lap of her tongue, a sharp, electric tug tightened his groin. His balls quivered and heat poured into his cock, filling it beneath the hand still poised to guard it from her explorations.

This shouldn't be happening. He'd been warned. His gut told him he'd already made one monumental mistake. Chessa would have his ass for sure, but he was convinced her anger wouldn't be the worst of the fallout from his moment of weakness.

Natalie shifted on the mattress, catching him unaware. Her knees nudged between his legs and he automatically shoved them apart, giving her space to kneel between.

Their positions reversed this time, his mind reeled as sexy, *innocent* little Natalie plied his flesh with her tongue, licking him ravenously—nipple to sternum, then on to the other throbbing nipple—her own swaying breasts searing his belly with licks of fire each time she leaned close.

The hand he used to shield himself wrapped around his cock, and he found himself gripping it hard to work the sex-slick skin slowly up and down the steely shaft. Again, he couldn't fight the arousal singeing every synapse.

When he scraped her inner thighs with the tip of his cock, he groaned and angled it straight at her core. Any thought of resistance his mind had harbored was swept away with a lust hotter than anything he'd ever felt before.

He had to fuck her again. Drive deep into her. Cram past her tight inner muscles to feel them squeeze around him and drench his skin with her cream. *Sweet Jesus*! It had to be now.

He gripped her hips and flexed upward to impale her, but she laughed and rose higher, escaping his straining cock.

"Not yet. I told you it's my turn." She slid down his body, pausing to push both plump breasts around his erection—the softest glove he'd ever worn.

The sight appeared to fascinate her almost as much as him because she stared as she squeezed and bobbed, playing peek-aboo with his cock. "Must be a million ways to fuck," she said softly, then looked up at him.

How had he ever thought he could resist her? Her eyes

shone bright in the lamplight, and her lips were wet and swollen. His cock peeked again from between her breasts, and he groaned. "Virgin-girl, you gotta nasty mouth."

"I like the act. The word feels . . . *powerful.*"

On her lips, it certainly was. He flexed his hips and fucked his cock between her breasts, desperate now to be enveloped in her heat.

On an upward stroke, her breath brushed the swollen head of his dick. On the next, her tongue glazed it with moisture.

Shuddering, he closed his eyes and stroked again, accepting her control of his arousal and hoping she wouldn't torture him long.

Her breasts fell away from the sides of his cock, and before he had a moment to regret the loss, her mouth swallowed him, her hands clutching his shaft as she murmured around his sex—sucking, licking, her head bobbing down and up, engulfing him in heat then abandoning him to the cool air with each sexy glide.

Not much finesse, but she was learning quickly what drove him nuts. Her fingers cupping and rolling his balls had him beyond speech in seconds. The hard suction of her lips had him groaning and straining to cram deep into her throat. He gripped her hair to pull her farther down his cock, but she scraped her teeth along his length in warning.

He needed more, and at the rate of her exploration his balls would be blue before she let him come. He caught her hands and wrapped them around the base of his cock and pushed them up and down, twisting slightly, showing her how he liked to be jerked off.

Natalie hummed her approval and came off his cock. "Will

you think I'm a wimp . . ." she said, gasping for breath, "if I tell you I can't do this much longer?"

He powered his hips off the bed, sliding his dick inside her circling palms. "Jaws tired?"

"My pussy aches."

A snort of laughter caught him by surprise. "Have you ever said that word out loud?"

She grinned. "Not once in my life—in this context."

He gave her a teasing smile. "Still wanna be in charge?"

"Please?" She sucked her bottom lip between her teeth, the two elongated fangs looking wicked yet innocent at the same time.

His cock twitched. "Then you fuck me." He grabbed the notches of her slim hips and helped her climb over him.

She spread her legs wide around his hips, her cunt lips leaving a slick trail along his shaft.

"Put me inside you," he said, his voice thick and harsh.

Her hands reached between her legs and grasped his cock, sliding the head between her wet folds. She gasped.

"You sure you're not too sore?" he said, while he stifled a groan of protest.

"Shut up," she said, gritting her teeth. "I can take this. I can take you."

Releasing her hips, he cupped the globes of her breasts and squeezed, lifting his head to latch onto a tight little nipple with his teeth and lips.

When he bit down, she shuddered and lowered herself on him, taking him inside a few molten inches. "Oh, God!" She planted her hands on the mattress and rotated her hips, screwing him, easing slowly down his shaft.

He opened his mouth, letting go of her nipple. "That's it, baby. Fuck me." He pinched her nipples between his thumbs and forefingers and lay back on the pillow, watching the expression on her face.

Her eyes squeezed tight, and her lush mouth opened around a moan.

"Take your time," he said, although all he wanted to do was grip her ass hard and force her faster down his aching shaft. He cupped her breasts and toggled her nipples as she rose and fell, a little deeper each time—a little wetter and a lot hotter.

Her head fell back, exposing the white skin of her long throat, and her gilded hair billowed around her shoulders when her movements quickened.

As soon as her breaths grew jagged, Rene slid a thumb through the crisp hairs covering her pubis and found her clit. He rubbed it in ever-tightening circles.

Natalie cried out and leaned over him, clutching his shoulders as she took him deeper, ramming down his cock, fucking him harder.

Her clit throbbed beneath his circling fingertip, and her channel clasped his shaft in rhythmic pulses that caressed and massaged his length.

He gritted his teeth, trying to hold off a little longer, but the heat building inside her core had him thrusting upward to meet her, spearing deep.

Just as his thighs and balls tightened, Natalie sobbed and her breath hitched, and then a whining, keening sound broke from her throat. Her orgasm rippled along her channel, tugging and squeezing—milking his cock.

Rene's head jerked back, and he exploded, pounding upward to drive himself deep with each jet of cum. He shouted and shuddered, fucking into her tight cunt, tunneling deep until he was spent.

When the roar of blood rushing through his ears quieted, he pulled Natalie down against his chest. For several moments only the sounds of their harsh breaths filled the air.

Natalie stirred against his chest. "You really shouldn't tempt me like this," she said, tonguing the side of his neck.

Too tired to be alarmed, he felt a smile stretch his lips. "What? You wanna bite me again?"

She pressed her lips to the place she'd bitten him earlier. "It seems I do have some control. I wanted to bite your cock."

He snorted. "Thank God, you had that much sense."

"Maybe you would have liked it," she said, her voice softly teasing.

"Trust me on this. It's not somethin' you wanna try on a man."

She yawned deeply. "Maybe next time . . ."

He didn't reply, knowing there wouldn't be one, but not wanting to spoil the moment. He'd never been much into aftermaths, but here he was, still tucked inside her warmth. He held his breath while he thought about that.

Twice now, he'd thrown caution to the wind—compelled beyond his willpower to mate with Natalie. It hadn't been anything approaching *love*making. What he'd felt had been primitive and urgent.

And while his earlier anger, most of it directed at himself, was tempered by how amazing the sex had been, he knew there was going to be hell to pay.

"You're thinking about her again, aren't you?" she asked, her voice muffled against his skin.

"Who?"

"Your partner."

"Her name's Chessa. Jealous?"

"I don't know. Disappointed, I guess."

"Natalie . . ." What could he say? This couldn't last beyond tonight. He wouldn't give her false hope it might. "You don't have anythin' to worry about th—"

"Don't." She pressed a finger to his lips. "I'm being needy again. I keep forgetting about the 'Big-Bad' out there. You should be flattered."

"Why?" He knew he was quickly becoming monosyllabic, but he was just too tired to follow her tangents.

"Because you make me feel safe enough to forget."

His arms tightened around her at the reminder of the dangers lurking in the darkness beyond the walls. "You should get some sleep."

She nodded against his chest. "This is nice," she murmured. "I can hear your heartbeat."

As rain renewed its patter on the tiled roof above their heads, silence fell between them.

Rene held her until she fell asleep, then lowered her gently to the mattress and covered her before dressing in the dark. He may have broken rule number one, but he'd be damned if he broke number two.

Rene wasn't going to lose someone on his watch.

# CHAPTER 5

A crunch sounded outside—a crisp scrape like a footstep on grit. A sound Natalie knew was distant, perhaps from the courtyard below the window, but it jerked her awake in an instant just the same.

And just as quickly, she knew something wasn't right.

The sound might have been the rustle of drying leaves as they tumbled across the paving stones, or a small animal slipping between the iron bars of the gate, but she knew that wasn't true.

She no longer questioned how she knew—she accepted the prickling warning the same way she did the fact she was a vampire. Instinctually.

The hairs on the back of her neck lifted, and alarm tensed her muscles, readying her for flight.

Only she wasn't the same frightened girl she'd been before tonight. Now, she'd gained a measure of personal power. She was becoming a monster in her own right.

And she had Rene.

Only he wasn't here, now. His musky scent lingered in the bedroom, clung to the pillow beneath her nose, but he'd been gone for some time.

Was he aware of the furtive movements outside his house? Had he left to investigate? Or had he tried to escape her once again?

She couldn't afford to wait for him to come to her rescue. This time, she'd be ready for whatever stepped out of the shadows. Refusing to huddle beneath the covers, she slipped from the bed and crept to the French window.

Standing to the side of the casing, she pulled back the edge of the hazy curtain and stared into the darkened courtyard below.

At first, it appeared empty. Wind whipped the tops of the short trees, stirring the leaves into an agitated whisper.

If she'd blinked, she might have missed the blurred gray shadows that streaked across the tiny courtyard.

Holding her breath, she willed her heart to slow its frantic beating so she could continue to listen above the rapid tattoo. Then she stepped toward her suitcase lying open on a small padded bench beside the door. She reached beneath wadded clothing until her fingers closed around the hard plastic grip of her handgun.

As she pulled it out, she felt a cool, fresh breeze lick across her bare skin and knew the window to the balcony had opened.

Natalie whipped around with the weapon pointing outward

to find a large male figure silhouetted by streetlight between the open doors. Not Rene's thickly muscled frame. This man was taller and leaner, with midnight hair that brushed the tops of his broad shoulders. His clothing was crisp edged—a long-sleeved shirt covered with a thickly padded vest, topping military style pants and boots. A holster rode along the side of one masculine thigh.

With her finger poised on the trigger, she drew a shaky breath. "You really should have tried the front door."

His head canted, and she realized that while his features were hidden in darkness, her pale skin was a beacon.

"I seem to have you at a disadvantage," he replied, French undertones cloaking his voice in silk. His tone was amused, his posture disturbingly relaxed.

"So, I'm naked," she blurted, "but I'm the one with the gun in my hand."

A soft snort indicated laughter, which only heightened her fear. "Even if you managed to hit where you're aiming, you can't win this battle, Natalie."

A shiver racked her body. "I'll manage just fine, but you might have a little problem finding me without a head attached to your shoulders."

This time the laughter sifted around her like a soft dusting of confectioner's sugar—delicious, light, tempting.

And before she could pull back on the 5.5-pound trigger, he was beside her, his hand wrapping around hers on the weapon. "Let go."

She whimpered from fear and a sudden, dampening thrill. "How?" she croaked, as curious about the speed with which he'd moved as she was afraid and aroused.

"I'm not going to hurt you, *mon enfant.*" He stepped closer and wrapped an arm around her back, then leaned down to nuzzle her cheek. "Just let go."

Her body betrayed her. But unlike the powerful lust that had driven her to take Rene past his good intentions, a strange, enervating lassitude had her leaning into his solid chest.

Had he done this to her with just his voice?

He tipped the nozzle of her weapon down and dragged it from her nerveless fingers. "There," he said, "no fuss. You're a brave girl." His chest rose beneath her cheek as he drew a deep breath. "And a naughty one, it seems. Good for you."

Was this how her friend Vicki had felt the moment before her throat had been ripped open? Resigned, relieved—*willing* to let death come without so much as a whimper?

But she wasn't ready to die. Not tonight.

With one last attempt to resist, she rallied her dulled wits and shoved at his chest, lifting one knee to ram between his legs.

He easily sidestepped her attack, then slipped a hard thigh between hers and pushed her against the wall, trapping her hands against his chest. One large hand gently cradled the back of her head; the other still held her weapon. He drew the cold metal slowly up her naked side, over her hip, letting it bump against each rib, one by one, and then follow the outside curve of her breast.

Natalie drew a ragged breath, knowing she was entirely at his mercy. The odd thing was all she could concentrate on was the rasp of the coarse fabric that clothed the muscled thigh pressed against her sensitive, heated flesh and the fresh-washed scent of the man holding her. "What have you done to me?" she asked, recognizing the familiarity of the words. Now she knew how Rene had felt. Compelled beyond his will to respond.

She sensed his smile against her cheek. "Just a trick. One I promise to teach you . . . if you're good."

The teasing note in his voice calmed her. His hand gripped her hair and he tilted her head to kiss her lips, then he released her hair.

She heard the rasp of Velcro opening and felt the sting of something sharp stabbing into her neck. She whimpered, but curved her fingertips into the stiff vest cloaking his chest and clung to him as darkness closed around her.

Rene prowled the house, sticking to the downstairs rooms this time. He'd checked his cell phone again and left Chessa a blistering message. What the hell was keeping her anyway?

Although his body still felt mildly drugged by his roll in the sheets with Natalie, his emotions felt edgy and alert. Standing at the sink in the kitchen, he ran cool water to wash his face—anything to stem the heat building again inside him.

He cupped water in his hands and stared at his palms, remembering the feel of her soft breasts with their erect little points. He muttered an oath and splashed the water into his face. If he dunked his whole head beneath the spigot, he still wouldn't clear the image or the feelings from his mind.

He was mad as hell at himself—and Chessa. She hadn't given him adequate warning. Partners didn't leave partners swingin' in the wind.

If he'd known what he faced, the potent, irresistible temptation she embodied, he might have stood a chance of deflecting Natalie's allure—hell, he'd have tied a knot in his cock sooner than fuck a vampire!

Sweet as she'd been, he didn't need that kind of trouble. Worse, he couldn't trust that what he was starting to feel for her was real.

But what exactly was he feeling? Desire? Certainly. Lust? Absolutely. Connection? That possibility terrified him. Natalie was quickly becoming an obsession.

He poured a glass of water and took a long drink, hoping the coolness slipping down his throat would somehow halt his body's arousal.

Even now, she lay naked in his bed. Moonlight bathed her curved body. The lemon and apple smell of her still scented the air—still clung to his own skin. He'd fled the room before the musky scent of sex overwhelmed him, hardened him—again.

Earlier, pale light had revealed his deepest fear. Natalie's eyes had glittered with longing and trust. That had been the scariest thing of all. Not that she was a vampire, but that she trusted him to keep her safe and not betray her heart.

He just plain couldn't give her what she wanted.

A floorboard creaked behind him, and he caught Chessa's reflection in the darkened window above the sink. She was dressed in SWAT gear. "It's about damn time you got back here," he growled. He placed the glass on the countertop and turned in time to catch Chessa's downward-sweeping glance.

His cheeks heated. Wearing only blue jeans and his shoulder holster, he knew she'd jumped to all the right conclusions as her lips thinned.

When her glance met his again, the stillness in her set his heart thudding with unease.

Then he heard footsteps coming through the hallway and saw several men dressed entirely in black, walking quietly through his house and up the stairs. He pushed away from the counter. "What the hell's goin' on, Chessa?"

She glanced briefly over her shoulder and then turned slowly back toward him. "We're taking her out of here."

"Let me go up to wake her. You're gonna scare her."

Her lips tightened. "And you'd care, wouldn't you?"

He heard a muffled whimper from above and stepped toward the doorway.

Chessa stuck out her arm, blocking his exit.

Close enough now that he could have pushed past her, he glared down into her face. "Chessa . . ."

"You can't help her now, *partner*." Her head tilted slightly. "Damn you, you can't even help yourself. You fucked her." She inhaled, her nostrils flaring as she sniffed. "Hell, you reek of sex. You couldn't keep away, could you?"

She didn't sound angry—which he would have preferred. Instead, he read disappointment and resignation in her tone.

Feeling off center and ashamed, he retorted, "You could have told me what I was facin'—spelled it out so this *human* would understand. Cheech, she was fuckin' irresistible."

"And now?" she said, her sharp gaze roaming his face. "What do you feel now?"

"Nothing," he lied. "Not a goddamn thing."

Another rustling sound came from above, and then a thin cry. He pressed against her arm.

"You need to let me handle this." Her eyes narrowed and

seemed to catalog every twitch he made that gave away his concern.

Rene fought against the overpowering need to surge past her and up the stairs. This was Chessa's business now, but he sure as hell hated not knowing what was happening.

"Did you come inside her?" Chessa asked, her voice dead even.

His gaze slid away from hers. He refused to answer. The shame burning his cheeks told her what she wanted to know.

"Of course, you did." She reached into a pocket on the top of her Kevlar vest and pulled out a syringe.

He eyed it warily and stepped back. "What the fuck's that for and what are they doin' up there?"

"We don't want her alarmed. Or harmed. So we're going to put her out for transportation."

"Are they stickin' her now?" he asked, anger stiffening his spine.

"Yeah, and this one's for you." She shoved her forearms into his chest, slamming him against the wall.

Rene roared and pushed back, but for the first time, he experienced the strength in her wiry muscles that could take down a linebacker. It happened so fast, he didn't have time to consider another strategy. He tried to pull back, but for the second time that night, he wasn't the one in control.

Her whole body strained against him, and she used one elbow to press into his neck so hard his vision quickly filled with prickling lights.

Her hand shot out, and she jabbed the syringe into his neck.

He pulled at her arm, but his already sapping strength was fleeing. His muscles felt more leaden by the moment.

As he found himself slipping to the floor, he heard Chessa mutter, "Dammit Rene, you really fucked up this time."

Chessa rode in the back of the panel truck.

Both Rene and Natalie, wrapped in sheets, lay in the center of the floor between the long bench seats flanking either side of the vehicle, snuggled close together.

The sight rankled.

"You don't look happy. Everything went according to plan."

She heard mockery in the voice of the man sitting across from her and wished Nicolas had chosen to ride in the vehicle with the rest of the security team. These two weren't waking up anytime soon—she didn't need help.

Worse, she hated his sharp-eyed perception. He'd read her interest as she'd cradled Rene's body on the floor and tenderly pulled out the needle from his neck after she'd shot him up with enough sedative to keep him down for the rest of the night.

"So, we have a baby vamp. That's cause for celebration, is it not?"

She leveled a glare at him, knowing he was only making conversation to annoy her. Her mind was still reeling, and she needed time to think. She'd taken a risk leaving Natalie with Rene, but she'd hoped he would be strong enough to resist her hormonal appeal.

Chessa'd had plans of her own for the Cajun. Four years of sussing out his strengths and weaknesses to determine whether he would be the right sort of man to enter her life. Four years of yearning for his hard, toned body, patiently learning the secrets that kept him from committing to a woman.

She'd been kidding herself there would ever be a time for them. He'd never really let her close, never shared the intimate details of his life.

Sure, they'd spent half their waking lives in each other's company. But she couldn't claim to really know him.

However, she did know he didn't particularly like preternatural creatures. He distrusted what he couldn't explain. Over time, he'd come to tolerate her well, despite the fact she had a second strike against her.

Rene hadn't wanted a female partner of any kind. Ever.

It had taken deliberately choreographed incidents to prove her physical abilities. Without revealing the true extent of her powers, she'd cultivated a relationship with him built on mutual respect. Eventually, he'd come to trust she wouldn't let him down or get in his way.

Tonight had dashed her hopes he'd ever see her as a potential lover. After this, he'd have eyes only for Natalie.

Over the years, she'd taken lovers for blood and sex, but she'd carefully avoided entanglement. Although the hurt that kept her heart apart and untouched was decades old, she'd been unwilling to risk it again.

Until Rene.

Despite his sometimes coarse manner, at the core he was a gentleman with a deep streak of integrity she admired. More than once she'd wished she had found someone like him for her life mate the first time around.

The truck slowed and bumped onto a gravel road.

"Almost home," Nicolas murmured. "Time to get these

two to bed. Sure you know whose bed you want him tied to?"

The sly humor in his voice set her teeth on edge while his words conjured a vision that pricked her sensual awareness, making her shift on the thinly padded seat.

The thought of Rene stretched across pale sheets, his hands and feet in manacles, tightened her body and sent a flush of heat across her cheeks.

Nicolas tsked. "He's not for you, but maybe you'd settle for something else, *eh chère*?"

Chessa stiffened and lifted her chin. "Why? You offering?"

A single eyebrow rose like a dark wing. "I'm not nearly so brave as that."

"You think a man needs courage to be with me?"

His glance swept down her body, and he lifted his shoulders in an indolent shrug. "I think he needs many things to take you on. Courage is only one of them."

Chessa snorted. "That almost sounds like a compliment."

"Just telling the truth." He tilted his head toward the floor. "Our baby girl's a lot like you. She's got courage in spades. She's not even fully cooked, and she tried to take me."

Chessa didn't want to hear about any virtues Natalie Lambert might possess. She was ready to hate the woman's guts. "Sounds like a fool to me," she muttered.

When his smile widened, she realized she'd given him exactly what he wanted. She bit back a curse at his soft laughter.

"I think it's a very good thing you're not the one charged with her safety."

"I know my duty," she bit out.

His smile dimmed, and his gaze bored into hers. "Yes, but you have yet to learn your place."

Pure, intoxicating fury blasted through her. "And where might that be?"

The white flash of his wicked smile had her wishing she'd bit her tongue rather than rise to his bait. "Princess, if I have to tell you, you're not ready for the answer."

His laser wit always had a way of flaying her self-control. Just once, she wished her temper wouldn't flare so readily in response to his jibes.

She'd give anything to be on the sticking end of the skewer. "Shut the fuck up, Nic."

# CHAPTER 6

As soon as the van pulled to a halt, the back doors swung open. Familiar faces appeared in the opening, but their gazes clung to the sleeping Natalie. They reached eager hands inside to pull at her feet, sliding her down the metal floor.

While they lifted the woman out and carried her away, Chessa braced herself not to feel. However, the cloying humid air with its accompanying scents of honeysuckle and roses was already stifling.

The view beyond the metal doors appeared no different than she remembered. The shining crushed shell and pebble driveway was perfectly edged with soft green grass and short shrubs. The tall oaks draped in Spanish moss shaded the pristine porches of the house, sentinels against the faint light of dawn glittering on dew-capped leaves and lush red blooms.

She hated returning to *Ardeal.* Resentment stiffened her shoulders, and a hollow ache settled in the pit of her stomach. She wanted to run, to get as far away from here as she could—back to New Orleans, another world away.

She especially didn't want to spend time with the residents from "beyond the forest."

Perhaps Natalie would draw everyone's attention away, and they'd leave her the hell alone.

"Let's get this one inside," Nicolas murmured. "Our girl might wake up in need of a snack."

Chessa lifted her chin and did her best to ignore his needling reminder of whose hunger Rene would serve.

Nicolas squatted next to Rene and lifted his shoulders from the ground, while another set of eager hands reached inside to grab his feet. Together, they carried the sleeping man away, leaving Chessa alone in the back of the van.

She peeled the Velcro tapes from the top of her heavy Kevlar vest and shrugged out of the garment, feeling only marginally lighter.

"Welcome home, *damu*," a soft, throaty voice called.

Chessa drew a slow, deep breath and turned on her seat to face the dark-haired woman with the infinite, soulful eyes. "Hello, *grand-mère*."

"Come," she said extending her hand. "We must get inside before the light becomes unbearable."

Chessa held out her hand and let Inanna help her to the ground. When the other woman's grasp tightened, she allowed her to continue to hold her hand as they mounted the steps of the veranda.

"The house is buzzing over the new arrivals. Such a miracle. Thank you for bringing her to us."

"You're welcome," Chessa said, although her throat closed so tight, she felt choked.

"I'm glad you're here."

"I'm not staying long."

Inanna's smile—secretive and sly—raised Chessa's hackles. "You're here, now. Perhaps you will find a reason to linger."

The heavy mahogany doors stood open, and Chessa let herself be swept inside. Nothing had changed here, either. Heavy, dark old-world furniture stood like sentries against cream-colored walls. High ceilings with lazy, lapping fans looked cool and elegant. Through open doorways off the marble-tiled foyer, the rooms looked inviting—large sofas, scrunched pillows in jewel-toned velvets and damask and plush pale carpeting. Everything bespoke money and privilege, but the message was subtly powerful.

This was Inanna's home—dark and light—as secretive as her existence, yet warmly inviting to her family—a very large and incestuous family.

"I have a job to get back to," Chessa demurred, feeling like a scruffy urchin next to the ancient one's easy elegance.

"But your partner remains here—"

"He made his bed."

Inanna squeezed her hand and led her through the dark marble-tiled foyer and up the curved iron staircase. "He will need a friend."

"He's got Natalie. She'll fill his life from now on."

"Since he's your partner, my guess is he's every bit as headstrong as you. He may fight his destiny."

"Then he'll be destroyed," Chessa said, trying not to let emotion block her throat, again. He wasn't her concern anymore.

Inanna paused on the upper landing outside the specially prepared room. "Nicolas is alone with them, now. Do you trust him to make them comfortable?" she asked, suppressed laughter sparkling in her black eyes.

Chessa gritted her teeth and tugged away her hand. "I'll just make sure he doesn't take a bite of his own."

"You do that. Join me for dinner tonight?"

Chessa's eyebrows drew together, and she didn't bother hiding her impatience this time. "I won't be here," she said, and turned on her heel. She shoved open the door to find Nicolas slowly unwinding the sheet from around Natalie's lush little body.

A low murmur of admiration escaped his curved lips. "Lovely—cream, tipped with berries. Delicious, don't you think? A veritable feast for our policeman."

"Just get her on the fucking bed," Chessa growled.

"Such an appropriate descriptor."

"Asshole," she muttered.

His soft laughter skittered down her spine, raising goose bumps. "A favorite destination—how'd you guess?"

Chessa clamped her lips shut—not willing to give the man any more ammunition. Instead, she knelt beside Rene, unsnapped his shoulder holster, and quickly stripped it away.

Next, she undid the button at the top of his jeans and slid

his zipper down, ignoring the slight tremor in her hand. Her fingers slipped between the waistband and his warm skin and pushed the pants down his hips and over his buttocks. If she lingered a moment too long, it wasn't because she enjoyed the hewn muscles of his ass and flanks.

When his flaccid cock was revealed, she swallowed hard against a moan of yearning. She raised her glance to Nicolas and found him staring back.

His cheeks were taut, his mouth a thin, tight line. "He's not for you."

"Never thought he was," she said, swallowing to moisten her dry mouth. "Besides, none of this is your business."

Nicolas fluffed a pillow at the head of the bed and raised Natalie's shoulders to slip it beneath her. Then he smoothed back the sleeping woman's hair from her face. His head canted and he combed his fingers through the ends. The blonde curls clung to his fingertips. He let them drop onto her breasts and arranged them to frame her pink nipples.

Chessa couldn't help noticing how attractive the other woman was. She was a perfect counterpoint to Rene's raw masculinity. Her stomach sank as she compared Natalie's body to her own lean frame.

"He'll enjoy all this softness," Nicolas taunted, drawing one long finger from her breast over the curves of her ribs and lower, finally twirling his fingers in the pale curls between her legs.

"Stop it."

Nicolas's eyebrows rose, but he drew back his hand. "Let me help you get him onto the bed."

Before she could utter a protest, Nicolas lifted Rene's naked body and deposited him beside Natalie. He made quick work of latching the manacles to his hands and feet.

Then he stood back and studied the pair lying side by side on the mattress. "Something isn't quite right." He knelt on the mattress and tugged Natalie closer to Rene, aligning her body so that her front draped his side. "What do you think? Better?"

"Quit being an ass. Let's get out of here."

"No, no. We want them too horny to think when first they awaken." He lifted Natalie's slackened hand and laid it over Rene's cock.

Chessa's back grew rigid. "I said that's enough."

"Too coarse, do you think?" He pushed Natalie's hand up Rene's belly to his chest.

Now, Natalie appeared to be caressing the solid muscle above his heart. He drew her knee over Rene's thigh and climbed back off the bed.

"What do you think, Chessa?" he asked, a devilish smile stretching his lips.

She narrowed her gaze at him. "I still think you're an asshole. Now, get out of here." She waited for him to precede her to the door, and then paused to look over her shoulder one last time.

Rene and Natalie looked like lovers. When they awoke that evening, they would start the journey toward being so much more than that together. She walked back to the bed and drew the cover at the foot of the mattress over their bodies, then left without looking back.

Chessa closed the door behind her and gasped when she was pressed back against the closed door.

Nicolas leaned over her, so close the musky scent of his arousal was impossible to miss.

For once, she felt an answering curl of desire deep inside her belly. It scared the shit out of her. "What do you think you're doing?" she said, gritting out the words.

"Nothing you won't enjoy. I promise."

Chessa was honest enough with herself to admit the thought of a mutual suckfest did have its appeal, but not with this man. He was too damn sure of himself. Too damn smug for a *Revenant*.

She shoved at his chest, but his heels dug into the carpet. As his head lowered toward hers a low groan escaped her throat.

His mouth was softer than she'd expected. His lips suctioned hers in drugging little circles that soon had her following his slow, sinful movements.

When his tongue licked the seam between her lips, she opened, eager to feel him stroking inside.

He tasted like toasted pecans and sweet maple syrup—well, not really, but he did taste like a rich dessert—*the kind that inspired toothaches.*

Chessa broke the kiss, keeping her eyes closed as she fought against her body's response to his lean, hard-muscled frame and the thick cock riding her through her trousers.

If she'd been looking for any old fuck . . .

"Let me go," she ground out.

Nicolas's hands stilled where they'd been massaging her ass. His lips glided along her cheek, then nipped below her jaw. The sharp edge of his fangs scraped over the pulse pounding at the side of her neck. "You sure, *petite*? I could be gentle . . . or I could be an animal. Whatever your desire."

The bastard hadn't a clue what she needed. His seduction was just another game. "Get your hands off me, or I'll break every bone in your body."

His soft laughter gusted against her hair, but he drew back, his body no longer plastered to her front, yet still close enough to heat the space between them.

She shoved him back a little further and wiped the back of her hand across her mouth, scowling at him the whole time. "I detest you."

"But Little Princess, you want my cock, don't you?" His gaze dropped down to the one place their bodies still met. He dipped his hips, lifting her momentarily off her feet, suspended between the wall and his hard cock. "So much anger inside you. You need release. Someone to tweak your valves."

Even with the rock hard pressure grinding into her pussy, she couldn't help the snort of laughter that caught her by surprise. "Tweak my valves?" She couldn't help it, laughter bubbled up inside.

"Not romantic, hmmm?" he said, a wry smile quirking one side of his lovely, symmetrical lips. How had she never noticed how perfect they were? His hands rose to flatten against the wall on either side of her shoulders.

Surrounded by him, she felt the crotch of her panties dampen, and her heart sped up. "I'm not looking for a lover, Nicolas," she said, so desperate now for him to release her, she let him see her trepidation. "Not now."

His head canted and his look turned probing. "When you are ready . . ."

She nodded quickly—anything to halt his efforts to seduce her.

He closed his eyes for a moment, then stepped back, letting her slide down and lifting his hands away in mock surrender.

Chessa swallowed hard and straightened her shoulders, wary of him as she'd never been before. Turning away, she raked back her hair, refusing to meet his glance. "The room is ready?"

"My team has everything prepared. Now it's all up to the baby vampire."

Natalie roused slowly and snuggled closer to the source of the warmth beneath her fingertips and cheek. It was Rene. Even before she opened her eyes, she knew she lay beside him. And in the moments before the muzzy grayness receded, she remembered.

After being accosted by the black-haired devil, she'd felt the sting of a needle entering her neck. She'd been taken from Rene's bedroom by a group of armed men, recalling hazy images of men wearing black masks, and then remembered nothing.

She peeked beneath her eyelashes to see whether they were alone now. Her eyes widened. She didn't recognize the bedroom or the bed they lay in. Dusty blue-glazed walls surrounded them. A canopy of gauzy white fabric obscured the ceiling. They lay on the softest cotton sheets she'd ever felt, covered with a pillowy duvet in the same cloudy blue decorated with purple flowers.

They appeared to be alone.

She rolled to her back and swallowed against a faint nausea—her stomach was a little unsettled, perhaps the aftereffect of the drug that had knocked her out.

Beside her, Rene hadn't moved a muscle.

She leaned up on an elbow and touched his face. "Rene," she whispered. "Wake up." Still, he didn't move.

She swept back the coverlet and was shocked to see they were both naked, and he was restrained by metal cuffs. Why wasn't she in a similar state?

Her stomach rumbled. Nausea raised bile in the back of her throat. She was ravenous.

Rene's throat lay exposed, his pulse throbbing softly as she brushed a fingertip over it. She remembered his taste and warmth slowly filled her.

Rene was still asleep. He might never know . . .

Alarm tightened a cold fist around her heart that her first inclination was to take her meal from him. She backed away from him on the bed. Although she'd done it before, she knew she'd feel as low as a snake later if she took him when he was completely vulnerable.

She crawled off the mattress and searched the room for something to cover herself. She pulled a lacy throw from the end of the bed and wound it toga-style around her body before padding toward the door.

Pressing her ear to the wood, she listened for movements on the other side, but found only silence. She wrapped her fingers around the doorknob and tried to turn it, but discovered it was locked.

She was torn. Although starving, she wondered whether she should bring any attention to herself. Their capture and Rene's imprisonment only emphasized the fact that danger was afoot.

She paced the room, searching for an exit, but discovered the only other door led into a well-appointed bathroom.

Back in the bedroom, she went to the small windows high on the wall opposite the bed and pulled back thick curtains. The windows were barred. When she shoved up the frame, wind whipped inside, but a glance outside revealed no nearby houses she might shout to for help—a brick wall lay in the distance beyond a wide green lawn below.

No help there.

A trembling shook her body as she realized they were trapped—at the mercy of whoever held them.

However, what frightened her most was the hunger that gnawed at her belly. Already, a tingling, prickling itch grew in the roof of her mouth, and although she tried to resist, her incisors slid down, the thin razor points biting into her lower lip.

She opened her mouth and dragged in a deep breath, tilting back her head to draw cooler air inside her mouth, hoping to relieve the ache.

Her tongue touched each sharp tip, scraping lightly, raising a droplet of blood—it was enough to cause a moan of want to tear from her throat.

She stumbled back into the bathroom and poured a glass of water from the carafe beside the sink. She drank it down without pausing for a breath, hoping to assuage her thirst.

As she lowered the glass, a glance in the gilt-edged mirror revealed a reflection she barely recognized. Her tangled hair framed a gaunt, strained face. Her lips were swollen and pink, and the fangs curving from beneath her upper lip extended below her gaping lower lip.

But the differences didn't end there. Her pale skin had acquired a faint, bluish tinge. She unwound the lacy throw and let it pool at her feet. Her body, always plumply curved, appeared to have lost a bit of flesh. Her breasts seemed tighter, the nipples drawn and pointed. The indention of her waist was a little more defined.

Then she noticed the dark brown smears on her inner thighs and remembered the powerful, sensual thrill that had gripped her body when Rene had thrust hard inside her the first time.

Her pussy clenched and a trickle of moisture escaped.

Her teeth sank into her lip, but she welcomed the stinging bite—anything not to think about what she craved most at this very moment.

Every part of her body ached to crawl over Rene's body, rub her swollen breasts against his chest and drive her hips down to take his cock deep inside—*while she drank her fill of his blood.*

She whirled toward the shower stall beside a large claw-foot tub and flung back the glass door, reaching blindly inside for the lever that controlled the flow of water. She pulled it out and spun it left, setting the temperature high.

Before the steam rose, she stepped beneath the scalding water, letting the searing pulses strafe her body. She sank on the ledge at the back of the shower and gripped the edge with her hands.

But the heat didn't relax, didn't help loosen the grip of her desires.

The pulses caressed her nipples, tightening the tips. She lifted her hands to cover them, but couldn't resist the urge to cup and massage the ache swelling her breasts.

She leaned back and opened her legs, letting the spray

sweep between her thighs. For a moment, it seemed to help. It was almost enough to appease the raging need.

Then a tension built in her womb, a slow, curling heat that forced her hands between her legs. She sank two fingers into her vagina, thrusting inside and withdrawing—again and again, until her hips moved on the slick tile beneath her ass to counter the movements.

Christ! It wasn't enough. She speared another finger inside herself and rubbed the top of her pussy with the ball of her palm, grinding hard.

When it hit, her orgasm had her crying out, shuddering as her frantic movements slowed.

Afterward, she wrapped her arms around her belly and cried, because she knew this was only a short respite.

She bathed herself, using a rough loofah to scrape the last of the tiny scabs from her arms and legs. The skin beneath the wounds was pink, but completely healed. One more question to be answered.

When she went back into the bedroom, Rene still slept, stretched across the bed. Like an offering. Hers to take.

She lay down beside him and curved her body close to share his heat. Her skin shivered, but deep inside the heat rose again to test her will.

# CHAPTER 7

Her body warmed as she cuddled closer. This close and this turned on, all she could do was stare at the virile landscape lying right beside her—right within reach.

Even relaxed, the masculine power remained leashed inside his form. His sheer size made her feel small and vulnerable. While they shared the same number of limbs and toes, the differences couldn't be more striking . . . or thrilling.

Dark hair peppered his arms and legs. An interesting arrow, thicker, softer darted down his stomach, opening over his groin. So unlike the sparse, pale hair between her legs.

Everywhere she was soft—he wasn't. Her breasts were pillowy, while his . . .

Unable to resist, she smoothed her hands over his chest, cupping and molding the firm, muscled hillocks. How would it feel to have the right to sleep with her cheek resting above his heart, the steady beat a constant life-affirming comfort?

Of course, she didn't linger there for long, not with the most interesting territory lying to the south. She swept her hand downward to follow the trail of dark hair beckoning her fingers toward his sex. His cock rested along the top of his thigh—partially erect.

She lifted her head, glad the daylight provided her first good look. A morning hard-on? She'd heard of them, but never actually seen the result.

She nestled closer still, sliding her thigh toward his cock, arguing with herself all the while about whether she should continue to explore uninvited. "Rene?" she whispered.

He didn't so much as twitch.

Tempted beyond shame, she reached a tentative hand for the part that fascinated her most. She lifted his penis and measured him with her fingers, the length and girth. Only partially filled, she could hardly believe her body had gloved him. The smooth-as-satin texture of the skin clothing his cock and the warmth pulsing inside her closed fist created a longing that cramped her belly.

Slowly, his cock began to fill and lift away from his body, growing harder, larger within her grip. Her heart thudded loudly in her ears. Now, he was firm enough to fuck.

Her mouth watered as she remembered his taste, and she scooted down the bed to nuzzle him with her nose—just to breathe in his scent. Maybe that would be enough.

But the softness of the skin that clothed his rock-hard shaft tempted her to trail up his length with her sensitive tongue. When she reached the ridged cap, she couldn't resist giving him a little kiss. Then she had to take him into her mouth, sucking, drawing on him until his sex grew even more rigid.

Her tongue licked down the outside, tracing the fat vein throbbing just under the surface. When she reached his sac, she tilted her head and licked the inside of his shaft, all the way up to the ridge that circled the plump head. She squeezed her hand around him, noting her fingers didn't touch, and licked the tip of him like an ice cream cone, lapping, swirling—until a drop of pearlescent liquid beaded in the tiny hole. Her tongue curved to take it, then returned to delve into the eyelet opening. The salty taste of his ejaculate left her hungrier for more.

Soon, the hunger gnawing at her belly was replaced by a visceral, cramping need to feel him plunging deep inside her body.

And even though she knew she was taking, again, she rose and straddled his hips, impaling herself on his cock. She worked him all the way inside her in short, bouncing strokes to ease him past the sore muscles, working up a creamy lather that soothed the hot, raw muscles of her channel.

Still he slept under the influence of whatever drug they'd used to knock them out. While a niggling inner voice scolded her, reminding her what she did was wrong, she remembered how he'd felt thrusting inside her. Remorse was momentary in light of her overwhelming need, so she sank on him, using his cock to feed the hunger moistening her channel already rippling along his length.

Awkward at first, she found a rhythm and angle to her up and down strokes that built the familiar friction.

Tentative at the start, soon she was thrusting hard against him, grunting softly with exertion as perspiration gathered at her temples and upper lip.

He started to make waking noises and stir beneath her so she hurried. She gripped his shoulders when her movements shortened, pushed off from his chest when she needed greater height. Up and down, up and down—until her whole body tightened and her pussy burned. Her breaths grew jagged.

Rene moved more restlessly beneath her, and her heart rate escalated. He wasn't quite wakening, not yet, still in the grip of the drug and his dreams.

Too far gone, she took advantage. She had to reach a climax. Closing her eyes, she leaned back and cupped her breasts, imagining his rougher palms squeezing them as she rode, jouncing hard against his hips.

She opened her eyes, and her breath caught in her throat.

He watched her.

She couldn't read his expression, but his jaw tightened, and his thighs trembled beneath hers. His hips lifted and he attempted to buck her body off. His teeth gritted as he tried to withhold his orgasm.

*Stubborn man.* The newly discovered part of her that relished her role as aggressor tightened her thighs around his hips and held him still. She wouldn't let him deny her release.

When he continued to resist, she did the one thing she knew he wouldn't be able to fight. She leaned over, capturing his wild gaze for a moment, and bit the top of his shoulder.

"Noooo!" he groaned, and his hips lifted again, this time

jerking up and into her, pounding in counterpoint to her downward thrusts.

The battle between them only fueled her excitement. She thrust hard against him, taking him, demanding his orgasm as her inner muscles clamped tight around his cock and her jaws gripped him tight.

Then the rapture swept over, filling her womb like his blood flooded the inside of her mouth. She drank and fucked, more slowly now, more deeply, murmuring her delight against his flesh.

After the last tremors faded, she lay over him, her legs spread wide around his hips, his cock still embedded deep inside her. As she fought to catch her breath, she didn't want to free him. Not yet. Instead, she lapped lazily to close the twin punctures on his shoulder.

When the deep shuddering tremors subsided in his body, she lay still, almost afraid to see his expression. Too late, she acknowledged remorse for her actions. While she'd been in the grip of the hunger, the only thing that had mattered was filling the overwhelming need. She recognized this might be a pattern. Emotionally, she prepared herself for many such battles and losses.

She leaned back and warily looked into his face.

Anger burned in his eyes, and he rattled the chains attached to his wrists. "Now that you're finished," he bit out, "do you think you can find a way to get these off me?"

"Good morning to you, too," she said, not able to hold back the bitchy edge that crept into her voice. Her body still trembled with delicious little aftershocks she'd have liked to savor.

Reluctance slowing her response, Natalie lifted up, letting his sex slip from her body.

The flaring of his nostrils was the only hint of emotion he let her see.

She clambered off the bed and dutifully followed the manacles on his wrists to the chains that draped over the end of the bed to the floor. The mattress was pulled away from the wall, and there was no headboard. The chains were soldered to metal plates bolted in the floor.

She tugged hard at the chain, but made no progress. "We'll need the key," she said.

"Well, find it, dammit," he said, his voice rising.

Natalie pushed a tendril of hair behind her ear. She still felt slightly dull, her body replete and sluggish as her mind. She looked at her hand and arm and noted her skin had lost its blue tinge.

"Sometime this year," he said, his irritation stretching out the last word.

She ignored his testiness. He had every right to be rude—he was the one chained to a bed. "Where should I look?"

"How the hell should I know?" he snarled. "Just start going through things. Begin with the dresser."

She went to the dark oak dresser, opening a little rosewood casket on top, but found it empty. All the drawers of the dresser were also empty. Nothing in the bedside table or in the bathroom cabinet other than toiletries.

When she came out of the bathroom, she shrugged. "I didn't find anything. Do you really think they'd put it somewhere we could get to it?"

His lips twisted and one dark brow lifted. " 'Course not, but looking kept you busy doing something else."

It didn't take a rocket scientist to figure out what he meant by "something else". Every time her gaze fell on him, she couldn't resist checking out his body.

"Well, we're going to have to wait to ask about a key."

Rene pounded his head once on the mattress, frustration evident in the tightening of his chest and shoulders.

Again, Natalie swept her glance over his body, feeling guilty about the secret pleasure of having him at her mercy. "Why would they put chains on you?"

Rene turned his head and glared. "It's kinda obvious they want to keep me here for you."

Only a little surprised, she replied, "You think they brought you here—for me? But why?"

His lips twisted in a mocking smile. "To screw, eat, drink—I'm your meal."

"Who brought us here, Rene? Was this Chessa's plan?"

His upper lip lifted in a snarl. "Yeah, her and her people."

Chessa and "her people" meant for her to use Rene? He was all hers? For the moment, she didn't care about the "why." Her breasts tightened.

Lord, how many times could she take him before her hunger was assuaged? She hid her excitement, pasting a concerned look on her face. "Are you uncomfortable?"

He rolled his shoulders. "A little stiff." His eyes narrowed as she pursed her lips to prevent a smile. "*My shoulders* are a little stiff. It'll get worse the longer I'm layin' here."

The smile she'd fought quirked up one side of her mouth.

"A warm bath might ease your muscles. Would you like me to bathe you?"

His glower grew impossibly darker. "Fuck no. Stay the hell away from me."

Disappointed, but beginning to enjoy the fact he was helpless, she walked around the room, aware his stare followed her. And if the sway of her hips was a little exaggerated . . . he deserved a little teasing. His surly rejection stung. "Why do you think they didn't chain me, too?" She wrapped her arms around her middle, pretending a chill while plumping her breasts above her arms.

Rene snorted, but his glance strayed downward. "Did they need to? You're stalkin' me, now!"

She realized with a start she'd walked around the room in ever-tightening circles, drawing closer to the bed. "I'm sorry," she said automatically, but not really meaning it. She was becoming such a liar.

The muscles in his neck and jaw tensed as he lifted his head. "You keep sayin' that."

She didn't blame him for not believing her. The excitement humming through her body, lifting goose bumps on her skin, found its center in her woman's core. "I really can't seem to help myself." The truth, this time.

Anger drained from his face. His expression grew bleak. "I know." He took a deep breath and relaxed against the mattress, his gaze lifting to the ceiling. "Natalie, I need you to think. You seem driven to fuck and feed. I get caught up in it, too."

She heard what he said, but had difficulty focusing to really absorb why he protested his fate so much. Her body's needs ruled her. Didn't he feel the same way? Didn't he share the elation—the passion that even now unfurled inside her?

That thought brought her up short. *It can't be happening this quickly again!* The acknowledgement had a sobering affect. When he looked at her again, his steady gaze only underlined the fact she was reacting to something she had no control over.

She had no real power here. She was ruled by her body and the moon—and *submitting* to her hungers.

"You can't have me," Rene said, his face hardening. "I'm not here of my own free will . . . and I would never choose you."

Natalie swallowed the bile rising in the back of her throat. The hope she hadn't even realized she harbored splintered like brittle glass.

"He's lying, you know," Nicolas said, wicked delight in his tone.

Chessa lifted her shoulder to shrug off Nicolas's hand as he played with a strand of her hair. She stood in front of the table with the row of monitors—all trained on various views into the chamber Natalie would share with Rene over the coming days.

The monitor she stared at gave a view of Rene chained to the bed that had ignited a slow burning fire deep inside her. His body, gloriously naked, was stretched, his sex the only part of him not horizontal.

"His cock says he's lying," Nicolas said, his words gusting softly into her ear.

She suppressed a frisson of awareness that raised the fine hairs on her neck. Rene was the man exciting her—never Nicolas! "Think I don't know it?" Chessa couldn't stop staring at Rene's gorgeous cock. Still glistening from his cum and Natalie's juices, his erection jutted above his belly.

She'd always known Rene would be a well-hung stud, but her gut clenched at the thought she'd never feel its bite. Her stomach had churned while Natalie had lovingly licked him like a lollipop—her own mouth had watered at the sight.

As though he read her mind, Nicolas pressed the long ridge of his cock against her hip. "I was going to tell you to wipe the drool from your lips—but I'd rather put it to better use."

"Cut it out," she said grumpily and turned down the volume on the speakers. She'd heard enough. Seen enough.

Her mission was fulfilled. She'd delivered the new vampire and her life mate to the coven. They could monitor Natalie's progress—and make sure she didn't kill Rene.

"I was surprised to find you here," Nicolas said, his silky tone her first warning he wasn't giving up.

"Erika needed a break," she said, not giving him so much as a glance.

"So it had to be you?"

No, it didn't—they both knew that. "He's my partner. I wanted to make sure he was safe." What really irked was she'd been so intent on watching the couple make love, she hadn't even heard Nicolas's approach. Damn him for being there to read the desire on her face. She wondered how long he'd watched.

"She's got great instincts, our little Lolita. Did you see how she teased him? It won't be long before he's begging her to take him."

Chessa stiffened, fighting not to react to Nicolas's digs.

"And that mouth!" He groaned. "Rene's very lucky she already has a taste for his cum."

His low masculine moan drew her nipples instantly erect. "Shut up, Nic!" Anger burning away her caution. "He doesn't have much of a choice, does he?"

He nestled closer, his warmth burning her from her shoulders to her toes. "Do you think he would fight his attraction if he were free?" he whispered. "That he might actually win—and choose you?"

How did he do it? How did he cut her right to the core? Chessa trembled with rage.

He tsked softly. "Bloodlust, especially the first taste, is a potent force. You should know."

Chessa's hands fisted. She didn't need the reminder. Watching the two inside the chamber had brought back her own bitter memories.

Watching had also stirred her lust. Rene's powerful upward, bed-shaking thrusts had soaked her panties. She had to get out of here. Had to find a meal and a fuck.

Nicolas's inhalation was soft, subtle, but she knew he caught a whiff of her arousal. "Let me feed you," Nicolas said, his hand smoothing around her waist and rising to cup her breast.

The flick of his thumb against her nipple, even through her cotton shirt, sparked a surge of lust that nearly buckled her knees.

*Not Nicolas!*

His other hand reached between her legs and cupped her through her jeans, massaging, grinding the ball of his palm into her pussy. "Just a quick fuck—and I'll let you drain me afterward. Let me feed you."

Not a slick line, but then, she didn't need much of an enticement to push her over the edge. Chessa sucked in air between clenched teeth, her body rigid with denial—but she widened her stance, giving him permission to continue. "You have such a way with words," she said, trying to keep her voice light, not let him see how much she needed this. "No wonder the women fall all over you."

"I don't need to charm—when I have this," he said, grinding his cock against her.

Shivering inside the circle of his arms, she closed her eyes and concentrated on the building sensations—not who was delivering them.

His teeth closed around the lobe of her ear and he bit.

She cried out, but burrowed closer to his body, her ass centering on his cock.

His hands got busy with buttons and her zipper. Soon, he was sliding her jeans past her hips, down to her ankles, only pausing to tug off her boots before drawing off the pants entirely and tossing them away.

Naked from the waist down, save for her panties and her gaping shirt, she felt at a distinct disadvantage. Her heart thudded loudly, waiting for his next move, which wasn't like her at all. Usually the one in charge, she waited on his pleasure, which should have rankled. Instead, eagerness flooded her.

When his fingers slid beneath the elastic band of her panties to delve between her lips, her pussy released a drenching wash of liquid that greeted his caress.

"Lovely, *Dieu*!" His clothed cock bucked against her ass, his fingers pinched her nipple hard, and he drove long fingers up inside her, stroking deeply, swirling in the moisture melting from her inner walls.

Chessa rolled her hips back and forward, over and over, the motion following the rhythm he set with his deftly stroking fingers. When her arousal began the climb toward release, she bit her lip and pressed the back of her head against his chest.

Suddenly, his hands left her and he pushed her forward, bending her over the console where the monitors rested.

One jerk and her panties tore away. She gripped the edge of the table and waited while the rustling of clothing behind her told her he stripped.

She pressed her hot breasts on the cool wood and dragged gulps of air into her lungs, trying to regain control, trying to break his lustful spell, but she nearly sobbed when his fingers glided down the crease of her ass and sank inside her cunt. "Fuck me!" she gasped.

One last rustle and Nicolas groaned behind her. His cock fell against her cool buttocks, hot and hard.

She rose on her tiptoes, straining higher to encourage him to come inside her.

He needed no temptation. His cock butted once against her slick folds, backed away and re-centered, then drove deep inside.

Chessa's mouth opened around a silent scream. Christ, how he filled her!

She waited for him to start the rocking thrusts she craved, but he leaned over her back.

"Does my size please you, Princess?"

Trapped against the table with his cock crammed deep inside her, she rolled her eyes. "I hate it when you call me that," she said, not liking the tremor in her voice.

"An answer, please. I won't move until you give it to me."

"You'll do," she gritted out. She should have known he'd never give her a straight fuck.

A soft tsk lifted the hair lying across her shoulder. "I don't like lies—or half truths. You have much to learn about me."

"I don't need to know anything except whether that cock of yours can do the job."

"That was crude, Chessa. Would you have me believe you're only using my body?"

"Asshole, get on with it!"

"I will. It will be my pleasure." He straightened, his cock surging deeper as he moved. His hands smoothed down her hips to her thighs. With a jerk, he lifted her off her feet and shoved her further onto the table.

Then he pulled out of her—slowly, inch by luscious inch—and Chessa's bottom wriggled, sure that now he'd give her what she wanted.

When he left her entirely, she raised up on her elbows to cast a furious glare behind her. "Quit with the games!"

"I'm not playing."

He cupped the cheeks of her ass and dropped to his knees.

"No!" she exclaimed, panic setting in. "I don't need that, Nic. Please!"

"You need to be pleasured—not just fucked."

"Don't tell me what I need, bastard," she shouted. "There are a dozen men in this compound who'd give me what I want and do a better job. You just happened to be here when I was horny."

"I know I'm your last choice. But one day you will beg me to love you, Chessa."

"I don't want love."

"You're a woman. Maybe one of 'The Born,' but at your core you're as needy as any female. Now, shut up."

Only being quiet was the last thing Chessa could manage. His lips closed around her clitoris and suckled. Chessa arched off the table, screaming for the first time in her life.

"I don't know 'xactly how this works," Rene said, his voice deepening with his urgency, "but I've only got so much blood. You'll kill me if you take too much."

The scents stirring in the air around Natalie—his musk, her arousal—teased her appetites. Her stomach burbled. "I wish you hadn't reminded me I'm hungry."

He blew out a frustrated breath. "At the rate you're feedin', there won't be much left of me."

The pulse at his temple throbbed, and her heartbeat quickened to match the beat. "I don't want to hurt you," she said, even as her nipples drew into hardened nubs. Her teeth lengthened inside her mouth. "But I don't think I can help myself."

"I think that's the point of our bein' here. Of me bein' chained. I can't fight you this way."

A creak sounded behind her, and she whirled in time to see the door opening.

A blonde woman carried a tray covered with a white linen cloth. "I should tell you up front," she said, her eyes and wide lips flashing amusement, "it won't do you any good to try to go through the door behind me. There's a guard in the hallway."

Natalie didn't return her smile. Despite the fact she was buck naked—she was too damn turned on to care. She straightened. "Why are we being held here?"

The woman's gaze swept over her, lingering for a long moment on her face. "It's for your own safety, Natalie."

Oddly, the woman's perusal didn't make her uncomfortable. She sensed no danger, no animosity or lurid interest coming from her. "What about his safety?" she said, lifting her chin toward Rene.

"He isn't nearly as important to us." The woman shrugged. "He's here to keep you company." She nodded to the tray. "I brought you food. You're going to need to keep up your strength. And there's enough on the tray for him, as well."

"When will you let him go?"

"Not for a while yet. You'll have to see to his comfort in the meantime. He's a stubborn one. They haven't had to use the manacles in quite a long time. Chessa suggested them last night, and I can see why. Nice choice." Her gaze swept him hungrily.

Natalie felt herself bristling at the woman's covetous stare. Not that she had any rights to him, but she didn't like the way the woman stared at the part of him that had so recently been crammed inside her own body.

"He needs a bath," Natalie said, irritation making her words sharp.

The woman's eyebrows lifted. "Shall I help you?"

"Natalie . . ." Rene's voice rose in warning.

Natalie shook her head. "I only meant bathing him without freeing him first will be awkward."

The woman gave her an amused smile. "Nice try."

Rene rattled his chains. "I wish the fuck you'd both stop talkin' like I'm not here. Where the hell is Chessa? I want to talk to her now."

"She's . . . occupied at the moment."

Her secretive smile had Natalie wondering what she meant.

"She will see you later," she said, giving him a last appreciative glance. "Be patient. We don't mean you any harm, Lieutenant Broussard. This really is for your own good."

"Who are you?" Natalie asked.

This time, the woman's expression looked a little brittle. "There will be introductions, again, later. Enjoy yourselves. If there's anything you need . . ."

"A key?" Rene growled and rattled his chains one last time.

A slim eyebrow rose in amusement. "Short of a key. You have only to knock on the door and someone will come."

Natalie tried again. "Why are we here?"

The woman glanced back over her shoulder, her mouth pursing as though she wanted to say more. "Natalie, embrace the changes that are occurring inside you. Don't question too closely . . . for now. When the time's right—"

"But I don't understand what's supposed to happen here."

With a hand on the doorknob, the woman's features tightened, her eyes appeared to glitter. "Sure you do," she said, her voice even, yet oddly lilting. "Follow your instincts."

Natalie instantly felt soothed, reassured.

"Feed your hunger. Can't you already feel your body growing stronger?"

Natalie stood still, absorbing what the woman was saying and trying to read what she hadn't.

"Eat all the food on the tray and try to limit the amount of blood you take from Rene. You don't want to kill him . . . yet."

# CHAPTER

# 8

*You don't want to kill him . . . yet.*

After the woman left, the words swirled around the room, like a noxious cloud.

Natalie felt chilled by them, but only for a moment. She found it hard to hold onto the alarm that skittered down her spine, plucking at her, to heed their warning. Already the warning faded, replaced by her heightened sensitivity to the man lying behind her on the bed.

Every rustle of the sheets as he shifted to ease an ache, the scents of sex and his sweat, even the faint sound of his heartbeat—something she just realized she could hear quite clearly.

How interesting . . .

Natalie was reluctant to look at Rene. Naked

and restrained—he was a potent stimulant to her hypersensitive libido. She could feel his blistering glare. "I guess we wait after all," she said quietly.

The chains rattled—his way of making his frustration known.

The sound made her smile.

"You didn't try very hard to get me out of here," he growled.

"What did you expect me to do? Tackle her to the ground? Then what?"

"I'm being held against my will!" he shouted. "And what the hell did she mean by 'don't kill him . . . yet'? Fuck!"

His anger reacted explosively with her desire. Already she could feel her teeth sliding down. He'd been brought here expressly for her. All his straining and thrashing against his bonds only increased her arousal. Fluid, slick and hot, trickled down to wet her thighs. She would have him.

Without looking back, Natalie straightened her shoulders. "Rene, I'm afraid we haven't any choices here." She shut out any empathy she felt for his predicament. A stealthy, twisting thought rose in the back of her mind. He'd been willing to let Chessa take care of their "problem"—her. If he'd had the choice, he'd have washed his hands of her, walking away without a backward glance—more than willing to abandon her to her fate.

Although she didn't know precisely what her fate entailed, she felt the changes the blonde woman had mentioned happening inside her. Besides the physical ones, she knew she wasn't thinking the same way she had twenty-four hours before. She wasn't afraid anymore. She wasn't hesitant or shy about her body, her needs, or her enthrallment over his body.

He was here for her enjoyment, to feed her appetite, and completely under her control. But what did she want with him, really? The first blush of wild attraction had passed. That hot, all-consuming need to "know" him had been sated, but there must be so many more acts and sensual experiences to discover.

Already her body warmed—the delicious, wet heat seeped from inside her. She wondered if he could be seduced without a bite . . .

She took a deep breath to fortify herself and turned.

Rene's gaze had fixed on her like a fly on wet paint.

Faltering inside, the aroma of roasted meat gave her an excuse to look away again and think. She picked up the tray from the table and walked toward the bed. "Are you hungry?"

His face closed up tight, his lips thinning, the muscles of his jaws flexing. He turned his head away.

His rejection stung—every time he did it, the wound felt fresh and raw. And it pissed her off.

Until she realized, she was just a convenient target for his anger. He couldn't take out his frustrations on the commandoes who had spirited them away, so he struck out at her—in the only way he'd allow himself.

That empathetic realization faded, too. The next moment, she wondered why she stood with a tray in her hands when they both needed sustenance. Her glance raked him and her breath caught, inspired anew to explore every inch of him. How easily she was drawn back again and again to pure, animalistic responses.

Brawny, defined musculature. Tanned, olive skin except for the pale stripe across his hips and groin. Crisp, curling dark hairs rose like a thin cloud across his chest, arrowing down his abdomen. Lord, his body was beautiful.

Even his defiant profile pleased her. Rough edged with dark stubble along his jaws and chin, wholly masculine.

"Get the fuck away from me."

This time she took no offense. As acutely tuned to his body as she was, she knew her own must have some appeal for him to feel threatened by her proximity.

She pulled the cloth from the tray and smothered a laugh. Rare steak, cut in bite-sized cubes so utensils weren't required. Melted cheese in a pot flavored with flecks of green and red bell peppers and the subtle scent of cayenne for her to dip the meat.

Finger food—playful food.

She swirled a finger in the hot cheese and brought it to her mouth. "Are you sure you're not hungry? I'll feed you."

His lips thinned, his defiance revealed in the straight, rigid lines of his body.

She shrugged. "I'm famished." She popped a piece of the meat into her mouth and chewed, closing her eyes to savor it. "You know," she said around the mouthful, "I'm as much at their mercy as you are . . . well, except for the chains. You could be a little nicer."

Rene's breath huffed, and he refused to speak.

Hurt mixed with anger at his rejection had her thinking that perhaps he needed reminding just how vulnerable he was. She placed the tray near the bed and climbed onto the mattress beside him.

He growled—an edgy sort of sound that only challenged her more.

She stuck her finger into the steamy cheese again and brought a dollop to his nipple and rubbed over it in a small circle.

Air hissed between his teeth. It was hot, but not hot enough to burn his skin.

She leaned over him and lapped it away with her tongue, finding the treat so much more delicious when flavored by his unique taste. "Is it too hot?"

Already she could see the tension that tightened his belly and thighs as he tried to reject her. But the little points of his nipples—stiff and erect as her own—told her not all of him was falling into line.

"Just try to resist me," she said softly. She put the tray down on the bed and picked up the pot of cheese. Then sitting cross-legged beside him, she began to paint his cock.

His shaft twitched, and his breath hitched. She guessed the heat and the pepper must sting his most sensitive parts—but she had his full attention now.

His cock jerked each time she trailed a finger along his shaft. His sex expanded and straightened, pointing toward the ceiling. As his erection grew, so did the angry tension that flexed his powerful shoulders and chest.

She smiled at his fury and continued to work, taking her time to stroke on the creamy treat.

When the upper part was coated, she leaned down and licked him, from base to head—long luscious laps, eating the cheese from him, curling her tongue around the ridged head so as not to miss a spot.

When she tongued the tiny opening at the center, she opened her eyes and glanced up into his face.

He stared back, rage and naked lust warring in his gaze.

She tilted her head and used her teeth to strafe his length, letting him see her fangs. She wanted him worried, although she was careful not the draw blood with the razor-sharp tips.

When she reached his soft crown again, she chewed it, causing him to jerk in alarm. She drew slightly away, letting her hair fall against his balls to tease. "You know, you really are going to need a bath," she said, keeping her tone lazy. "Would you like me to do that for you, Rene?"

"Get away," he said, his voice ragged.

"Is that really what you want?" she asked, reaching between his legs to cup his balls.

Air hissed between his teeth, again. She painted his taut testicles with the cheese then drew them into her mouth and suckled until his thighs trembled.

When she'd finished her snack, she released his sac and grasped his shaft in her hand, pumping slowly up and down. The heat of his skin and the humid moistness she'd left behind created friction that burned and had his hips rolling to stroke his cock inside her curved palm.

Keeping her grip firm, she leaned closer to his cock, breathing in his musky scent, letting it build her hunger. "You know you aren't being fair to me. I'm not here willingly either. That's your fault. You gave me to them." She paused to lick the crease between his thigh and scrotum. "I think you're lying to yourself. I think you want this."

"Let go of me and get away," he said from between clenched teeth, only this time his command lacked any real fury.

She tongued his inner thigh, finding a throbbing pulse beat. She knew precisely where to bite.

When her teeth pierced his skin, his hips reared off the bed. "*Merde!* God, sweet, fuck . . ."

She gripped his cock hard in her hand and continued to slide up and down his shaft as cum spurted to stripe his belly and her hand.

When he finished, she crawled up his body and lay over him like a blanket, embracing his heat and his wet lies. She wrinkled her nose. "You know, you really need that bath now."

Rene eyed this Natalie with suspicion. The scared, lonely woman he'd comforted the night before had disappeared. Now, a woman with a feral expression stalked him.

To her, he was nothing more than a rare steak with a dick. He desperately needed her to remember who she was, lose whatever power trip she was on, or he was toast. "I don't understand how this is happening," he said, as she kissed his chin and rubbed her face against his sprouting beard. "I thought vamps were made by bein' bitten, but you're transformin' into one. Do you think it's possible to halt the process?"

She paused and her eyebrows rose. "Why would I want to? I'm stronger than I was."

"There are consequences. Do you wanna be a parasite? You'll have to live off blood—fresh blood. You won't be able to walk in daylight without the risk of fryin'."

She shrugged and ran a finger along his lower lip. "So I'll learn to love moonlight. I'm stronger. I'm in control."

The frown he aimed at her could have stripped paint, but she smiled, confounding him.

How could he make her understand? "You control nothing, Natalie. You can't even keep a handle on your desire. You fuckin' raped me."

"Raped?" Soft laughter gusted against his lips. Her smile was easy, not the least ashamed. "*Maybe* at the start, but you wanted it. You came for me." Her eyes narrowed, and she inserted a hand between their bodies, pushing it down between her legs. Moist, succulent sounds followed before she brought her fingers up to paint his lips. "Wanna taste how hard you came?"

The scent of their sex nearly undid him. However, the stubborn tilt of her chin kept him on task. "If I'd had a choice, I never would have fucked you," he ground out, hoping to wound her—anything to get her off him before his dick recovered. "From the first moment I touched you, something drew me to you. But it wasn't natural. I'd never have chosen to be with you."

She flinched. He could tell his words pelted her like tiny stones. Her eyes lost a little of their flinty spark.

"Natalie, don't play their game," he pleaded his case. "We need to get out of here. I need your help to do it."

Along with her shoulders, her gaze dropped. "Why should I help you?"

"I saved your life."

She blinked, as though rousing from a dream. "It's strange. But I almost forgot about that . . . I'm forgetting about anything . . . before."

"It's this place. It's us in here together. But we have to fight it. We have to get out."

Her eyebrows drew together, and she shook her head. When she rose to straddle his hips, his heart pounded. Was she going to take him again—because dammit, he wouldn't be able to fight her allure.

Instead, she slid off his body, still not meeting his gaze. "I need a bath."

Rene gripped the chain and pulled with all his might, but it didn't budge.

Watching Natalie withdraw, first inside herself, then into the bathroom ate at his gut. Not that he hadn't meant every word he'd said. He just wished he hadn't hurt her.

She'd started this journey as an innocent. Even now, after everything she'd done to him, he knew instinctively she hadn't any more choice than he did.

However, time was running against him. The longer he spent in her company, the more certain he became that he was a dead man if he didn't find a way out.

First, he had to get out of these cuffs. Trussed up like a Thanksgiving turkey, he was at a decided disadvantage every time Natalie's libido kicked into high gear.

He had to figure out a way to keep her far away.

The sound of running water slowed, and he could imagine her lying in the tub, water covering her body to her shoulders, the scent of perfumed bubble bath hanging in the air. His body hardened, as he imagined how sweet she'd smell, warm and moist coming from the water.

Lord, he couldn't seem to veer from the topic of sex any more than she could. Only, she didn't have any incentive not to follow her hunger. He did. He didn't want to die.

Maybe they intended for her to turn him like the poor bastards who hung out in the blood banks just outside the French Quarter. He'd watched Chessa stop for a bite on a couple of occasions when her hunger made her too grumpy and edgy to be safe to be around.

She'd disappear into one of the seedy backrooms for a while, only to return with a haunted look on her face.

For the first time, he wondered how Chessa had become one of the walking dead. Funny, he'd never thought to ask. Had she been like Natalie? Alone and confused? Hunted by unnatural creatures and not understanding the changes occurring inside her?

If he ever got out of here, he'd make damn sure he knew.

Natalie sank below the surface of the water and stared through the water at the ceiling. Maybe if she held her breath long enough, she'd just fade away.

She'd forgone the array of bath salts that lined the ledge next to the large claw-foot tub. She didn't want cloying scents to lead her thoughts down another tempting path.

All the changes occurring inside her hadn't made a damn bit of difference in her life. She was still alone.

Rene was right. She needed to get out of here. Return to the French Quarter and her search for her mother.

When she'd first discovered evidence of her adoption amid the papers in her father's lock box, she'd felt betrayed somehow. Like her whole life had been a lie. Neither her birth mother's nor her father's name appeared on the document. However, she knew where the adoption had been recorded—New Orleans. She also knew her true birth date. With those clues to work with, she'd come here determined to find her family.

But now, knowing what little she did about herself, she realized the Lamberts had likely protected her all along. The mother she thought had abandoned her at birth might actually have done her a favor.

The menace stalking her in Memphis had followed her here. How much sooner might it have found her if she hadn't been hidden amid the normal trappings of a human family?

Her lungs burned and finally she gripped the curved edge of the tub and hauled herself up. She didn't want to die. She still had a purpose. Two actually, if she counted thwarting her stalker.

She'd like to forget him. For long periods over the last twenty hours, she almost had. The muzziness that had followed the blonde woman's suggestions dissipated, and she realized she might have been under some hypnotic spell—the same as she'd received the night she'd been taken by the dark Frenchman from Rene's bedroom.

Their low, seductive urgings had fed right into her fantasy of having Rene for her own.

With Rene, she felt safe. Even chained, he radiated strength of will and a steely confidence. She'd like to aspire to an ounce of his courage.

But he didn't want her—didn't want the trouble that having her would entail. He thought her a freak of nature. A parasite, he'd said.

Well, he needn't worry again that she'd drain him dry. If she had to suck on steak for the rest of their imprisonment, she'd give him what he wanted—his freedom and his life.

She owed him that much.

Rene didn't realize he'd dozed until the mattress sank beside him. He jerked awake to find Natalie kneeling beside him, a basin of steaming water held between her hands.

One glance and he knew something had changed.

Gone was the sly, sensuous creature that had tempted him beyond his ability to resist.

A subdued aura of sadness clung to Natalie, as her glance met his then darted away. "I know you're going to object, but let me do this for you. Afterward, I'll see about someone helping you relieve yourself."

Her blush confirmed that whatever had had a grip on her was gone, at least for now.

"I'd like that," he said softly. "Whatever was in that cheese is still burning my skin."

Her lips curved at the corners. "Cayenne pepper."

Relieved to see that hint of smile, he drawled, "That wasn't very nice of you."

"At the time, I thought you deserved it."

He relaxed, sensing no imminent threat to his manhood, and gave Natalie a reassuring smile. "Don't be shy now. It's not like you haven't touched everything I have already."

She blinked. "I can think of a couple of places . . ."

His lips stretched wider into a rueful grin. "Don't go there."

Her cheeks bloomed with color. "I won't. I promise."

He liked the light teasing and relaxed a little further against the mattress. "My arms are killin' me. Is that water as hot as it looks?"

She nodded and waited for his response.

"Start with my arms and shoulders then, before it cools. Wring out the cloth and just lay it on the muscle."

She did precisely that, following his direction, letting him take the lead. In a way, giving him back a measure of control.

As heat penetrated his sore muscles, he studied Natalie. Her pose was non-threatening, submissive even, but there were clues her body wasn't truly subdued.

As she reached over him to lay another cloth on the opposite shoulder, he noted her nipples had spiked, the areolas a bright, hectic pink—a sure sign of sexual excitement.

She swallowed, the sound audible as she stretched the fabric to cover as much of his shoulder and upper chest as possible. When she sat back again, her breaths were shallow. A pink blush flooded her forehead and cheeks.

Her smell was the clearest indication of her growing arousal. Beneath the fresh soap and water scent that clung to her skin, the faint, lush smell of her musk rose to tease his nostrils.

His groin tightened, his balls drawing up hard as hockey pucks, his cock jerked in time with his heartbeat—filling so rapidly his teeth ground against the urge to rut upward.

Natalie swallowed, holding his gaze for a long moment. "Remind me . . . *often* . . . why we shouldn't do this. I'm starting to shake."

"Because I want to live, Natalie."

She closed her eyes and drew a deep breath. "It's not working."

"Put a cloth between your legs."

She blinked again and reached for one of the cloths draped across his skin and plunged it into the water. She didn't even wring it dry before she balled it up and stuck it between her legs. Her breath hissed and as her lips drew back, he saw her teeth glide into place.

When she opened her eyes, the feral hunger was back.

Rene made a quick choice, knowing things were going to get out of hand in a heartbeat. "Put the cloth in your mouth and straddle me, baby. Fuck me—but bite the cloth."

Natalie pulled it from her crotch and opened wide, biting down so hard water gushed onto his belly. She swept away the basin to the floor with a splash and climbed over him.

Her fist closed around his cock and pointed it right at her entrance. Emitting a strange, breathless wail, she sank, circling her hips to work him quickly all the way inside.

Surrounded by heat and her strong, clasping muscles, his cock felt moments from explosion. He wished he could grip her hips and force her hard against him. He wanted to fuck her deep and hard, pound away at her pussy. Natural or not, he'd never been so far gone. He didn't care about the why—he needed release. Now. "I'm gonna come fast, baby. Move!"

He didn't wait for her to adjust, he arched his back, seeking as much leverage as he could manage, pressing shoulders and feet into the mattress. He pulsed against her, driving shallow thrusts to aid her movements.

She planted her hands on either side of his shoulders and worked her hips, pumping up and down, grinding hard when their pubic bones met, clamping her inner muscles so tight that when his orgasm did begin to jet cum inside, she milked him, dragging her pussy along his dick, squeezing so hard he gritted his teeth against the need to shout.

"Fuck!" he gasped, almost blinded by the strength of his orgasm. His whole body convulsed, shuddering as he spurted inside her again and again.

She spat out the cloth and rubbed her tongue across the tips of her teeth. Red tinged her teeth, and he realized she'd cut herself rather than feed off him. She swallowed hard and closed her eyes as she circled her hips, grinding down. At last, finding her own release.

When she slumped against his chest, he wished he could have folded his arms around her and hugged her close. "Thanks."

She nodded, dragging deep breaths into her lungs. "You were there, too, weren't you?"

"Yeah, I get it now."

"It's not that I want to hurt you," she said, a hint of tears in her voice.

"I get it." He really did. This time their furious coupling had been mutual—evenly desperate. "We have to try to fight it. We're in this together."

She nodded and her hands slid along his chest and side to hug him.

Rene knew their fates were somehow bound to one another now. That knowledge scared the shit out of him.

# CHAPTER

# 9

Natalie finished bathing him and pulled the sheet up over his body—less tempting that way.

Rene had dozed while she quietly tended to him, and she'd been careful not linger over parts that would have aroused them both.

At the last, he'd confessed he needed to relieve himself.

Deciding to find out whether the woman had told her the truth, she wrapped the lacy throw around herself and approached the door. She knocked softly.

It swung inward almost immediately. The young man on the opposite side smiled politely. His gaze remained on her face rather than trailing down her scantily clad body. She appreciated his manners.

"I'd like someone to unlock Rene's handcuffs. He needs to go to the bathroom."

He nodded, the sides of his eyes crinkling in the beginning of a smile. "I'll see what I can do."

Seeing as he looked far from intimidating, she stuck her head out the door and peered to the left and right, curious about the rest of her prison. Just like her bedroom, soft colors—decidedly feminine ones—made up the décor. It looked like any other well-heeled Southern home. Hardly the kind of place to have a prison cell.

"Someone will be sent to help you," the young man said, a polite way to tell her to get back inside.

Natalie wrinkled her nose, but he just grinned. He was kind of cute—lean, tall, broad shoulders almost too wide for his slender hips. His hair was light brown, straight, curling at the ends where it met the top of his shoulders. Almost feminine. His nose helped tremendously to dispel any effeminacy—it was a little wide, with a bump at the top.

She wondered why she'd even noticed. Or why his scent, so different from Rene's, appealed.

"I'm not one of them," he said, "if you're wondering."

A blush heated her cheeks when she realized she'd been staring. "One of them?"

"A *Revenant*. I haven't been turned. The others like to nap during the afternoon."

"A *Revenant*? That's a kind of vampire?" She had so much to learn, but already her stomach burbled, distracting her again.

"Yeah." His head canted and his gaze sharpened. "If you're hungry," he said, his voice lowering to just above a whisper, "I can feed you. I haven't been tapped in a while."

"Tapped? You mean, like . . . bitten? You'd do that willingly?"

"Sure." He flashed a quick smile. His teeth were a little large and very white. "It's pleasurable . . . for both of us."

It dawned on her that he was so comfortable flirting because no one was likely to check on him. Could she somehow catch him unaware and arrange an escape? Excitement kicked up her pulse rate speeding warmth south. She pushed her hair behind her ear and leaned indolently against the doorframe. "Are you supposed to do that?" she asked, giving him a slow smile.

"Uh . . . actually, no." His hand braced against the wall next to her, and he crowded closer. "I'm not supposed to even talk to you," he whispered.

Perhaps, she could kill two birds with one stone. After all she'd be less tempted by Rene if she did have a little snack. "But you'll let me feed?" At his nod, she touched her upper lip with her tongue. "Um, how?"

"You just suck," he said, his voice purring.

She almost laughed and didn't bother hiding a grin.

He pulled aside the neck of his black T-shirt. "We'd better get out of the hallway. However, I keep the key to the door. No funny stuff."

"Sure. Nothing funny about it," she murmured. She opened her door wider and let him step inside, her pulse pounding at the delicious thought she could have him and escape, too. She hoped like hell Rene didn't waken before she'd had her fill, because she didn't know how she'd explain her compulsion.

She latched onto the young man's arm and pulled him into the room.

He turned to lock them inside and deposited the key into his pocket. When he straightened, he flashed a quick glance at Rene still sleeping on the bed and lifted an eyebrow.

She pressed her finger to her lips to tell him they'd have to keep quiet. She clasped his hand and pulled him deeper into the room. "You're too tall," she whispered. "Would you kneel down?"

He shrugged and knelt in front of her, just the right height for her to snuggle close to his neck. An eager supplicant.

Nervous about what came next, she lifted a shining strand of his hair to give her something else to concentrate on rather than his warm, male musk and sweet breath. "What's your name?" she whispered. "I think I should know since I'm about to eat you."

His white teeth flashed again. "Gerard."

"I like that." With her hands resting on his shoulders, she leaned over him and licked his neck, feeling with her tongue for just the right spot. When she found his strong, thudding pulse, she let her fangs descend and quickly punctured his skin.

His breath gasped, and then a low groan followed.

Thick, hot blood spilled into her mouth, almost too fast for her to swallow.

His hands reached for her hips, and she realized he was turned on by her bite—and that she was also becoming aroused. As he sank on his haunches, she let him guide her down onto his lap, spreading her legs wide to straddle him as she continued to drink.

His groans grew louder, harsher. His hands tightened and he pushed her forward and back on his lap, dragging her over the ridge growing at the front of his trousers.

With his clothed cock grinding into her sex, and his rich, delicious blood filling her belly, she let herself enjoy the moment. She pressed closer, tugging down the edge of the throw to rub her bare breasts against his chest. She couldn't get close enough, couldn't get her fill of him.

When his hands slipped away from her hips, she barely noticed.

The door slammed against the wall behind her, but she continued to feast and rut. Only when strong arms encircled her belly and squeezed the breath from her, did she open her mouth to gasp.

The red haze subsided. In its place rushed a dawning horror. The insistent throbbing between her legs dulled as she stared at the blood sluggishly streaming down the young man's neck to soak his T-shirt.

A hand gripped her jaw and forced her head to turn.

Chessa leaned close, disapproval drawing her brows down. "Lesson number one—you don't kill your meals!"

"He's dead?" Natalie asked weakly.

"He will have to be turned," said the man holding her against his chest—the Frenchman. "Lesson number two?"

Rene had rolled to his side as far as his chains would allow when he'd been woken by groans and gurgling sounds within the room.

Silent throughout, he'd watched Natalie astride a young man, dry-humping while she'd fed until he passed out. Hot fury at her betrayal seared through him. He didn't know why he hadn't let them know he was awake, maybe he'd been curious to see how far she'd take the other man.

When the door burst open and Chessa and a dark-haired man rushed inside, he lay back and pretended to sleep, curious to see what would unfold next.

He felt like he was watching his own fate play out. That might be him the next time Natalie lost herself in bloodlust.

Chessa knelt on the floor and propped the young man against her chest. "Natalie. *Natalie!*" she called again when Natalie continued to stare at the blood soaking his clothes. "Pay attention, we haven't time, his internal organs are shutting down. You bit him—you save him! Those are the rules."

"How?" Natalie croaked, unaware smears of blood remained around her mouth and chin.

She looked like a goddamn zombie.

"Open your wrist," the dark-haired man said. When she still didn't move, he brought her hand to his mouth.

A cry of pain had Rene wincing along with Natalie as her wrist was slashed and then placed to the mouth of the dying man.

But he didn't move. Didn't drink. His lips remained slack.

Chessa tilted back his head and pinched his chin to open his mouth wider. Then she rubbed his throat, trying to force him to swallow the blood.

Rene thought for sure the bastard had bought it. The blood pooled in his mouth and overflowed his lips. Chessa and the dark-haired man shared a tense, charged glance.

Finally, the younger man's hand twitched on the floor.

"That's it," Chessa crooned, stroking his hair as he started to drink. "What's his name, Nic?"

The dark-haired man's jaw tensed. "Gerard," he said, his voice thick.

"That's it, Gerard. Drink. You want to live, baby? Drink!"

Slowly, one tiny swallow at a time, he regained strength, gurgling at first as he fought down the blood dripping steadily into his mouth, choking, and then drawing ravenously against Natalie's wrist.

His parchment-pale features regained color until at last he opened his eyes and jackknifed out of Chessa's arms to curl into a ball, whimpering with pain.

"Nicolas, get him out of here, he'll need time to recover."

Nicolas put his arm beneath the young man's shoulders and hefted him into his arms to carry him out, leaving Natalie and Chessa kneeling there, blood trickling now from Natalie's arm into the carpet.

"Inanna's not gong to be happy," Chessa said, her gaze on the dark, stained carpet. Looking pissed off, her eyebrows nearly meeting, Chessa lifted Natalie's arm and placed her lips around the wound on the younger woman's wrist. She sucked and licked until the wounds closed.

Throughout, Rene had barely breathed, observing the transformation from dying to dead, and beyond. He shuddered at witnessing the birth of another unnatural creature and wondered how he'd ever look at Natalie quite the same way. She was no longer an innocent, but a demon.

Chessa turned his way and caught him staring. She must have read something in his expression, because she stiffened. "Natalie, go get a shower and stay there until I come for you."

Natalie, her face pale and fragile, followed the command like an automaton, shuffling toward the door and closing it quietly behind her.

Chessa dug into the pocket of her dark trousers and pulled out a key. "I think you know what's going to happen here now, don't you?"

"Cheech, get me the fuck out of here, now," he said, letting her see the tension and desperation in his face. "You know that's not what I want. You know I don't want to die like that."

Chessa leaned over him to unlock his handcuffs, one at a time. As she reached, her small, firm breasts rubbed against his chest.

Rene's arms were already screaming with agony. Too much so to fully enjoy the softness pressing against him. He was afraid to move his arms because he knew he wouldn't be able to hide his pain, so he kept them in place as she circled around the end of the bed to release his feet.

When at last the chains dropped to the floor, she lifted his foot and started to massage it, working her way up the calf, then helping him bend his knee as he gritted against the agony.

Her gaze averted from the part of him he couldn't control as he reacted to the ministrations of an attractive woman, someone he'd wondered about from time to time and had, in his weakest, horniest moments, considered as a sexual partner.

"Must be a bitch, not being able to hide a single thing you think," she said, as she gently placed his leg back on the bed and reached for the next.

His lips twisted in self-derision, not bothering to deny he was hard because she touched him. "Yeah, kinda makes a guy vulnerable."

She took a deep breath. "What you saw before—"

"I saw Natalie fuckin' kill that guy."

"*What you saw,*" she repeated slowly, "doesn't happen often. We have rules. We learn discipline."

He turned away his face.

"Usually, we only do that when we are asked, and only when someone's proven their loyalty to the coven. The reason Gerard was at that door was because we were ready to turn him and bring him into our security team."

Rene gave her an incredulous stare. "You aren't worried about the fact he disobeyed an order?"

"That's something we'll work on. We're not really worried about that—he was under the spell of our little Jezebel in there."

Under the spell? Was there more at work than just an attraction, something mystical? The thought encouraged him. He might be able to fight this.

"You wanna try sitting up?"

Rene blew out a breath and nodded.

Chessa put her arm beneath his shoulders and helped him to sit. He lowered his arms, gasping at the pain shooting through his shoulders and upper back. Once the worst had subsided, he opened his eyes and gave her a weak grin. "Now I really am gonna need to piss. And no, you're not holdin' it for me." He swung his legs over the side of the bed.

"Darn. You just crushed my dreams."

Rene laughed, and then groaned in agony when his feet finally met the floor, but he stretched, forcing blood into muscles that had been asleep.

He glanced down at Chessa standing next to him. Her glance slid slowly over his naked body. "You know, Cheech, if things had been different before I met you . . ."

She shook her head, a hint of regret shadowing her gaze. "I don't understand, Rene," she said, her face uncharacteristically somber and sincere. "I know your wife died in a car crash. Not by a vampire's bite. You have to let go of your guilt sometime. You deserve happiness."

He blinked hard and looked away. "Whatever. I still have to piss."

Her back straightened. "Come with me." Chessa led him out the room and across the hallway to another bedroom.

He glanced around another comfortably appointed bedroom. "What, no bondage equipment here?"

"No, we save that for assholes."

Glad the old Chessa snapped back, he gave her a crooked grin.

She opened an inner door and stood back. "Don't bother trying to go out the window. The grounds are patrolled by some really nasty creatures."

"Werewolves?"

"No, mastiffs." She gave him a saccharine smile. "You change your mind about me holding it?"

He narrowed his eyes and entered the bathroom, locking the door behind him. Although she could bust it down in a heartbeat, it still felt good to lock her out.

Chessa slumped against the wall and sucked in a deep breath. She could have waited a month of fucking Sundays for a day like this.

She'd been pulled away from her nap the moment Gerard was seen entering the bedroom. Natalie was way ahead of schedule. A chip right off the old block. Her mother had never learned to regulate her hungers.

The door clicked open and Rene walked out, still naked. He hadn't availed himself of any of the towels hanging from the rack. "Must be really comfortable in your skin," she said, dropping her gaze down the front of his body.

"It hardly matters. The whole point is for me to have sex with her twenty-four-seven—until I'm bat food."

"If things got out of hand, we'd step in."

"Like you did for old Gerard."

"That was unexpected."

As she escorted him back to his room, he hesitated at the door. "Are you going to chain me, again?"

"You gonna miss having an excuse not to give it up?"

His gaze narrowed. "Fuck you."

"You'd like that?" She lifted one brow to mock him. "Want us both?"

The force he used to open the door slammed it against the wall. She must have struck one helluva raw nerve.

Once inside the room, Chessa reached up and tilted back his head, surprising him with the strength of her fingers—she knew by the way he sucked in his breath. But he didn't step back out of her reach.

She traced the slight indentations left from his first bite. "I hate to tell you this, partner, but your life is forever changed."

"Nothing's changed—I'm just takin' a vacation. I'm goin' back to my life when this is over."

"You really think you can leave her—walk out of this house and not look back? You're bound to her."

"I'm not turned yet, and I won't ever be." The vehemence in his tone relayed a stubborn resistance to his fate.

"You'll beg for it in the end. The blood bond between a Born coming into her season and her first mate is strong—stronger than either of you. You don't need the cuffs anymore. You're already chained to her, tighter than any steel."

Rene's tense jaw and bunched shoulders didn't worry her a bit—he was fighting himself.

Chessa locked him inside the bedroom, without the manacles, just as another of Nicolas's team reported for duty at the door—this time a seasoned man, a vampire.

She gave him a nod and continued down the hallway, down the curved staircase, shoving the maelstrom of emotion roiling inside her deep down where it couldn't touch her. Where it wouldn't show on her face.

Dinner was being served in the dining room. There was no getting out of it. She'd taken so long with Rene, she was already late. Inanna'd had plenty of time to play with the seating arrangements.

She entered the dining room and quickly noted only two empty seats. All heads turned toward her, and she stifled a curse.

Candlelight lit the room from wall sconces and the ornate candelabrum placed near both ends of the long, ebony table. The place settings and the guests reflected Inanna's preference for ceremony. The long dining-room table gleamed, and the scent of beeswax lay beneath the savory aroma of roasted meats.

Everything looked so perfect and civilized. Succulent roasts, seared on the outside, bloody on the inside. Enough to whet an appetite, but nothing as garish as a blood-host sitting next to a vampire to supply the main course. Carnal appetites were meant to be appeased in private.

Inanna waved her to the chair beside her. "Come, dear. Come sit beside me. It's been so long, we have lots to catch up on."

Dragging her feet, she made her way toward the head of the table to the seat directly across from Nicolas.

Erika sat beside him, her blonde hair piled high. Small diamonds in her ears sparkled as brightly as her smile.

Everyone, it seemed, had dressed for the occasion, except her. If they didn't like it, fuck them. She wasn't going to play dress up. She wasn't here because she had any real choices.

Inanna had dressed in bronze silk that draped one shoulder and left one bare. Around her throat was her primitive carnelian cabochon with its carved phoenix on a braided gold cord.

Chessa remembered playing with it as a child as it dangled between "Nanna's" breasts.

Inanna's eyes sparkled with mischief. "So, it appears we have a new member of our family."

"Are we talking Natalie or the *Revenant*?" Chessa growled. At Inanna's disappointed moue, Chessa shrugged. "What? Should I call him 'the walking dead'? It sounds more polite in French."

"You've offended Nicolas," Inanna said. Her tone was soft, chiding.

"She hasn't offended me," Nicolas murmured, his dark gaze resting on Chessa.

She shifted in her seat, wishing he'd look anywhere but at her. She could still feel the bruises on her bottom where he'd gripped her hard as he'd taken her.

Inanna sat back, sly amusement glittering in the glance she swept between the two of them. "Ahhhh, I suppose any barbs she throws your way this evening will be deflected, *eh*, *cher*?"

Nicolas didn't comment, but the look he shot Chessa confused her.

There was no triumph, only a question.

One she wanted to avoid at all costs. *Would she seek him out again?*

# CHAPTER 10

Mercifully, Inanna veered the conversation another way. "Erika, what did you think of our baby girl?"

Erika's mobile face lit up. Her brown eyes and lips widened as she enthused, "Isn't she beautiful? I never would have expected blue eyes. I wonder where they came from?"

"Her father's side, perhaps," Inanna murmured, taking a sip of wine from her crystal glass. "It's not as though we knew that much about him."

Erika's smile dimmed, and she glanced away. "Well, it isn't as though he could introduce us to the rest of his family once he'd joined us. I suppose we will never know." She speared a bit of prime rib with her fork and popped it into her mouth.

Chessa's already fading appetite fled completely. Rene had no extended family. He was a perfect candidate for mating with a vampire. No blood ties to pull at his loyalties. Once he committed to Natalie, he would have no reason to regret the decision—nothing else to lose beyond his life.

"You aren't eating," Inanna said.

"I'm not much into nibbling."

"You're such a city girl now. Into all that fast food."

The others sitting around the table laughed, confirming in her mind that she was the evening's entertainment. They'd spoken only in hushed whispers since she'd entered, waiting for whatever amusing or shocking thing would come out of her mouth.

She'd thought a decade might have dimmed their memories.

She picked up her fork, deliberately choosing the useless salad fork and reached across the diner beside her to spear a slab of lamb.

Her cheeks burned at her rudeness, but she wanted to make a point. She didn't belong here. She wasn't staying. They were welcome to their civilized trappings—she lived the gritty reality of their existence.

"Did you see the way she went after Gerard?" Erika said, this time her voice hushed, almost awed.

"Perhaps she already has a reason for her precocious appetite," Inanna murmured.

The hand raising her fork stopped halfway to her lips. Chessa laid it back on her plate and placed her hands in her lap below the table, fisting them tightly out of sight.

A supreme act of will forced her to raise her head.

Inanna's gaze was resting on her, glittering, watchful—like a cat waiting to pounce upon a crippled bird.

Chessa met her gaze, emptying her expression of any emotion. Now, she knew Inanna's intentions for tonight's entertainment.

Inanna was destined to be disappointed.

"Do you think she's already pregnant?" Chessa asked, her voice carefully neutral.

"I'm not sure. But I will visit her tomorrow. As voracious as her appetites have become, it is entirely possible she has already conceived."

"You'll have to send me an invitation to the baby shower. Be sure she registers at Wal-Mart. Remember, I live on a cop's salary."

More laughter rang around the table, but Chessa didn't bother to give the others a quelling glance. Her gaze remained on Inanna's, answering her challenge.

Inanna took another slow sip of wine. "Her policeman is a surprise. Such a handsome brute of a man. Most young women would set their sights on someone . . . prettier and younger."

"He was just in the wrong place at the right time when her pheromones kicked in," Chessa murmured.

"It's a pity they weren't introduced first. It's always easier if a relationship already exists. And his age is a problem. He is mature enough and stubborn enough to resist her."

Chessa waited, knowing Inanna was getting to the point of this conversation. She demurred to fill the silence, "He is only human. Eventually, he will fall in line."

"If he already loves another, he might be strong enough to

fight her allure. I think we should offer him the choice. Don't you?"

Chessa held her breath, afraid to show a single weakness.

But Inanna wasn't finished yet. She sat forward, triumph in the glitter of her eyes. "If he has already served his purpose, perhaps you should take him home when you leave."

Chessa sat, fighting the urge to lurch to her feet. The bitch had read her interest in Rene and used it like a whip to strip her flesh from the bone.

Instead of giving her the reaction she wanted, Chessa nodded. "We'll wait until tomorrow. After you've determined whether she's conceived. If not, I'm not hanging around any longer than that. I have a job to get back to."

Inanna stared a moment longer, then shrugged and lifted her glass for another sip. The other diners took their cue and conversation resumed.

Beneath the table a foot nudged hers.

Chessa met Nicolas's gaze as he raised his glass in salute.

She'd survived Inanna's volleys without going ballistic herself. Maybe she had changed in more ways than one over the years.

Inanna looked toward the entrance of the dining room and a smile wreathed her features. "Ahhh, I'm glad you were able to join us."

Simon Jameson, Natalie's next-door neighbor, appeared in the doorway, his hair still spiked. His damnable bird perched on his sleeve. He'd dressed in casual khaki pants and white shirt, the sleeves rolled to his elbows.

"Please come join us, Mr. Jameson, and bring the bird, too. You can feed her from your plate. We don't mind."

Simon bowed to the group and took the last remaining seat. When he was seated, he gave Chessa a challenging glare.

"What's he doing here?" she asked Inanna, her tone deliberately belligerent.

"He called me." At Chessa's surprised look, she added, "He very astutely guessed her destination."

"Still doesn't explain what the fuck he's doing here. Thought his kind wasn't welcome here anymore."

"He's our guest, Chessa. Behave yourself," Inanna chided softly. "As he has knowledge of Natalie, he's here for us to pick his brain."

"I do apologize for being late," Simon said, giving Inanna an apologetic smile. "That storm's kicking up. There was a downed tree between here and New Orleans."

"You couldn't have left that damn lice trap at home?" Chessa bit out, impatient with the small talk and Simon's ingratiating good manners.

Simon lifted one brow, and his lips twisted in a tight smile. The bird ruffled its feathers and rubbed its head beneath his chin, all the while staring at her with its fierce golden eyes.

"You shouldn't insult Kestrel," he said softly, the warning cloaked in barely veiled menace. "She's very sensitive, you know. She doesn't like you very much."

"She doesn't know me." Chessa folded her arms across her chest and sat back in her chair.

"I think she does," murmured Nicolas, a hint of a smile curving his lips.

"So, what's with the glamour? You are among *friends*," Chessa said.

Simon sighed and waved an indolent hand in front of his

face. One moment he was the youthful video-store manager, the next a shimmer muted the sharp edges of his face, blurring blue and white, like moonstone, before reforming. Gone was the skinny young man with spiked hair and lazy, insolent features. In his place was the true Simon—the broad-shouldered warrior monk with light brown hair brushing his shoulders, and a moustache and beard framing his lush mouth.

Kestrel appeared to approve the change. She hopped up on his shoulder and nuzzled behind his ear.

Inanna clapped her hands in delight. "Lovely!"

"I'm gonna barf," Chessa said.

Inanna leaned forward in her chair, resting her arms on the table. "So tell us, Simon. Why your interest in our Natalie?"

"She found me one day while she was canvassing the French Quarter for a summer job. I found her shy, but highly intelligent. She walked into my shop and took an instant liking to Kestrel as Kestrel did to her, which piqued my interest. Kestrel is very discerning," he said, giving Chessa a bland glare. "We discovered an affinity, and I hired her to work in my shop."

"Did you know right away that she was Born?"

"Only after I knew her well enough to learn intimate details of her life and discovered she had the characteristics. I wondered how she had remained on the loose so long."

"It's a sad state of affairs," Inanna said. "When we fostered her out, we lost track. As you may know, we try to keep the locations of our progeny secret. Fewer opportunities for anyone to discover their whereabouts."

"It's a difficult path you travel these days."

"For us all, *non*?"

Simon bowed his head. Kestrel nipped his ear and he laughed, reaching for a slice of roast beef. For long minutes, he carefully cut the meat into strips, then lay aside his utensils. "How are things going between Natalie and her policeman?"

Chessa stiffened. "How do you know he's here?"

Simon's smile was cunning. "I could read the interest between the two back at the apartment. There was something charged, even . . . inevitable in the air. When I found feminine products in her bathroom the night of the break-in, I knew I needed to keep a closer eye."

"Were you keeping a closer eye yesterday when she was attacked by pigeons in Jackson Square?"

"Pigeons?"

Inanna cleared her throat, a pained look on her face. "Have you noticed any unusual occurrences around her recently?"

"Unusual? You mean, other than her coming into her season?"

"Yes, anything else . . . of a sinister nature?"

"No, but then again her season had only started."

Chessa knew she wasn't always quick to pick up on undercurrents—subterfuge just wasn't her way of getting things done. However, she noted the desperate way Inanna deflected the conversation away from the attack. Perhaps, she was reluctant to bring up directly the subject of the attack in front of the whole group—or maybe just in front of Simon.

"Will I be able to see Natalie while I'm here?" Simon asked.

Inanna nodded. "I think that would be a good idea. She likely needs comfort from someone she trusts."

He lifted an eyebrow. "Her policeman isn't providing that?"

"She 'killed' her first meal," Chessa broke in. "She's having difficulty controlling her bloodlust. Rene's a little wary of her now."

"Wouldn't anyone be?" Inanna said with a little laugh. The rest of the table chimed in, a nervous edge to their laughter.

Simon didn't comment as he fed Kestrel bits of meat that she plucked daintily from his fingertips.

Natalie listened to the sound of running water in the bathroom. She stood just outside the door, her ears tuned to the sounds inside, her nose drawing in Rene's scent. More than anything, she wished she could go to him and try to explain what he'd seen. But really, what could she say to make him understand she hadn't been herself? Did she really know who she was anymore?

A cleaning crew had come into the bedroom to do their best to clean the blood soaked into the carpet and to remove her bloodied throw. They'd freshened the bedding, too.

She'd had a shower while Chessa occupied Rene. She'd lingered a long time, scrubbing her body over and over, trying to rid herself of the scent of the blood. While it had horrified her at one level, it also seemed to hone her craving even more. So she'd scoured her skin to remove any hint that might tempt her to violence again.

When she came out of the bathroom, Rene shouldered past her without a word, locking the door behind him. Telling her just how soundly he rejected her and what she'd become.

She didn't blame him one bit.

What future could they share? She didn't really know him. He didn't know any more about her than he'd observed. What she'd demonstrated had to be frightening.

She didn't have any control over the changes happening within her, no control over the impressions she gave Rene, and no control over her growing attachment. She was beginning to need him, not just as assuagement for blood and sex. She needed his strong arms, the low rumble of his voice. She longed to see acceptance in his gaze.

Not likely to happen after he'd seen what a monster she'd become.

Before she'd bitten Gerard, she thought she could take a little sustenance from him and stop when she'd satisfied herself. But once she'd pierced his skin, drank his gasp and his blood, felt him harden between her thighs—she'd been lost.

She'd felt outside of herself, like she was watching another woman straddle him and grind her sex against him. All within a whisper's distance of Rene. What must he think? He hadn't been asleep the whole time she was with Gerard as she'd thought at first. Not by the condemning look he'd given her as she'd shuffled past him to the bathroom.

Exhausted beyond anything she'd ever experienced, she lay down on the bed and pulled the covers over herself. But she couldn't escape into sleep.

Not with the memory of the hunger or the life she'd taken so fresh in her mind.

The need to linger in that moment of purest ecstasy had drawn her, seduced her past her natural abhorrence of the act—allowing her to draw out the exquisitely pain-filled moment.

While she'd held Gerard in her fierce grip, she'd felt his orgasm as though it had been her own, seen the blackness that devoured his thoughts grow like a large nimbus cloud to fill his mind, felt him falling toward it until he'd ceased to exist on any plane.

Never mind that Gerard was recovering, or so the team had told her as they cleared away her mess. But she hadn't known when she should stop or understood what needed to be done to save him in the end.

If she could do this to a total stranger, how might she behave if she were making love to Rene? Would she stop herself the next time?

She sat up at the side of the bed and eyed one of the manacles Rene had been forced to wear. With a shaking hand, she slipped it around her wrist and closed it.

While the others lingered over drinks, Chessa excused herself to follow Nicolas as he headed back toward the security barracks.

Outside, the wind had whipped up, tearing at her hair as she moved swiftly down the graveled path through the garden, past the gazebo, and beyond to the old horse stables that had been converted for the team's use.

As she passed through an arbor gate, a dark figure stepped out of the shadows.

"Are you following me?" Nicolas asked, his low, rumbling voice nearly carried away on the wind.

Chessa's breath caught. The storm building around them hadn't a tenth of the ferocity of the one growing inside her. Dinner had scraped her emotions raw. "I—" Her throat closed around her words, forcing them back. Why had she followed him? She didn't want to look too deeply inside herself for that answer.

"Why are you here, Chessa?"

He wanted to hear the words, but her tongue refused to form them. Tears filled her eyes, and she blamed the wind that cut like a sharp knife.

Nicolas remained still, buffeted by wind that molded his shirt to his lean torso. He stood stoic and solid in a long night that threatened to unleash her inner demons and memories.

With an inarticulate cry, she launched herself into his arms, winding hers around his neck, climbing up his body, needing to be closer to take his strength, drink in his scent and essence until he filled her.

His arms closed around her, and his hands grabbed her buttocks in a bruising grip as he lifted her higher against his body.

The violence of their kiss ground her lips into her teeth, raising blood they both drank. Muscles like hardened oak flexed beneath her hands and within the tight grip of her thighs.

Nicolas drew back his head and dragged air into his lungs. "I want you," he said, his voice raw with need.

Chessa drew a ragged breath. "Take me."

"Here."

"God, yes."

He walked with her deeper into the garden to a raised grass-covered bed and knelt, lowering her to the ground with a hand cupping the back of her head.

Chessa still held him in the circle of her arms and thighs, unwilling to let him go. She reached up and kissed his chin, and then scraped her lengthening teeth along his neck.

"I want you naked."

She nodded and nipped his throat, drawing blood that she immediately licked away.

Soft laughter shook his chest. "You have to let me go."

"Nnnnnhh," she murmured against his skin, rolling her hips against him.

Nicolas grasped her hands and pinned them to the ground beside her head. He settled over her, letting his weight hold her still beneath him. When he had her attention, he shifted his thighs on either side of her hips and sat up.

His fingers made quick work of the row of buttons on her shirt. He tugged it from the waistband of her trousers, and then raised her up to strip it away. She didn't give him any more help with her pants.

Laughter, tense and harsh, gusted from him as he fought the button and zipper and then shoved her legs from his waist to draw her jeans down. His fingers plucked her underwear, tearing them away.

Then he stood and quickly stripped away his own clothes, until the only thing clothing him was the dim light from a faraway lamp.

Chessa lay still, her womb clenching around an empty ache, unable to look away. The moment felt charged, pregnant with promise. His dark, hooded eyes, so intent and piercing, thrilled her, opening a dam of moisture that flooded her vagina in liquid anticipation.

With the wind caressing their bare flesh and flashes of lightning to add to the fierceness of the moment, he knelt between her legs, his hands gliding up her sides and over her breasts to plump and caress them.

His mouth closed around one spiking nipple, and Chessa

cried out, arching her back to drive it deeper between his lips.

He suckled and tugged, until her legs moved restlessly along his sides and her head thrashed side to side. When he gently chewed the peak, she keened and urged him to the other nipple.

Nicolas licked his way across her chest, curling his tongue around the ripened bud, flickering it with his tongue then suctioning hard.

Chessa's pussy tightened, cream seeping from inside to ready her for his invasion. She dug her heels into the grass and lifted her hips to rub against his hard shaft, inviting him to take the plunge.

But he released her nipple only to glide his mouth down her belly, pausing to nip the curve of each rib, sucking her skin to raise love bites along his path to her mound.

Her belly quivered with each shallow breath she struggled to take. "Nooooo!" she gasped.

She'd known he wouldn't go straight to the finish. And in her soul, she gloried in his determination to wring every last gasp, every drop of cream from her body.

When at last the clouds released their rain, she opened her arms, letting them fall to the ground above her head in acceptance of his gift.

# CHAPTER
# II

Chessa stared into the stormy sky as rain began to fall. Cooler than the humid heat around them, drops thudded against her skin to shatter in tiny wet explosions.

Rather like the sensation of Nicolas's kisses that drew steadily nearer her pulsing cunt.

She spread her legs wide, unable to hide the trembling of her thighs.

As he bent over her belly, his hands caressed her legs. To soothe her? His touch did nothing to lessen the quivering that had her jumping, gasping as he tongued her belly button, rimming it with the hardened tip of his tongue. When he pressed the button at the center, it was as though the spot were an ignition switch.

She half-raised off the ground, crying out only to fall limply back to earth when he roamed lower.

"Easy," he crooned. "Sweet, so sweet." He slid his lips across her lower abdomen, nipping the skin between his teeth, then soothing it with a lazy lap of his tongue.

Chessa thrust her fingers into his thick hair and tried to guide him lower. Her pussy pulsed to a slower beat than her heart, opening, gasping like her mouth, clasping air. Dewy cream slid from inside her, trickling down her cunt between her buttocks to waste itself in the grass beneath her bottom.

When at last he touched her swollen outer labia, she tried to hold herself very still, hoping not to distract his attention from the center of her torment.

He spread her plump lips and licked the edges of the thinner pair between, teasing her with occasional forays that delved into her opening, only to dart away again.

A thick, calloused thumb drew back the hood cloaking her clitoris, and he blew air over the hot, engorged knot, causing her belly and thighs to spasm and tighten. Then he drew her thighs over his shoulders and cupped her buttocks to bring her closer to his mouth. Her fingers tugged hard on his hair, trying to guide his mouth to her clit to ease the ache quickly consuming her mind.

When at last his lips closed around the knot of bundled nerves, Chessa issued a strangled scream as her pussy convulsed with the first spasm of an orgasm. He held her still as she writhed against his mouth, drawing out the moment with the increasing suctioning of his mouth.

When she lay spent, sobbing, only then did he rise over her and thrust his cock deep inside her.

He lay on top of her, shielding her from the rain from chest to toes. He kissed her, his lips softly gliding over hers. Then he rose on his elbows to look into her face. "This is how I want you. Always. Spent. No strength to argue or throw up barriers. Mine."

Chessa blinked against the rain and the intensity of his stare. She shook her head. "I c-can't. I don't love you."

His smile held no trace of humor and his gaze seared. "We have forever to correct your misapprehension." With that, he thrust his knees between hers and pulled up her hips on either side of his, arranging her for his pleasure.

"For now, remember this." He drew out his cock and slammed back inside her. Again, he pulled out and thrust back with more force, his cock driving toward her womb, each thrust that followed harder, sharper, driving the air from her lungs with each deep stroke.

His anger rolled off his body in hot waves that threatened to drown her in remorse. But the friction he built inside her reignited her passion, and she ground her heels into the mud to parry his thrusts, working in opposition to stoke the flame higher.

His shoulders bunched beneath her hands, his breaths gasped between his clenched teeth, and still he hammered harder, pistoning against the cradle of her sex, his fierce thrusts shoving her across the bed of grass, until she splintered, shattering into a thousand shards of brittle glass, keening as she was thrust beyond herself into darkness.

When she opened her eyes, Nicolas glared down at her, still seething with anger although his slowing motions told that he too had found release.

"Why are you so angry? This is all we can have," she said. "I won't stay here. You won't ever leave."

"You don't love him."

She didn't pretend not to understand who he meant. "How can you know that?"

"Because you didn't seek him out when you were hurting."

"I'm not hurting!"

He shifted and slowly withdrew from her, closing his eyes briefly when his cock slid completely free. "No? That wasn't pain that nearly knocked me off my feet?"

She lifted her shoulders, pretending a nonchalance she couldn't really feel when he surrounded her still. "It's just sex, Nic. That's all."

His gaze nailed her to the ground beneath him. "Then why didn't you drink from me?"

Damn! She hated his perception. "You think that means anything?"

"*Not* drinking certainly does."

Shock at his perception took her breath away. Like a whore who refused to kiss, she'd held back a part of herself.

Nicolas's breath huffed and he shook his head as though clearing away a fog. He rolled to the side and lay with the rain washing his body. After a long moment, he turned his face toward her and offered her a crooked smile. "I didn't mean to spoil the moment."

Chessa blamed the rain for moisture filling her eyes. He'd backed off for now. Given her space when he could have pushed and maybe forced her to admit more than she was ready. She rewarded him with at least part of the truth.

"You didn't spoil a thing. Knowing you give a damn means a lot."

Rene paced the bedroom, too edgy to rest. He did his best to ignore Natalie huddled beneath the covers on the bed.

He knew she was awake. Her breaths were too shallow. But he didn't care about her deception, was glad she didn't want to talk, didn't even look his way. His cock already tented the towel he'd slung around his hips after the shower he'd taken when Chessa left.

For whatever reason, close proximity to Natalie equaled arousal.

The fact she lay still and silent with the blankets up to her ears caused him a pang of sympathy, but he didn't care enough to do anything about it. Certainly didn't want to get into bed with her again.

To keep his mind busy and off the ache in his groin, he circled the room, looking for any possible means of escape. He wasn't going to wait for anyone to spring him. The longer he remained here, the better the likelihood Natalie would take another bite. If he didn't put some distance between them, his days were numbered.

Unfortunately, the soft, feminine-looking room had reinforced concrete walls, a solid oak door, and steel bars over the windows. Digging a tunnel out of this prison wasn't a possibility.

Which meant he had to go out the door. With only a towel around him.

Rene smothered a curse as he circled the room one more time, wishing he could break something, but not wanting to alarm Natalie. Just for the satisfaction, he lifted a lamp and hefted it like he was going to send it smashing against the wall. He wound up like a baseball pitcher—he was midway through the mock-toss, when he noticed something dangling from the base of the lamp.

He held it up closer, his blood starting a slow boil when he realized what he was looking at.

It was a goddamn camera—the kind vice cops used when setting up a sting. A tiny lens on the end of a cable.

He set the lamp down quickly, hoping he hadn't already given away the fact he was onto them. He circumnavigated the room again, this time more slowly, pretending to stretch his muscles and never letting his gaze rest too long on one spot when he found another lens.

By the time he'd finished, he'd counted five. Fuck! Every word they'd spoken, every time they'd screwed, someone had been watching. Rene fought the urge to curl his hands into fists, but he couldn't fight the simmering rage.

He wasn't so much angry for himself as for Natalie. She'd paraded nude around the room, *explored* his body with an innocent fascination for their differences, *serviced* him with an enthusiasm that made his body ache every time he closed his eyes, *fucked* him with a quiet desperation that tugged at his heart—even when he refused to acknowledge any feelings existed at all.

She didn't deserve this, but she did deserve to know.

He approached the bed intent on telling her. When he got close, he noticed the chain snaking up the side of the mattress, disappearing under the blanket beside her.

Fury flooded his body. "What the fuck do you think you're doing?" he shouted.

Natalie jerked up in the bed, the blanket pooling at her waist. Wide-eyed, all color drained from her face. "What?"

He planted his fists on his hips. "That goddamn handcuff! What's it doin' on your wrist?"

"I-I'm trying to protect you. If we are going to share the bed—"

"I'm taking the floor. Just give me a pillow and a blanket."

"But you don't have to this way."

"I can take care of myself," he bit out between clenched teeth. Her delicate wrist was already red beneath the metal cuff.

"Oh, really?" she said, her voice rising along with a flood of anger to her cheeks. "Like you had any choice coming here? Fighting me off? When I wanted you—I took!"

Anger burned white-hot inside him. It was all he could do not to put his hands around her neck and squeeze. "If I hadn't wanted to screw you in the first place, none of this would have happened."

"So you did want me." Her eyes shone.

Her response cut him short—doused the anger like a splash of ice water. The way she looked at him—her quiet intensity told him how important his answer was. Despite knowing it was a gross tactical error, he couldn't lie. "Yeah. I wanted you."

"Still do by the looks of it," she said, her glance dropping below his waist. A small smile tugged at her lips.

His cock jerked beneath the towel. "Some things I can't control. But now that I'm not chained, I can choose whether to act on it."

"What if I told you," she said, pausing to swallow, "that I'm doing this so you can choose me. For now."

Stillness seized Rene, holding him frozen for a moment. He could have her—for now—without risking his neck. His body hardened. "There are still two little problems," he said, staring at her mouth, fighting his building reaction.

"Oh!" She blinked and cleared her throat. "Um, stuff something in my mouth to keep me from biting. A gag maybe?"

The thought should have sickened him, but he wanted her too much not to consider the solution. "I'd have to chain your other arm, too," he said slowly, part of him not believing he was actually going along with her. "You might take off the gag otherwise."

"Do it." She lay down on her back and stretched her arm across the mattress to the other side. The movement pulled the blanket beneath her breasts.

Then he remembered the cameras. "There's one more problem."

"What? It doesn't matter, we'll find a solution."

He crawled onto the bed and leaned close to her ear. "They're watching us. I found hidden cameras all over the room."

Natalie's breath drew slowly inward and her eyes teared up as she stared back at him. "They saw everything?"

"Yeah." He smoothed back her hair then laid his palm along her cheek. "I'm sorry."

Her eyes closed and a tear leaked down the side of her face. "Rene?"

"Yes, *chère*?"

"Get away from me now. If you don't want to give them a show, move off the bed now." When her eyes opened, desperate longing tightened her face. The lust was rising fast inside her.

His balls hardened. His cock twitched. His breaths deepened as he realized he was quickly approaching the same point of no return. "Do you care what they might see?" he whispered.

She shook her head. "God help me, no! Fuck them. Fuck me, please! I can handle fighting only one of these hungers at a time."

There really was no choice. Not for either of them.

Rene reached beneath the bed for the second manacle and clamped it around her wrist. Then he emptied a pillow case and shredded it with his bare hands. He held up one long strip in front of her face and she nodded, opening her mouth.

He tied it tight. "Can you breathe?"

She nodded, her nostrils flaring, her chest rising and falling faster.

"Any bad moments, you make a lot of noise, you hear?"

A smile wrinkled the corners of her eyes and she nodded.

"Do we keep the blankets over us?"

She leaned up and rubbed her covered mouth over his. When she lay back, she shook her head side to side.

Rene's mouth stretched into a humorless grin. "Then let's make sure we fog up the bastards' screen." Rene pulled away the covers from her body and tossed them off the end of the bed. Then he sat back on his haunches and stared. He understood the temptation he'd posed for her.

Spread eagled, her body open and vulnerable to his whims, she was more than a temptation. She was a feast. And all his.

Her round breasts were stretched, nearly flattened by her arm's reach. The pink nipples already tight little points, spiking from the soft round pads of her areolas.

Skin stretched over each of her ribs, and her soft belly dipped between them and her woman's mound. He could start anywhere he liked, take her in whichever way he wanted.

A slow-burn heat pumped his muscles, filling him with an animalistic need to take and conquer. Is this what she'd felt? Christ, he could understand, his hands unclenched as he reached to cover her breasts.

She murmured behind the cloth, pressing her chest up and into his palms, inviting him to caress.

Rene pulled the towel from his waist and straddled her hips, hyperaware of her soft skin beneath his balls. He stroked his cock, watching her watch him as he gripped it hard and pumped.

Natalie wriggled beneath him.

"Want it, don't you? Want me fuckin' deep inside you, *chère*?"

She gave another feminine little murmur and arched her back, pulling at the chains.

"Rattle all you like. It's my turn."

He slipped his knees between her legs and leaned over her, rubbing his cock along her slick folds. He liked the wet sounds they made together. "Fuck me, you're hot."

He bent to tongue a nipple—just the tip, using the flat of his tongue to move it around in circles.

Natalie's knees rose up either side of his hips, and she ground her open cunt along his belly.

He cupped the breast he worked on, plumping up the side, enjoying the softness and the clean scent of her skin. He nuzzled her, breathing her in, using his tongue to taste and tease. The velvet-soft areola invited his kiss, and he sucked it into his mouth, drawing hard as she made those kitten sounds that turned him on like nothing he'd ever heard before.

He suckled and tugged, and finally, bit.

Her shrill little scream only encouraged him to torture her other breast.

Soon, her body writhed beneath him, bucking up, grinding hard. Perspiration dotted her forehead, and he reached up to lick it, using his weight to hold her down, reminding her who was in charge this go-round.

Her wild-eyed gaze pleaded for release, but he wanted more. Would accept nothing less than mindless want.

He scooted down her body and shoved up her thighs, exposing her sex to the cameras and his gaze. He rubbed his face and chin around her cunt, coating himself in her cream, scraping her tender flesh with his beard until she keened and begged, the muffled sobs only driving him harder.

When he licked between her slick folds, her hips jerked up, her thighs trembled around his head, cupping him, drawing him closer.

He needed no encouragement. The taste of her, the slippery feel of her pussy pressing into his lips and tongue tore groans from him which he muffled against her flesh.

One hand cupped her ass and raised her, so he could explore the soft and sensitive skin just below her folds. He sucked it, rubbed it with his tongue, and then licked lower to circle her delicate little asshole.

Natalie's whole body quivered with shock. She was coming unglued as he teased her and pressed his thumbs on either side of the tiny hole to slip the tip of his tongue inside.

Her head thrashed on the pillow, her body shivered uncontrollably. *Christ*, he was so hard he could drill a hole in the mattress if he didn't fuck her soon.

Rene slipped two fingers into her cunt and pumped them in and out while he continued to tongue her asshole.

Her vagina clamped around his fingers, squeezing, and his cock twitched and jerked. He drove it into the mattress, pumping the bed to ease the ache.

He thrust another finger inside and drove his fingers deep, her buttocks flexed, lifting off his cupped hand as she strained upward to take him deeper.

How much could she take? How much longer could he keep her on the edge and ease her higher without giving her release?

He licked his thumb and rubbed around her asshole, then slowly pushed it inside.

Her screams, shrill, broken, told him she was close. Her pussy pulsed around his fingers, but her breathing only escalated—didn't catch. He had more to go. Only his own arousal was impossible to ignore a moment longer.

He withdrew his fingers and kissed her pussy one last time, before hauling up and over her, settling his cock against her entrance.

He kissed her closed eyes and pulled back his head.

When her blue eyes blinked open, he said, "I'm gonna fuck you into oblivion. Ready?"

With her breaths ragged little sobs, she shook her head.

"Too bad," he whispered.

He reared back and knelt between her slackened legs, his cock fully engorged and pointing at her cunt.

Her wild gaze widened as he stroked himself. "You're gonna take it all. No holding back. Ready?"

Again, she shook her head and the trembling started anew, causing her soft belly to quiver and her thighs to jump.

"Too late." He shoved his arms under her thighs and hooked his elbows beneath her knees, lifting her ass off the mattress.

With her doelike gaze watching, he centered her pussy on his cock and drove his hips forward—all the way inside her.

She came. Her body undulated wildly even before he pulled out to thrust inside again.

He didn't care. He was past thought. Past control.

He hammered her cunt. Fierce, sharp strokes that tunneled his cock deep into her hot pussy. Her inner walls clenched around his cock like a wet fist. He forced feminine grunts from her muffled lips that echoed in the room with his harsher sounds.

When at last his thighs and balls tightened painfully hard, he shouted, his cock erupting deep inside her, cum jetting in powerful spurts to bathe her womb.

Afterward, he continued to rock against her limp body, unwilling to stop and lose the waning ripples caressing his shaft.

When at last it was over, he collapsed onto her, dragging air into his starved lungs. Drugged with sex, his muscles quivered with weakness.

He nuzzled the corner of her shoulder and kissed her, falling asleep in the next breath.

Once again, Rene had surrendered to his desire—acquiesced to Natalie's hunger.

Chessa watched him settle over, limp from exhaustion and

an orgasm that had racked his whole body. His shout at the end still rang in her ears.

After she'd showered Nicolas's scent from her skin and changed into dry clothes, she'd come back into the security control room. When Rene'd clipped the cuff around Natalie's wrist, she'd ordered the grinning guard from the room, unwilling to let anyone else witness their lovemaking.

She'd watched it all, her own body clenching, her pussy dampening as she stood transfixed by the look of unadulterated need that passed between the couple writhing together on the pale sheets. She hadn't been able to look away until Rene's flanks shuddered as he poured himself into Natalie—

—ripping apart the last of Chessa's dreams.

She resigned herself to leaving the next morning—returning to work without her partner. Once upon a time, she'd entertained the thought of taking him as her lover, a *complete* partner. She'd waited a long time to make sure he was strong enough, right for her. They shared so much in common—more than Rene could ever know.

They'd both suffered painful losses. They'd both foresworn ever loving so completely again. Yet here he was sinking deep into Natalie's web, thrusting into the depths of her body.

"If you love him, you will stay."

Inanna's voice jolted Chessa back to the present. She hadn't heard the ancient bitch enter the room.

"While the rest cosset our baby vampire, he will need a friend to guide him or he may not survive."

"Who said anything about love? He's just my partner."

"And that's why you can't take your eyes off him?"

"I'm just making sure she doesn't drain him."

"He is beautiful, *non*?" she said, her melodic voice a deepening caress. "Like a lion—all rippling muscle and roar."

"She's not woman enough for him."

"She will not be the same woman once she becomes what she is destined to be."

"And I could have gotten that bit of wisdom out of a fortune cookie. At least then, I'd get the egg roll first!"

"So much anger." Inanna's hand caressed her stiff shoulder. "Stay. One more day. If only to make sure in your mind you have lost."

Chessa threw a glare over her shoulder. "Cut to the chase, will you? You don't give a damn about me. You just want me back, so you can play with me—spider to the fly."

"I'm not sure what that means, but I see you don't trust me. You know, I only ever wanted what was best for you."

"You think throwing Nic in my path is best?"

"You think I have anything to do with that? By the way, he's spectacular, *non*?"

"He was convenient." Guilt hit her at her lie.

"If that was true, you wouldn't be so angry."

"Leave it, will you? I'm not staying."

"One more day. If only to make sure Rene stays safe. Besides, the storm outside only strengthens. You might be stranded on the road."

Chessa turned back to the monitor. Rene's hands cradled Natalie's body as he slept atop her, his sex still crammed tightly inside her.

"She will need blood. They will both need release. Perhaps you can tempt one while you feed the other."

For a moment, a ray of hope shone through the darkening clouds. Chessa bit her tongue at the woman's suggestion, rejecting it, not wanting to hold onto an impossible dream. They were bound. She'd lost.

A crack of thunder nearby rattled the windows, reminding her of the ferocity of the storm she'd already weathered.

"I'll stay. But only one more day."

Inanna's soft footsteps retreated.

No doubt she'd cackle to herself outside now she'd gotten her way. Chessa had once loved her, or at least the memory of what she had been to her a long time ago.

However, Chessa'd grown up, suffered disappointments, and sought a life outside the enclave. Inanna never stopped trying to draw her back. Her bribes were sometimes ridiculous, her vengeance vicious when she lost.

Chessa'd stopped trying to figure out what drove her when she realized it really didn't matter. Inanna never changed, but she had.

Not that there wasn't a greater purpose to be served if she stayed. But saving the human world from the demons that populated the shadows wasn't her thing anymore. That was Nic's mission. Hers was more prosaic. Serial killers, cop killers—that was her fight now. If every once in a while a case smelled like a creature-feature, she was in the right place to stop it before it reached the light of day and the front page of the *Times-Picayune*.

Rene's breaths had slowed and evened as he rested with Natalie. Soon his cock would wake him, drenched in a fresh wash of carnal cream, and he'd be driven again to fulfill his destiny. Could she bear to watch them make love one more time?

Perhaps Inanna's suggestion wasn't so improbable. The couple might need a little help to dull the edge of desperation. She'd stay one more day.

# CHAPTER 12

"Damn!"

Natalie awoke with a jolt. The room was dark except for a sliver of light from the bathroom door, and she wondered whether someone had entered while they slept, still joined, or had somehow remotely turned off the overhead light.

Not that she needed much light to see into the dark anymore.

Rene knelt beside her and thrust his hands beneath her head, struggling to untie the knotted gag. It eased and he dragged the cloth away. As she pushed the bunched fabric from her mouth, he stayed beside her. "Sorry 'bout that, baby. I fell asleep."

So had she. But despite the cottony mouth and the tightness around her jaws, she wasn't about to complain. Rene had forgotten himself inside her. He'd fallen asleep with his head pillowed against her breasts. Her arms screamed with agony for having slept in the same position for a couple of hours, but Rene's arms had cuddled her close.

He brushed back her hair with his fingers. "I'm going to get you a drink of water, then I'm gonna find someone with a key to take those cuffs off."

She nodded, watching as he retreated to the bathroom, her eyes clinging to his tall, sturdy frame. Then she ran her tongue over her teeth and determined she was in desperate need of a toothbrush.

When he returned, she lifted her head from the pillow as she drank. The water was less than satisfying—unlike the concern in his eyes.

He drew the covers from the floor over her body, and then went to the door and knocked. It opened a crack and he murmured to the guard outside.

Now that he'd done everything he could, it appeared he didn't quite know where to look, which struck her as funny given where he'd rubbed his face just a little while ago.

Natalie cleared her throat and swallowed to bring moisture to her mouth. "That worked nicely," she said, giving him a smile.

Rene's startled glance landed on her.

"The gag."

A slow sexy smile curled the corner of his mouth. "Yeah, it did."

She tried valiantly to keep her gaze glued to his, but however long they remained in each other's company she didn't think she'd ever get blasé about being naked with him.

Her glance swept down his body.

Everything about him was oversized. From his shoulders to his massive thighs and the heavy cock that even now rose from his groin as he stared back. "You have to stop lookin' at me like that, *chère*," he growled. "You'll have me worn down to a nub."

She blinked, not so much in shock for his coarse comment as for the wicked humor glinting in his eyes.

The door swung open and Chessa strode inside, a stack of clothing in her arms. Natalie didn't know her well, but the crimped corners of her lips and her unnatural pallor said something was wrong. She gave Rene a quick once-over and laid down the clothing at the end of the bed.

"Tired of lookin' at my dick?" Rene asked, his tone belligerent.

Natalie wondered about his edginess.

Chessa ignored him and circled the bed to unlock Natalie's cuffs. "You're both going to have company today. Natalie, you need to get up and get dressed. Someone'll be coming in a little while to escort you."

"What about me?" Rene asked, his arms crossing over his chest.

"You and I are gonna take a walk."

"Am I free to go?"

"Not quite yet. We'll talk."

Natalie watched the byplay between the two, more curious than jealous. Excited about the possibility of getting out, she rolled up to a sitting position, ignoring the pain shooting through her arms and shoulders and went to the bathroom to shower.

When she returned Rene was alone, sitting on the bed, his elbows resting on his thighs. "I'm just about goddamn starving."

"Me, too. You should have eaten the cheese," she said, waggling her eyebrows.

His gaze narrowed. "Well, don't you be lookin' at my neck."

She flashed her fangs. "Who said I want to bite your neck?"

"Fuck!" he said and retreated in a hurry to the bathroom.

Natalie giggled at the horrified look on his face. She liked his sense of humor and liked even better how easily she could get a rise out of him. She must be getting to know him.

She dressed in a silky, robins-egg blue robe. No underwear. No shoes.

She wondered if they intentionally wanted her "commando-ready" at all times should she have the urge to jump someone.

Feeling famished but lighter of spirit than she had in a long while, she finger-combed her hair in the mirror above the dresser. She'd have given her new eyeteeth for a little makeup, but still thought she hadn't looked so well in a long time. She'd lost more weight, which hollowed her cheeks and gave her hips a sexier flare.

Was it the sexy workouts or the liquid diet?

A soft knock preceded the opening of the door. Simon Jameson stood in the entrance.

"Simon!" she exclaimed, a rush of relief washing over her at seeing someone dear and familiar. "What are you doing here? Did they take you, too?" She rushed to give him a hug, flinging her arms around his neck.

He squeezed her hard and set her back on her toes. "I came on my own. Wanted to make sure you were doing okay."

Natalie let his comment and steady gaze sink in for a long moment. "You know?"

"That you're a vampire?" His grin was strained, not a bit of humor in it.

"How long?"

He shrugged.

Natalie felt a chill prickle her arms and hugged them to her belly. Was she the last person on the planet to find out?

Simon cast a glance at the closed bathroom door and the sound of running water. "Your policeman in there?"

She nodded, a blush heating her cheeks. He probably knew exactly what he was washing off. "Yes."

"Is he treating you well?"

Still feeling a glow from Rene's tender care, she nodded.

"Good. Or I'd have to kill him."

The thought of Simon killing anyone surprised a laugh from Natalie.

"Don't think I could?" he asked, quirking one eyebrow.

She shook her head. "Nothing would surprise me anymore."

"Hold that thought." Simon crooked his elbow. "Let's take a turn around the house."

"They're letting me out?"

"In my care. There's someone I want to introduce you to."

She slowly slipped her hand inside his arm, unsure now about their friendship and his loyalties. Everyone, it seemed had secrets. "You know the people who live here?"

"Not well. And only the oldest inhabitants. It's been a while since I was welcomed." He patted her hand on his arm. "Stop thinking so much. It'll all work out."

She gave him a quizzical glance, but he shrugged. Glad to see the rest of her prison, if only for a quick "turn," she didn't press. Maybe she could learn something useful—like how to spring Rene and herself.

"Her policeman" might think he was going to leave her behind, but she'd be damned if he did. At that moment, she realized she already thought of them as a couple. Bound together. She knew he was far from feeling the same, so why would she entertain such a fanciful thought?

Maybe because she knew it was true, the same way she knew how to find the right places to bite.

She gave a glance over her shoulder at the bathroom door, unsure about leaving him alone.

"He'll be okay. Chessa will look after him."

That was hardly reassuring. She still had the niggling feeling Chessa wanted Rene, but she didn't really have any rights over him.

So they'd slept together. She wasn't sure what constituted a relationship in Rene's mind.

However, she followed Simon out the door, feeling as though she was entering Oz as she crossed the threshold. Instead of a yellow brick road, pearl gray carpet cushioned her bare feet.

She walked toward the end of the hall to a long staircase that curved down to an open foyer tiled in black marble shot through with veins of gold. A massive chandelier suspended above was made of wrought iron twisted into vines, frosted glass globes, and cylindrical crystals.

She didn't have time to catalog the rest of her surroundings. Simon pulled her into a parlor with cream-colored walls, velvet-upholstered camelback sofas with lots of plush, colorful pillows in an erotic mix of maroons and golds. Thick velvet drapes covered the floor-to-ceiling windows, but the centerpiece was a black marble fireplace with a portrait above it.

Curious, she walked closer to study the painting. Splotches of vivid red and gold surrounded the stunning woman at the center of the portrait—blood red lips, black hair, black eyes, a sallow cast to her skin—Middle Eastern or Indian, she thought. Her gown was rendered in gold foil and a gold necklace with a large red stone carved into the likeness of a creature with outstretched wings rested between her breasts.

"She's beautiful," Simon whispered very close to her ear. "But when you meet her, beware."

Natalie drew back in surprise, glancing at him over her shoulder. "She lives here?"

"This is her house."

His expression seemed to be schooled, reserved. Far from the open, fun-loving person she had thought him to be. "What's her name?"

"She has many," he murmured. "But here, they call her Inanna. She's your grandmother many, many times removed. In fact, every one of The Born who lives here is descended from her."

"That term, 'Born'—"

One side of his mouth quirked up. "Not for me to explain."

She didn't bother to hide her frown of frustration. "All right, can you tell me how many Born are here?"

"I don't know. In the past, when I was a regular visitor, they came and went frequently. This was a kind of social center. Now, it seems more a military compound than a residence."

"I don't understand."

"Neither do I. And you're not expected to. You've been out of the fold. So have I. I'll let them explain it to you. I just wanted to give you a little warning." He leaned close again, his voice dropping. "Don't trust. Follow your own path."

She dropped her hand from his arm and stepped closer to be sure he could see exactly what she thought. "Stop going Yoda on me. I'm twenty-five, not five. And I'm getting pretty sick of everyone knowing what the hell is going on around me!"

"Natalie." He reached for her arms and gripped her, giving her a little shake. "Just be careful. Nothing is ever as it seems on the surface."

"Perhaps you should let her see beneath your own surface, Simon," came a melodic, singsong voice from behind them.

Natalie turned to find the woman in the portrait—Inanna. She looked as though she had just risen from bed. She was dressed as Natalie was in a long, silky robe, only hers was a deep crimson shot with gold thread that made the gown shimmer as she walked toward them. Her dark hair fanned around her shoulders and she didn't wear a trace of makeup. Still, she was the most beautiful woman Natalie had ever seen.

"It's well past time we met," Inanna said, holding out her hands, palms up. The tilt of her head relayed a challenge.

Although she was reluctant to touch her, given Simon's warning, Natalie reached out and her hands were enfolded in warmth—and surprising strength. Inanna tugged her closer, until Natalie stood close enough to smell the other woman's minty breath.

This close, the woman's eyes weren't black at all, but a liquid, bottomless brown, her pupils surrounded by a surprising golden aurora. Her skin was a creamy café au lait—and for a woman who was supposedly her grandmother "many times removed," dewy and youthful.

Her lush red lips curved as she returned Natalie's stare, seeming to inspect each feature. "There's little of your mother in you," she murmured. "The same blonde hair, the same coloring, but I see more strength. That bull she chose was an excellent choice after all."

Her mother? Natalie felt her pulse throb at her temples. Somehow, it didn't seem the right time to pursue the topic. Not standing this close. She felt almost light headed from the effort of keeping her expression neutral.

"Natalie, you are breaking free from a chrysalis—you are only half-formed. Soon you will be magnificent—blessed to be among us. Powerful in ways you cannot conceive."

Somehow, the words didn't sound ridiculous. Not in Inanna's melodic intonations.

A shiver bit the base of Natalie's spine.

Inanna released her hands and turned to walk toward twin sofas that faced each other in front of the fireplace. "Please, have a seat," she said, settling gracefully onto the cushion. "Lunch is coming. While we wait, we can get acquainted. I'm sure you have a million questions."

Shaking off her fascination, Natalie lifted her chin, refusing to follow her to the sofas. "I do. For starters, why were we brought here?"

Inanna's smile didn't reach her eyes. "It was a bit dramatic, *non*? But it was for your protection. It seems you've had a bit of excitement in your life lately. We wanted to make sure we spirited you out of the city without anybody getting wise to your existence. A quick surgical extraction. Nicolas's idea. Were you frightened?"

As she glared back, Natalie found herself unwilling to express her fear. "Of course not. I slept through the whole thing."

Inanna's smile held approval. "Are you comfortable in your room?"

"I might be more so if the lock was on the inside of the door."

"You are blunt. As I said, we only want to keep you and your . . . friend safe."

"We'd like to leave."

Inanna's smile seemed more genuine this time. "I know you would. But it's out of the question for now. It's not safe for you outside of these walls. There are those who would kill you for the promise you hold in your body."

"What do you mean?"

"Your child."

"What?" A chill spread through her.

"You may have been a virgin yesterday, but you may already have conceived. You are in your season. In a very short span of time you've managed to mate frequently. We've been monitoring your progress."

"The cameras."

Inanna's eyelids lowered slowly then rose again. "Your Rene is very clever," she murmured, then her gaze drifted beyond Natalie's shoulder toward the door and she relaxed deeper into the cushions. "Our meals have arrived. Do have a seat, *damu*."

Natalie looked behind her and stiffened. Two young men entered. Surely, she didn't mean . . .

"Simon, you may leave us now," Inanna said, her gaze hardening.

Simon's back stiffened, and then he bowed his head and departed the room.

But not before giving Natalie one last warning glance.

"Pasqual, please help Natalie to her seat," Inanna said, waving her hand toward the younger of the pair. He was swarthy skinned, his eyebrows dark slashes above his hooded eyes.

Pasqual gave Natalie an easy smile and extended his hand.

Again reluctant to touch, this time for a very different reason, Natalie lay her hand in his and let him guide her to the sofa. He sat next to her, his thigh sliding snug against hers.

Natalie didn't glance his way, holding herself rigid.

"Come here, darling Sergio," Inanna said to the light-haired man. "Sit beside me." The smile she flashed at Sergio had his cheeks heating. "This is small, intimate," she said, never lifting her gaze from Sergio. "I thought the setting might help in introducing you to our customs."

"Introducing whom," Natalie broke in. "Sergio?"

Inanna's gaze swung her way at last, and she laughed. "It was rude of me not to look at you. But he is beautiful, don't you think?"

Natalie was quickly becoming irritated. The warmth along her thigh, and the lovely cologne emanating from the man beside her, had her salivating. "What's the point of my being here? In this room?"

Inanna's eyes widened in mock innocence. "We are becoming acquainted, and you must begin your training. Your hunger should be a private thing. Since I am your grandmother, I thought I'd provide the lesson myself."

"Lesson? I've already had enough education today," she said, thinking about Gerard.

"Our hungers ought to be mastered—and they shouldn't be a public thing. And despite your attachment to your policeman, you really must look farther afield to feed yourself, or you will deplete him. I take it you have already discovered how to find a vein?"

That only served to ratchet up her awareness of her grumbling stomach. Natalie licked her lips with her tongue, aware the man next to her stared at her every movement. "Um, I can feel a pulse beat beneath my tongue." Her breasts beaded beneath her thin robe.

"Very good. You can also listen for the beat or feel for the greatest warmth beneath the skin. Be very careful about how you bite—if you intend no harm. You mustn't bite too deeply as you did with Gerard. His blood flowed too quickly for you to track his progress. You need to be supremely aware of every heartbeat so you know when he's given all he can."

Pasqual shifted on the seat beside her and his breaths grew more shallow. Was he aware of her growing arousal? Could he smell it as distinctly as she did? Desperation had her blurting, "A question? Do you just keep meals like this about the place?"

Inanna's smile widened, tilting her eyes upward at the corners like a cat's. "These men aren't human, *damu*. They're vampires, *Revenants*."

"That word again," Natalie said, feeling breathless.

"They are a form of vampire. It will all be explained. Right now, the important thing to learn is that once vampires have fed from a human host, you can in turn feed from them. You can continue the cycle without fear of doing harm. With humans, you can't continue to go back to the well, or you will drain them to the point of death."

"Pasqual and Sergio are both vampires?" she asked, feeling herself lose intellect as each second passed. Knowing the men were here to drink from loosened the leash on her hunger.

"Did I not just say so? For this lesson," Inanna said, her eyes glittering, "you will not have to worry about going too far."

Inanna reached for Sergio's hand and brought his wrist to her mouth, giving it a delicate lick.

"May I touch you, Mistress?" he asked in a reverent tone.

"Of course you may," she crooned to him as she held Natalie's stare. "Put your head to my breast."

He knelt on the floor in front of her and opened her robe, nuzzling her breast with his lips while she bit into his wrist.

His groan stretched, and his back grew taut.

Shock had Natalie gasping at their public intimacy. She'd wanted to find family—but this wasn't what she'd had in mind. Despite her revulsion, liquid seeped from inside to wet her sex. She gave Pasqual a nervous glance.

His answer was a player's smile, one corner of his mouth quirking upward.

Natalie didn't know quite how she felt—equal measures

of revulsion and sensual excitement making her hot and cold all at once.

Watching Sergio as he suckled Inanna's breast, had her own nipples ruching, drawing painfully hard beneath her robe.

Inanna's gaze held hers, glittering fiercely, triumphantly as Sergio's hand crept beneath the hem of her robe and his hips pumped against the sofa. Inanna's robe rustled softly as she parted her legs allowing him greater access.

All the while, she drank, her eyes glazing, her murmurs against his skin quickening in cadence.

When she'd had her fill, Inanna licked his wrist to close his wounds and drew him close for a moist, noisy kiss. "Thank you for the gift."

Then she glanced beyond his shoulder at Natalie and smiled. "You need not feel disloyal to your policeman. Your *Revenant* will spend himself in his trousers. Just from the taste and feel of you. You can take your fill and provide him pleasure, without betraying your lover. Pleasure is the price of the transaction."

Pasqual's hand had crept to her thigh and Natalie pressed her legs together to shut him out. Still, her body trembled with pent-up lust. She needed to get out of here, needed to find Rene before she succumbed to Inanna's planned seduction.

For this was a seduction.

"When you take a human host," Inanna crooned in her melodic voice, "it will be the same. They can be brought to orgasm, just from your bite."

Inanna nodded at Pasqual and patted the seat beside her for Sergio to join her. Sergio collapsed beside her, a damp spot on the front of his trousers.

Natalie started when Pasqual knelt before her. Her wild gaze returned to Inanna who gave her a nod and a calm smile. "You must take the edge off your hungers, for Rene's sake."

The soothing tone of her voice settled Natalie's nerves, and she watched Pasqual as though she stood outside herself while he unfastened the silk frogs at the front of her robe and bared her breasts to the room's occupants.

"Lovely," he murmured and leaned toward her.

She knew she'd been watched before—by cameras when she'd made love with Rene. Still, it was a little alarming and a lot arousing, knowing the couple seated on the opposite sofa watched Pasqual fondle and suckle her breasts.

"Go on and pet him, darling," Inanna crooned. "If he's willing to submit to your bite, shouldn't he be rewarded? Meals should be lingered over. Appreciated. They should be pleasurable and sensual."

"You make it sound like we're having sex," Natalie complained, even as she gasped at the pleasure heating her body.

Inanna lifted both eyebrows, her expression amused. "If you desire it, you may. That's entirely up to you and your appetites."

Natalie drew a deep breath, trying to draw back from the edge. She reached out to push Pasqual's head away from her breast, but he clamped his lips around her nipple and drew so hard her toes curled into the carpet.

Instead of repelling his advances, she thrust her fingers into his hair and held him hostage.

The part of her that remained an observer was shocked by her behavior, dismayed by the pleasure she took from a stranger and the eroticism of allowing others to watch.

That niggling voice whispered in her ear, telling her she could take one quick bite, assuage her hunger—and stop.

She licked her lips and drew a deep breath. "I think I'd prefer your neck, Pasqual."

He laughed against her breast and gave her spiked nipple one last flicker of his tongue.

"Just . . ." she gasped, ". . . just lean forward. I don't need you to touch me."

Pasqual grinned and grabbed the hem of her robe, sliding it upward with his palms. His smile dared her to object. "I think you like it like this, don't you?" he whispered as hands closed around her hips and pulled her off the sofa to straddle his hips.

"You watched the damn tape," she growled, leaning toward him to slide her cheek against his, "when I killed Gerard." But he was right, she did like it just like this.

Her teeth slid from her gums, and she sank into his neck, drawing hard against his skin to bring his blood into her mouth.

"Look at me," Inanna said.

Natalie opened her eyes and found Inanna poised on the edge of the sofa. "You will not lose yourself."

*Easier said than done, bitch.*

Pasqual's broad hands palmed her buttocks and dragged her forward and back over his clothed erection.

The heat between her legs and flowing down her throat was too much. She rubbed her naked breasts against his shirt and ground her hips down, seeking release, seeking satiation.

Inanna's laughter, light and musical, rang in her ears.

Natalie knew she was letting the moment get away from

her. *This is betrayal. If I care so much for Rene, how can I do this with another man?*

As though she read her mind, Inanna said, "We don't live by the same rules as humans. Our definition of fidelity isn't as narrow. You'll learn to accept this in time."

Pasqual moaned and his body shuddered, his hips lifting to center his erection between her labia. He jerked against her, fucking her through his clothes.

Just when the familiar blackness swept over her, she opened her jaws and withdrew her teeth, mewling as she came hard.

Her body shivered and twitched, and Pasqual rubbed his hands down her back to her bottom and back up.

"Thank him for the gift, *damu*," Inanna said.

Natalie pressed her face into the corner of his shoulder, stifling a sob. "Thank you for the gift," she repeated, understanding the significance of the blessing.

"You see? He's taken the edge off your hunger. Your skin is glowing and pink. You don't feel as desperately hungry now, do you?"

Natalie's arms snaked around Pasqual's waist, needing to hold onto something solid. "How often? How often will I have to do this?" she asked, hiding her face against his broad chest.

"Right now, in your season," Inanna said, "you will have to feed often. At least once a day."

Natalie straightened away from Pasqual, who gave her a soft smile. His pleasure appeared to have dulled his wolfish smile.

*I should feel guiltier than I do.* But Natalie acknowledged that her stomach was full, and she could go back to Rene and perhaps make love without worrying about overindulging.

Would he know what she'd done? Should she tell him?

A soft, embarrassed giggle sounded from the doorway.

Natalie jerked away, rising and pushing down the hem of her robe.

The blonde woman who'd brought her food before smothered another soft laugh. "I'm sorry. I should have made a noise or something."

Natalie's cheeks flamed. "I should get back to Rene," she said, shame making her voice husky.

"But you must stay," Inanna said. "I insist. Your mother has been very anxious to make your acquaintance."

# CHAPTER 13

Chessa sat on the edge of the bed when Rene came out of the bathroom. Which was too damn bad so far as he was concerned.

The soft training trousers she'd brought for him to wear did little to hide the erection no amount of masturbation seemed to relieve. He placed his hands on his hips and dared her to drop her glance.

He should have known Chessa wasn't the least bit shy about checking him out. Her glance slid south in a slow, sexy crawl that caused his cock to pulse.

He cast a quick glance around the room for Natalie.

"She's not here. She won't be back for a while."

Rene didn't like the fact his disappointment

stung. He didn't want to care. And he didn't like the husky quality of Chessa's voice.

His hands fisted at his hips.

She sighed. "Partner, you're all ate up."

"Unless you have the key to get me out of here—now—fuck off!" Restless, he prowled the room.

"No need to bite my head off. I'm just the messenger."

"Just the messenger, huh?" Rene gave her a nasty scowl. "Been enjoyin' the show?"

Chessa eyed him warily. "I can understand how you'd be pissed at me."

"Oh? I don't know. What the hell do I have to be mad about? I'm living any guy's fantasy. First, you leave me holed up in my house with a virgin vampire. Then you shoot me full of shit to kidnap me. You top it all off by chaining me to a goddamn bed in a room full of hidden cameras. If I wasn't so flattered by your interest in my love life, I'd probably tear your head off."

"Grumpy," she muttered.

That capped it. Rene sprang on her, forcing her back to the mattress. "Not grumpy, you fuckin' bitch—I'm going out of my mind!"

Chessa had the strength to fling him halfway across the parish if she wanted. Instead, her lips curved in a feral smile. "Horny, too."

There was no denying that fact, when his cock rode her cunt. Rene growled, but didn't pull back. Not when his cock craved the warmth of her pussy.

He ground himself helplessly against her. All fight draining out of him. "Chessa, get me out of here," he said against her hair, his voice hoarse.

Her arms closed around him. "It's okay," she whispered. "Tomorrow. I'll take you out before dawn. Be ready."

"Everything's changing," he said, rocking slowly into the cradle of her thighs.

"Doesn't have to be that way," she said, her lips next to his ear. "We can go right back to the way things were. If you want."

"I don't know if I can—if I can forget."

"Does she mean that much to you?"

"I don't want her to." Rene's buttocks flexed and relaxed, continuing the rocking motion that gave him some relief. "Make me stop, Cheech."

"Why?" Her lips slid along his cheek. "Your little virgin is downstairs getting it on with her next meal."

Rage, red-hot, flowed through him. "Doesn't matter," he ground out, his cock pointing through his trousers, finding the outline of her cunt lips through her clothing. Christ, release was right there!

"Sure it matters," she said softly, lifting her hips and circling, helping him find her center. "She won't be able to stop herself, anymore than you can right now. Don't you get it?"

"Fuck!" He got it all right. He'd screw a knothole right now, just to relieve the ache. "Stop me, Cheech. You can make me."

"I don't want to. I can help."

"Won't change how I feel." And he felt like a beast, his muscles tensing, bulking out, every part of his body straining into her.

"Let me be your friend," she whispered.

Only their friendship was getting too damn "friendly" by

the second. How would he ever be able to pretend nothing had ever happened when he got back to the real world? "Fuck buddy, you mean?"

"No. I'm not that much of a masochist." Her body tensed beneath him.

It was all the warning he got. She rolled him, trapping his body between her steely thighs.

"Cheech?"

She gripped the top of his pants and pulled them down his hips, uncovering his cock, which sprang straight up. Then she reached for his balls and shoved the elastic beneath them. "I'll give you release. No fucking to it."

"Using the presidential definition?" he said, trying to make it light, but hurting too bad to make it work. His cock was heavy, filled to bursting.

"Yeah, I'm gonna blow you, buddy." Her hands closed around his cock.

He squeezed his eyes shut, too far gone to think of any lie to make this not his choice. "Damn!"

"Pretend, if you have to."

Pretend it was Natalie? He couldn't. Not when Chessa's hands were so much stronger, her body lighter and her scent—not Natalie's.

Her breath brushed his lips a moment before her mouth opened over his, her tongue thrusting inside.

Rene's arms crept up to close around her—but it was gratitude, not anything deeper, urging her closer. He moaned into her mouth, not liking the needy sound tearing from his throat. Unfortunately, he figured he'd be whole lot noisier by the time she finished with him.

Chessa sucked on his tongue, her lips promising heaven if she ever used them on his dick.

His fingers threaded through her soft hair, and he pushed her away and down.

She let him guide her mouth, licking his skin as he shoved her toward his cock, until her hot breath blew over his sex. But she ducked lower and opened her mouth to suck his balls.

He shouted something incoherent and dug his heels into the mattress, bucking against her, knowing she could take his rough strokes and not be unseated.

She mouthed him, her tongue flicking his balls, tugging so strong he was coming unglued. Her hands closed around his dick and squeezed hard, just shy of agony, ringing him and shutting off his building orgasm. "Cheech! Let me fuckin' come," he gasped.

But she had other ideas. Her mouth sank over his cock, her throat opening to let him slide deep.

No gurgling or choking, she swallowed hard and the back of her throat constricted around him like a cunt—hot, wet, massaging his shaft.

His hips stroked upward—sharp, frantic thrusts. If she'd let go of the base of his cock for even a second he'd explode like a bottle rocket.

Fingers rooted below his balls, sliding between his buttocks, caressing his asshole, making him so crazy his head thrashed on the mattress and his whole body shuddered so hard the bed shook.

Still, she didn't let him get off.

When one slender finger breached his ass, he roared, his

hips bucking, pistoning upward, his hands clutching sheets, his breaths so jagged he felt like he'd run a marathon.

"Chrissake, Cheech! Let me come!"

At last, as her finger stroked inside his ass and her mouth slid up and down his shaft. She eased her tight hold around the base.

His instant orgasm sucked the air from his lungs, and he heaved his hips upward, spearing relentlessly into her hot mouth. "Fuck, fuck, fuck!" he chanted.

When at last the tremors racking him faded, he dropped his ass to the mattress and lay sprawled, weak as a rag doll while Chessa licked him, her tongue soothing him now, lulling him.

"Tell me you've had better," she said, her voice thick.

"You know I haven't."

"Then why?"

"I don't love you."

"Do you love her?"

The automatic denial stuck in his throat.

Chessa raised her head from his belly. Her lips were reddened, swollen, but all color drained from her cheeks. A hollow, haunted sadness filled her eyes.

"Doesn't change a damn thing, Cheech. I gotta get out of here." He raised his head to capture her gaze. "You still gonna take me?"

A pain-filled grimace crossed her face as she pressed a kiss to his belly and the head of his cock. Then she was on her feet beside the bed—the movement too quick for him to see. "I promised. I won't go back on my word."

Rene held her gaze for a long moment. "Thanks."

She shrugged and gave him a tight smile. "What are friends for?"

He shut his eyes rather than watch her leave. He'd fucked up—more ways than one. Broken another of his cardinal rules. He'd gotten too close to Cheech. Cared about her. He hurt because he knew he'd caused her pain.

Worse, he'd betrayed Natalie. Not that he'd made any promises. Tomorrow, he'd compound the wrong by leaving her behind.

"This is awkward."

Natalie gave Erika a sideways glance. The situation was beyond awkward and nothing like she'd envisioned when she originally set out to find her mother.

For one thing, her mother was a vampire. Had caught her having sex in front of an avidly watching audience.

Erika had handled it all in stride, leading her to a bathroom to clean up and acting like this sort of thing happened all the time. Which apparently it did at *Ardeal*.

That was the name of this place—Inanna's home. And her mother's. Unlike the ghouls who came and went that Simon had mentioned, her mother had stayed.

They strolled in a courtyard with a rock wall that only partially blocked the fierce wind whistling past. The furious storm echoed the one brewing inside her.

She'd found her mother, but not the family she'd lost. This vapid creature held no welcoming warmth in her curious gaze. Yet she'd given her birth.

Disappointment tasted like a bitter pill in Natalie's mouth. "Who was my father?"

Erika sighed and glanced away, looking as though the question had drawn her far, far away. "Just some man. I was brought here when I was much younger than you. When my time came, I wasn't given a choice. Inanna chose my mate and locked us up together until she was sure I was pregnant. Robert was his name. He was very handsome."

She'd been confined, too? "What happened to him?"

Her soft snort of laughter held the edge of a sob.

"You killed him, didn't you?" Natalie couldn't help her bitchy tone.

Erika didn't seem to notice. She shrugged. "I didn't mean to," she said softly. "But I don't seem to have much control. I'm weak that way. It's why I stay here."

"You're afraid to leave?"

Erika sat on the edge of a stone fountain and trailed her fingers in the water, watching the swirling waters. "I'm afraid I'll do harm if my hungers aren't fed in strictly controlled conditions. I do get out, though." She glanced up at Natalie. "I'm part of the security team."

"Were you one of the goons that kidnapped Rene and me?"

"I'm sorry about that." Only her expression held no true remorse. Only emptiness.

Natalie's glance swept her from head to foot. Her frame was petite, hardly what she'd consider suitable for a . . . commando-SWAT-whatever their "security force" really was. "I know I'm staring, but you seem so frail."

"I'm not. You have a ways to go yet. The full moon cycle has only started. By the time it ends, you'll be fully transformed. Stronger than you can even imagine."

The strength she wouldn't mind. But something else did bother her. "Will I feel different?" she asked, pulling her hair from her face as the wind whipped it wildly.

"How do you mean?"

Natalie looked away. "Will I be the same person—inside?"

"Change is inevitable," Erika said, her voice sounding dreamy. "The power you'll gain, the things your body can do—you can't be the same person you were before."

Natalie sat beside her and folded her arms over her chest. A chill worked its way down her spine. She wanted to know more, but even Erika, her mother, couldn't just spit everything out. This game of twenty questions was wearing thin—and she missed Rene. "I don't know anything about vampires other than what I've seen in movies and on TV," she said, trying a less direct tack.

"Then you know our secret handshake."

Natalie glanced sideways and caught Erika's little smile. Oh, she was joking. "I just want to know if I'm going to become a soulless bitch like Inanna."

Erika's wide blue eyes saddened. "Oh, Natalie. You misjudge Inanna. I know she seems harsh, but she has her reasons."

Natalie snorted. "Whatever."

"I'm not sure what made Inanna the way she is, but she's incredibly powerful and very, very old. If she's not among the first, she's very close to the first generation of vampires."

"You don't know?"

"She doesn't talk much about her past before the Dacian kingdom."

"That's supposed to mean something to me?"

Another shrug. "What did you study at Tulane, anyway?"

Natalie's lips curved ruefully. "Would you believe journalism?"

"You wanted to be a reporter?"

She shrugged. "Doesn't matter now."

"No, I guess not." Her mother's smile was a vapid stretch of lips. "This certainly isn't anything you can write home about."

Like she had a home anymore. Did the woman have a clue? "It would make a helluva fiction book, though."

"Want to be a novelist?"

"No. I just want this to be over." Enough circling the tiger. "Can you tell me about the people who killed my parents?"

Erika's lips tightened and her gaze slid away. "Were they good to you? Your parents?"

A direct hit and still she evaded. Natalie's frustration was quickly nearing her limit. "They were the best. They were always there for me. They didn't deserve to die that way."

"They weren't the first to be attacked, you know."

"And there I thought I was special," Natalie mumbled.

"We've been fostering children out since the first known attack. Putting them with human families to hide them."

"Who wants us dead?"

Erika shrugged, her expression unconcerned. "Who doesn't? Most of the world's religions consider us demons, a plague. They hunt us."

"Knowing what I do now, I can't believe humans did that to my mom and dad."

"Probably not. Chessa thinks it might be rogue *Revenants*."

That word again. "What's a *Revenant*?"

"One of the walking dead. We make them, but they aren't

like us—born into it." Her mother's words held a note of condescension.

"How'd you piss them off?"

"By not sharing power. Inanna and the other ancients, all Born vampires, hold all the seats on the council. They govern as they see fit, negotiate for territory with other . . . communities. They also set the rules and police accordingly. Some folks resent the fact they have no voice."

"But why go after the Born children?"

"Genocide." Erika's lips tightened. "They figure they might win influence and power through attrition as our ranks diminish."

"Are there many of us?"

"Born? No. We are the source. The death givers. We made the first *Revenants* to serve us. They're forbidden to procreate and make more of their kind."

"What happens when they do?"

"We destroy the newly raised and the *Revenants* who made them. That's my job, actually. I troll the blood banks to make sure everyone's playing nice."

"Blood banks?"

"They're safe places we can go to feed. Humans come for the pleasure we give."

"The gift," Natalie murmured.

"Right. Kind of like what you gave Pasqual," she said, her sly smile making her relationship to Inanna all the more apparent.

Natalie hoped like hell she hadn't inherited the "bitch" gene.

"He looked very satisfied with the transaction."

Natalie stood, feeling sick to her stomach. "I need to get back."

"To Rene?" Natalie didn't answer, but Erika nodded anyway. "There's some talk about your stud."

Natalie turned back at the note of caution in her mother's tone.

"He may be leaving soon."

All sound seemed to grow fainter around her as her heart beat quickened, thudding dully against her temples. "When?"

"The morning. Prepare yourself. He's done his part and doesn't want to stay. Inanna's giving him the choice."

"Done his part?"

"Made you pregnant."

Her mouth grew dry, and her hand went to her belly. Pregnant? "How can you know that? It's only been a day."

"Inanna knows. She says if he can resist your allure, he may leave."

"What if *I* don't want to stay?"

Erika's eyes widened. "But you must. You need us to protect you."

"And the baby." Natalie was surprised by the bitterness in her tone.

"Especially the baby. She's precious to us. Our future."

"And I'm not?"

"Of course you are," she said, her answer coming too quickly to be sincere, "but you will only have this one child. Once you complete your transformation, you won't be able to have another."

"So I'm to stay until the baby comes? What then?" She was

almost afraid to ask, because she knew she wasn't going to like the answer.

"She will be fostered out—just like you were. In a safer place."

No wonder Natalie didn't feel an ounce of connection. Erika wasn't family—wasn't anything approaching human. Despite the dryness and the lump forming at the back of her throat, she asked, "And I won't ever see her?"

Erika shrugged, her expression free of all remorse. "It's too dangerous. You'd draw attention to her. You must give her up—for her sake."

"You're so sure it'll be a girl?"

"We only bear girls. A male would be the equivalent to the second coming and that's never going to happen."

The nonchalant way she said the last—like she had the inside scoop—had hairs prickling on the back of Natalie's neck. She turned away. "I have to get back."

"Savor your time with him. If you want him, try to make it impossible for him to say good-bye."

# CHAPTER 14

Chessa tracked Nic down to his quarters in the barracks. From the looks she was given by the members of the team she passed, either it was unusual for him to be there at this time of night or someone had already broadcast the news of what she'd done with Rene.

Not bothering to knock, she opened his door a crack and slipped inside the darkened room. Sparse as a monk's cell, she didn't waste a glance on the contents. Her gaze went straight to Nicolas, who sat on his cot with his back to the wall, a sheet draped over his lap. Lit only by moonlight filtering through his narrow window, his hair was a soulless black against his naked silvered shoulders.

"Chessa, get out."

So, he knew. If his voice had been rough with anger, she would have brazened it out. However, his tone was flat.

Hesitant to approach, she leaned against the door and searched for something to say to fill the silence that stretched between them. "The storm's nearing landfall."

His legs shifted, one knee coming up under the sheet. "You came to give me a weather report? Thanks. Now leave."

Feeling inexplicably anxious, she blurted, "Erika said you'd be departing after it hits to check the river beside the graveyard." Damn, she sounded inane, but she had to keep the conversation going or her ass would be tossed out the door.

He blew out a long breath. "That's my job." He rested an elbow on his knee and pushed back his long hair. "And not something everyone here doesn't already know. Now, will you get out?"

The last sentence held a hint of irritation—something she could work with. "I came to tell you I'm leaving before dawn."

"With your *partner*."

"I'm taking Rene to his home."

"Is that all the taking you'll be doing?"

His silky tone sent a melting shiver down her spine. He didn't like the thought of her with Rene. "I don't know," she drawled. "Depends on him, I suppose. But he doesn't love me."

"Isn't that what you wanted?"

Despite the fact she recognized her words were at odds with her actions, she said, "Sure. It's exactly what I want."

"Then why are you here?" he asked, his voice dropping to a graveled bass.

Chessa's breath hitched as she fought the urge to leap at him again. "I just wanted to say good-bye."

His lips thinned. "At least have the courtesy not to lie to me."

She held up a hand. "All right. I was hoping . . ." She bit her lip, not wanting to say it.

"What? That we could fuck? Since your policeman didn't seem so inclined?"

Anger, fresh and cleansing, swept through her. She stood away from the door and put her hands on her hips. "Oh, he was 'inclined,' all right. I didn't want to take advantage."

"But you would take advantage of me?" Again, that nasty edge crept into his voice.

Chessa quit trying to figure him out. She lifted one eyebrow. "Do we have to talk?"

"No," he said, pointing toward the door, "you may leave."

She resisted the urge to stomp her foot—just. "I'm here because I want you."

"Not good enough, Chessa."

This time she did stomp her foot. "Dammit, Nic. So, I had sex with him—"

"You gave him a blow job," he bit out.

"*All right, I went down on him!*" She took a deep breath and glanced away. It looked like she wasn't going to break through his anger without anything less than the truth. "The whole time I was doing it . . . I realized I was only there because I didn't want to lose."

"What was the prize?"

She blinked ruthlessly at the moisture welling in her eyes. "There's not any. I wanted someone in my life who couldn't really touch me. I like him—even love him a little—but I'm not obsessed with him."

"Then why take him home?"

She brought her face around slowly, lifting her gaze to let him see . . . more than she was comfortable admitting. "Because he doesn't want to be like us. I'm taking him back to his life—that's all."

"So, we are back to why you are here. You wanted to say good-bye."

"You know damn well I want more than that." Her voice shook and Chessa clamped shut her mouth.

There followed a long, pregnant silence and she had just decided she'd been an idiot to come, when Nicolas shifted.

"Then why are you still clothed?" he asked softly. "I've been waiting for you."

Chessa's breath hitched. He'd been waiting for her? Even after he knew where she'd been—whom she'd just left?

Her whole body suffused with heat and tremors of excitement. Her nipples beaded into sharp, tight points that scraped against her shirt.

She stripped, leaving her clothes in a puddle on the floor next to the bed. Her eagerness had her wet before her knee touched the mattress.

Nicolas flung aside the sheet but reached to grip her shoulders, preventing her from climbing onto the narrow mattress. "I want you to blow me, Chessa. Just like you did Rene."

Her heart stilled. He wasn't over being mad, and something darker, even more intense, brewed beneath the surface of his harsh expression. Was he jealous?

"You'll need to lie down," she said, pretending she wasn't feeling uncertain.

"First, turn on the light."

"You need one?"

"Since this is likely to be the last time we see each other for another decade," he said, dryly, "I want to savor the experience."

"Sure." She reached for the lamp on his bedside table and flicked on the switch. Golden light flooded the small room, striking shadows over the sharp angles of his face and body.

He lay down, shoving a pillow beneath his head, reaching up to fold his arms underneath it and raise his head further. He wanted to watch. His dark eyes glittered. His features were taut and stark.

She wasn't sure now what was going on, but she walked to the bottom of his bed and crawled up the mattress between his spread legs.

His cock lay curled along his thigh. *Flaccid.*

So he wasn't in the same place she was. *Horny as hell.*

She worried for a moment over where she should start. Nicolas had centuries more experience than anyone she'd ever had, and she didn't want him to find her lacking. She wanted him to think of her often, because after this, she knew she wouldn't get him out of her mind for a long time.

She glided her hands up his calves and thighs, lingering over his hewn muscles. Her excitement grew at the thought of all that power flexing as he thrust his cock inside her.

She stroked over his skin, skimming upward. The sparse hairs covering his thighs were soft and curling, just the same texture of the hairs surrounding his sex.

She bypassed his cock and smoothed up his belly, bending over him to follow her fingers with her tongue and lips.

The taste of him reverberated inside her, shocking her with the pleasure. He tasted of old-fashioned bay-rum soap and his own unique flavors—almonds and masculine musk. A taste she acquired in a hurry and wasn't likely to forget. She pressed wet kisses on his belly and licked up his chest to circle his flat nipples.

She nibbled at the tiny erect points and rose to look into his face. His arms were still beneath his head, as though he was unhurried, maybe even bored with her progress.

She was melting inside, and he was bored? Chessa leaned closer and kept her eyes open as she kissed his lips, tracing the seam of his closed mouth with her tongue. His nostrils flared slightly against hers, but his lips remained still. She sucked his lower lip between hers to nibble some more.

His face remained unchanged, his breath slow and even. Hers grew sketchy, and her pulse hopped. Ending the kiss, she narrowed her eyes and decided to get straight to business.

She scooted down the bed and bent over his cock. He said he wanted exactly what Rene got—but Rene had been hard and ready for it. She'd been caught up in his excitement and hadn't needed a strategy—she'd gone on instinct.

How to get Nic to that same place presented a challenge. She cupped his balls and rolled them in her palm, planning her next move. The velvet softness of his sac distracted her, drawing her down. She licked the soft skin, tracing the faint seam that separated his balls. She cupped them and bent closer to kiss the tender skin directly beneath his scrotum, suctioning gently and leaving a small love bite.

All the while, Nicolas displayed stubborn, rigid control—but cracks were beginning to show. His legs shifted wider, and his cock twitched.

Chessa urged his legs farther apart and slipped her hands beneath his knees, encouraging him without words to lift them.

This tilted his hips slightly giving her greater access. She suckled the skin beneath his scrotum again and lapped lower, pressing her thumbs between his buttocks to part them so she could delve between.

Nic didn't protest, but the muscles of his thighs tightened.

When her tongue flicked the puckered hole, his hips jerked.

Chessa sucked on two fingers and worked them between his cheeks, circling his little hole, prodding it in teasing forays that had his full attention now.

She kissed his balls and continued to finger him while she moved up to glide her mouth and tongue along his shaft. His cock was slowly straightening, filling with blood as his body heated.

Still soft enough to curl, she tucked his whole cock into her mouth and began to tug at it with her lips, pulling blood upwards to fill it, rearing back her head as it overfilled her mouth, until at last, it was rigid, thick, and long—ready for her to fuck. Only he'd demanded what she gave to Rene.

"Nic?"

His fingers curved around her skull and pushed her back to his cock. He wasn't giving her a reprieve.

Was this her punishment? To give him release and leave,

aching worse than she had before? She bobbed over him, gliding her lips down his shaft, sucking hard when she came up.

Lord, he had a lovely cock. Dense, straight, ruddy—with veins that felt like ridges beneath her tongue. She wanted to savor each inch as it crammed deep inside her.

But she wasn't likely to know that pleasure any time soon. Not when Nicolas was intent on punishing her.

How could she have let things go so far with Rene when she'd had Nic right here—ready to give her exactly what she needed?

The answer left her squirming inside. In Inanna's garden, he'd fucked her like he meant it—and that had scared her spitless.

Now, she'd willingly risk exposing her heart, just to have him make love to her one last time. But first, she had to give him what Rene had gotten.

While he watched, she clasped his cock between both hands and stroked them up and down his length, sliding in the moisture her mouth had left. She bent and laved his plump, purple head, paying special attention to the slit at the center, pointing her tongue to dip inside.

Nicolas's fingers tightened in her hair.

Closing her eyes, she licked him, dragging her tongue in slow swirls around his crown, then opening wide her mouth to take him inside, sliding down to meet her joined hands before coming up, then sliding down again.

As she suctioned, her cheeks hollowed and billowed, up and down, she rose and sank, opening her throat to take him deeper, twisting her hands around him as she pumped.

His hips lifted from the bed, thrusting gently at first, then harder and deeper as she quickened the pace until he stroked so deep she fought the urge to gag.

Just when her jaws began to ache, he grasped her hair hard and pulled her off.

His expression said it all. Taut, reddened cheeks, flexing jaw, nostrils flaring with his quickening breaths—he pulled her by the hair, bringing her up his body.

She didn't mind his roughness. She deserved it—wanted his punishment. Her nipples scraped his belly and chest. Moisture flooded her channel, seeping out to slick her folds.

When her face lay beside his on the pillow, he tugged her hair harder and his lips lifted in a snarl. "You shouldn't have come to me with the smell of him on your skin."

She mewled, arching her body against him. "I couldn't wait, and I wasn't going to lie."

"You wanted my anger?"

"Yes!" she rubbed on him like a kitten, sliding her cheek on his bristled chin, pressing her breasts against his chest.

"I won't be nice," he growled. "I won't consider your pleasure . . . or your pain."

"Just do it!" she gasped. "Come inside me, now."

He kissed her hard then shoved her back. "Get on your knees."

"Yes! Anything, please!"

He let go of her hair and sat up beside her as she knelt on the mattress, bracing herself on shaking arms.

His hands cupped her buttocks and squeezed. "I'm going to take your ass, Chessa." He squeezed again and slapped both cheeks.

The thought of all that cock cramming inside her caused

her whole body to shudder. When his palms slapped again, her head dropped between her shoulders, and she tilted her ass higher, giving him access and permission to continue.

Hard, sharp—each slap struck a different spot. His punishment only spiked her arousal. Her back arched, her belly quivered, and she widened her knees in invitation.

His palms continued swatting her soft skin until her whole bottom burned. When his strikes neared her pussy, her breath caught.

The first moist slap made her groan, and she shifted on her knees. The next caused a ripple along her inner channel. "Nic, oh God, please!"

His laughter was deep, dark. His hands landed on her one last time and stayed, gliding over her skin, soothing her now, squeezing hard. He left her gasping against the ache and knew he'd left the mark of his hands on her flesh. Then he spread her cheeks.

When his breath flowed into the crease of her ass and lower, her pussy clenched.

His mouth opened over her cunt to suck on her labia. She jerked against him and sighed, her belly and thighs quivering, her hips circling.

His tongue licked the length of her furrow, lapping at the moisture coating her lips and slicking her thighs. While his mouth and tongue labored over her sex, his fingers crept between her buttocks and prodded her asshole again.

Slowly, he worked a finger inside her, stroking in as he thrust his tongue into her pussy, until she was mindless, moaning with pleasure. She undulated her hips, trying to deepen both penetrations.

When he drew away, she whimpered, but he centered his cock between her folds and she quieted, breathing hard now. As the thick, blunt head pressed into her, she reared back to take him deeper.

His hips screwed his cock into her, twisting, stroking forward and back, building the heat and friction between his cock and her inner walls. His hands smoothed over her back and around to cup her breasts. His fingers flicked and pinched her nipples.

Desire curled tighter in her belly, arousal winding tighter and tighter until she squirmed on his cock, clenching her inner muscles hard around his shaft. "I'm close. Jesus, Nic. Fuck me harder!"

One hand left her breast and glided down her belly. His fingers delved through her hair to the top of her pussy, finding her engorged clitoris. He pinched it while he pounded faster, powering into her so hard each stroke drove the breath from her lungs.

Just when her orgasm rushed up to capture her, he pulled out.

"Noooo!" she keened, her head sinking to the mattress. Her whole body quivered, and her pussy clasped wetly around air.

His hands squeezed her buttocks and drew them apart. Moisture dropped between them and a fingertip rubbed it around her tight hole. Then the blunt head of his penis pressed against her anus.

"Oh, God, no!" she cried out. But she really meant yes. The painful pressure had her hands fisting in the bedding, but she didn't try to draw away. She braced herself, holding still, not breathing as his huge cock pressed hard and met resistance from the strong muscles guarding her entrance.

His thumbs pressed either side of the hole, opening her slightly, and he pressed forward again. The pressure grew as he continued to push forward, circling, prodding, until the tight ring finally eased and just the head of his cock slipped inside.

"*Dieu*," he muttered, and his hands gripped her ass hard.

Chessa's breath rushed out, chopped and jagged. She tried not to move to keep him from driving deeper. She wasn't ready for this. She didn't know if she'd ever be.

More moisture dropped, and he used his fingers to smear it around her opening and pulled out slightly and pushed back inside, this time deeper than before.

She burned. The tightness and pain didn't relent. "I can't take it. I can't, Nic," she moaned.

"You will." His fingers found her clitoris again and he scraped it with a calloused finger, sending sparks of electric shock that reignited her orgasm and had her squirming despite the painful fullness.

"Oh God, oh God!" She pressed her forehead against the cool sheets. "Please. Christ, Nic?"

Nicolas leaned over her, his belly covering her back. "Yes, Chessa," he whispered in her ear. "Tell me."

Chessa drew a harsh breath. "Move! Oh, God, please move. Fuck meeeeeee!" she keened as he surged inside, gliding into her, stroking deep, his fingers pinching her clit hard.

When the first powerful wave crested over her, his mouth closed on her neck and his teeth sank deep, piercing the vein. Her pussy spasmed, deep rolling convulsions that tightened her asshole around him.

He drew blood, a cool rush flowing from her head while her orgasm shook her entire frame. She would have fallen to the mattress but for the gentle hands that surrounded her, supporting her while his hips continued to pump against her bottom, and his lips suckled at her neck.

When he finished, slowly lapping the blood from her neck, tears trickled down her cheeks to fall to the bed.

He slowly withdrew his cock and pulled her up until she sat on his lap. As his breaths slowed, his hands caressed her breasts and his cheek slid alongside hers, soothing her.

"I'll miss you," she whispered.

He kissed her cheek. "I'm a patient man, and we have time. As much as you need. When you're ready to return . . ."

"Why do you want me?" she asked, her voice cracking.

A soft snort gusted against her cheek. "In you, I find the challenge I've been missing."

"You only want to conquer me?"

"Partly," he answered. "You excite me on so many fronts. You're very like me, Chessa. Lonely, alone—unwilling to compromise."

"When I stop running, won't you be bored?"

His soft, delicious laughter warmed her. "That will never happen, Princess."

A smile tugged at her lips. "What? You getting bored?"

"You standing still to let me catch you."

"Maybe," she drawled. "Until then?"

"I wait."

When the door creaked open, Rene stiffened.

Natalie slipped inside and closed the door. She stood with her hand around the knob, not turning.

For a long moment, he stared at her bent head. "Did you enjoy your meal?" he asked quietly, wondering at the low, deadly anger that filled him.

Her shoulders straightened, and she glanced back, her gaze falling short of his. "It took the edge off."

She didn't say of which hunger. Dammit, she'd filled both. Rene closed his eyes. "I'm leaving. In the morning."

"I heard," she whispered.

"You'll be okay here. Safe."

"And if that isn't enough?" She turned and leaned back against the door. Her blue eyes were moist. Her mouth tight.

Inside, Rene groaned. The way she looked at him, like he was her sun and moon, made him even madder. "I can't be what you need. I won't die for you."

Her chin wobbled. "I'm not asking you to turn. I'm asking you to be there for me and your child."

Ice-cold shock stiffened his spine. "What?"

She pulled away from the door and walked toward him, a scowl drawing her golden brows together. "Feeding my stomach wasn't your purpose in coming here. Giving me a child was. The bitch who owns this place seems to think I'm already pregnant."

"It's been one fucking day—"

"And night. Apparently, long enough for her to know."

He raked a hand through his hair. "What does it matter if you are?" Even while the words pushed through his lips, he knew he sounded like a complete ass, but he felt like he was strangling.

"You'd still leave me with them?"

Her incredulous expression had him feeling even worse. Still, his inner demon shouted for him to cut and run. "Will you both be safe here?"

"What about the part where I'm supposed to be happy?"

"Well, that sure doesn't have a damn thing to do with me."

She came closer. "I'm not staying," she whispered. "If you don't take me back with you, I'll walk. I'm not asking for you to be with me. Just get me the hell away from here."

Rene could empathize with that statement. The longer he stayed the less of himself remained. Like a slow-working poison, the house and the inhabitants turned his insides out. "I don't know if I can help you," he admitted, pitching his voice low and hoping they didn't have better sound equipment than the vice squad. "Chessa has clearance to take me back."

"Figure out a way to smuggle me out, too," she whispered back. "Take me back to New Orleans. Maybe Simon will help me get away."

"Simon?" Just the mention of the name struck a raw nerve. "What exactly is he to you?"

"Just a friend, I thought." Her eyebrows drew together in a perplexed frown. "I'm not sure now. He's mixed up in this, too."

Rene dragged in a deep breath. He couldn't leave her here—but he wasn't ready to think too hard about why. He knew he wasn't ready to know. "When Chessa comes, we'll figure out a way," he said, reluctance already making him itch. "If you don't want to stay, I won't leave you here."

"How long do we have?"

Rene shrugged and walked to the window. "I haven't a

clue," he said, more loudly this time, not wanting the watchers to get too suspicious. "Maybe a couple of hours." He pulled back the curtain. Clouds obscured the moon and stars. He wasn't even sure he'd be able to tell when dawn arrived because the cloud cover was so heavy.

Keeping his gaze on the trees, bending in the wind, he asked, "Did you fuck him?"

She drew a deep breath then released it. "No. It went pretty much the same way as with Gerard."

He was glad she didn't lie, but his body still rejected the thought of her that hot and close to another man. "Did you kill this one?" God help him, he hoped so.

Her footsteps drew close, stopping just behind him. "Not even a little bit. I think I'm getting control."

"Maybe next time you won't have to get off with him," he growled.

Natalie's arms encircled his waist, and she hugged him. "I'm sorry about all this."

"We're getting out. It'll all be over soon." Only each step he took away from her seemed to draw them closer. He had the sinking feeling he'd never truly be free.

Her hands glided up his chest, and she snuggled closer to his back. "We still have a little time together. Do you want to . . . ?"

He closed his eyes. Hell, his cock was already rubbing his belly button. "Yeah. Have to make sure the goon squad doesn't think anything's up."

# CHAPTER 15

Silence stretched between Nicolas and Chessa as they each dressed. Deep inside, a knot of some emotion she wasn't willing to acknowledge tightened her stomach. She closed the last button to her blouse, rolled up the sleeves, and finally raised her glance to meet his. "Guess this is it."

Nicolas gave a sharp nod. "That storm's going to wreak hell all over this area. I need to get my team organized. Make sure the compound is covered and get with The Mausoleum team." His jaw flexed. "You haven't been to one of our briefings in a long time. There are many new faces. Would you like to come?"

Was he trying to draw out their parting?

She shook her head. "No, I need to get back to

Rene. We have to get on the road soon so we can make New Orleans before dawn."

She felt awkward, unsure how this parting should go. She cleared her throat—and then she had a thought. "You mentioned The Mausoleum. I need for you to do something for me."

He lifted an eyebrow.

She hesitated to voice her suspicion. One possible explanation for the bird attack was something so horrible she didn't want to say it out loud.

Chessa raked a hand through her hair. "Something odd happened the day we picked Natalie up. I need to know if it's possible that small animals have access to the crypt. They swarmed her. Attacked her. I want to make sure that our 'guest' isn't causing problems."

"We go over that thing with a fine-tooth comb on a regular basis." His dark brows drew together. "Of course, we aren't looking for things going in. I'll check it myself."

"Good enough." She'd run out of things to say. "Well, I guess this is it."

"I think you said that before." A lopsided smile curved the corner of his lips.

"Yeah, I guess I did." She lifted her gaze and didn't attempt to mask the longing she felt inside. "I don't know how to say good-bye. I'm not very good at it."

"You don't have to say anything." He opened his arms. When she walked to him, he gathered her close. His kiss was soft, a soothing glide of firm lips that seemed to tug at hers when he pulled away. "Just stay safe. And think about me once in a while."

She lifted her hand to caress his cheek. It was crazy—they had no chance for a future together—zippo, nada. But . . . she felt like she was leaving part of herself behind. "I think you've made it impossible for me to forget you," she said faintly.

"That was the plan, *chère*."

The door creaked open and Natalie lifted her head from Rene's naked chest.

Chessa strode inside, dressed in her usual somber colors.

Natalie jiggled Rene's shoulder. "Wake up. Chessa's here."

Rene stretched, his powerful arms bulging. He blinked once before coming fully alert. "Cheech." He pushed aside Natalie's arms, still draped over his chest, and sat up. But not before he checked the sheet to make sure it covered his lap.

That seemed odd to Natalie considering the fact they'd both paraded nude in front of his partner before—even if only in defiance.

Chessa's glance dropped momentarily, skimming the sheet, and she gave one of her smart ass smirks. "You still want to head back, partner?"

"Yeah, but we've got a slight change of plans."

Chessa eyed him warily.

Rene gestured for her to come closer. With Chessa standing between Rene and the camera that watched the bed, he said softly. "Natalie's comin' too."

Natalie was surprised he blurted it out that way, like a command.

Chessa's head swiveled toward her, but her gaze didn't accuse. Instead, she looked troubled.

Natalie rose from the bed, unconcerned with her nudity, and lifted her chin. "I'm not staying here."

"Have you thought about what's going to happen when you get back to New Orleans?"

She shrugged. "Not really. I'm hoping I can get help from Simon."

Chessa nodded slowly. "He might be willing. He's not beholden to Inanna."

Natalie tilted her chin higher. "Like you are?"

Chessa's lips tightened. "You might be able to lie low and avoid detection by *Revenants* for a while, but what about—"

"The creature attacks?"

"Plural?"

"Locusts came after me, too."

Chessa's eyes widened. "What next? Is the Mississippi gonna run red?"

Rene snorted.

Chessa's concern mollified Natalie's irritation somewhat. "I was in the open both times," Natalie said. "If I stay inside as much as possible and don't draw attention to myself, they shouldn't find me either."

"Are you willing to take that risk? Are you going solo?" She glanced between Rene and Natalie.

Natalie nodded, her throat tightening. "I'm on my own."

"Well, shit. You guys sure don't know how to keep things simple." Chessa crossed her arms over her chest. "I'm not sure how I'm going to get you out of here, but if Nic hasn't left yet, he might be willing to help." She straightened. "Both of you, get dressed."

She left them long enough to dress—Rene in his sweat pants, Natalie in her robe.

"We'll have to hit my place for more clothing for you when we get to town," Rene said, pulling his drawstring taut and tucking it inside the waistband.

"I don't see the problem," Natalie said. "I'm heading back to my place anyway, aren't I?"

"No. If you want to see your Simon, you'll have to let us contact him for you. We'll find you a room somewhere."

"It's nice to know you don't plan to dump me at the city limits," she said, keeping the tone light—if a little acidic.

Rene's scowled. "I'm not dumping you."

"No, but you're also not sticking around. I'm not sure I see the difference."

"If you really are pregnant—"

"Don't worry about it," she said, impatient with his resistance. "I'm not asking you to play daddy."

"I wouldn't be very good at it."

"You've tried it before?"

He shook his head. "I'm just not a family guy."

Natalie thought about that for minute. "You've been married before, haven't you?"

"Yeah. I was a lousy husband."

The door opened, and Chessa waved them toward her. "We have to go now. The security team's finished their meeting, but Nic's got those on patrol around the house in a pow-wow. We have five minutes tops. My car's in front."

"Would they really try to stop us?" Natalie asked, worried she'd put them in danger.

Chessa's expression turned from dour to amused with a slow grin. "Yeah, they really would."

Once out the door they raced down the hall to the long staircase and out the foyer to the front porch. Rain pelted them as they stepped off onto the pebbled circular drive.

Chessa lifted her remote entry and clicked open the locks to her sedan. "You take the backseat, Natalie, and keep your head down."

Natalie dove into the back and lay across the seat while Chessa started the engine and pulled away.

"The storm's getting' nasty," Rene muttered. "Sure the road's still open?"

Chessa flipped the switch of the police scanner. "We're gonna play it by ear. For now, let's just put some miles between us and *Ardeal*."

"That's the name of this place?"

Natalie realized Rene hadn't been apprised of any of the history or the people who lived here. Not that they'd spent a lot of time talking. "*Ardeal* means beyond the forest. It's the original homeland for the vampires here. For me, too, I guess."

"All except Inanna," Chessa murmured, keeping her eyes on the road. "We're nearing the gate. Almost in the clear."

There was a bump as they left the private road for the blacktop. From her position stretched across the backseat, she saw Chessa give a small wave to somebody just beyond her view. "All right, we're cool. The only thing we have to worry about now is that damn storm."

Natalie sat up in the back seat. Within the thick walls of the house, she'd been unaware of just how strong the storm had become over the last night. The tall oaks that lined the main road like sentries bent sharply in the wind. Long strands of Spanish moss littered the surface. Rain fell like a thick curtain distorting their view ahead.

"Damn, I'm chilled," Rene said, turning down the AC.

Chessa gave him a sideways glance. "We'll have to stop and buy a T-shirt for you. If we can find any place open."

Natalie cleared her throat. When both gazes swung her way, she shrugged. "I'm hungry."

Chessa settled back in her seat and glanced at her in the rearview mirror. "That's gonna be tricky, but I'll keep an eye out."

"Will they try to follow us?" Rene asked.

"Nic will keep them busy with storm prep for now. He promised we'd have a bit of a head start."

"What's he to you, anyway?" Rene asked, his gaze on the road ahead.

He'd asked the same thing about Simon—in the same possessive tone.

Chessa shrugged, but didn't answer.

Rene's gaze stayed on her as though picking apart clues in her appearance and expression.

Was he jealous of Chessa as well? Natalie wished she didn't care so much what their relationship really was, but she sensed that something had changed between them over the last day.

The convenience store they pulled up to was in a small town, an unmapped blip on the road. Fish bait, along with cigarettes and beer, was advertised in the sign on the glass door. The windows had all been boarded shut in preparation for the coming storm. However, the only thing that mattered was the little cardboard sign that read "Open."

Chessa cut off the engine and turned to Natalie. "You stay here. I'll signal when you should come inside."

Natalie looked at Rene. "Are you sure you don't want to come in, too."

He shook his head. "Just don't forget that T-shirt. I'm cold."

After Chessa had gone inside, Rene said, "I don't suppose you're goin' inside for a doughnut."

Natalie looked away. Her stomach already felt like it was eating itself. Acid boiled so hot and sharp. "You know I'm not."

Chessa appeared in the doorway and waved for her to come inside.

Natalie fumbled with the door handle, so hungry and desperate she'd become clumsy with it.

Inside the shop, she blinked against the dim light. The interior of the shop was grimy and smelled of cigarettes and spilled beer. Behind the counter stood a grinning man with his dark hair pulled back in ponytail. The uniform shirt he wore bore the embroidered name "Arno."

"I've been talking to our friend Arno here," Chessa said, a smile pasted on her face, "and he says he's up for a little fun." Chessa's steady stare told her to go along with her.

Still smiling, Arno lifted his chin. "I've got a gun under the counter if either of you two try anyt'ing funny," he said in his deep Cajun drawl.

Chessa held up her hand. "My friend's in a bad way. You don't mind . . . being nice to her, do you?"

Natalie's stomach churned. The asshole must have thought she was some kind of nymphomaniac. She was going to have to kill Chessa. Later.

Arno looked Natalie over from head to foot. "She's a pretty t'ing. What she need with me?"

"Do you care?" Chessa asked, lifting a brow.

His gaze fell to Natalie's breasts. "Guess not." He lifted the folding counter top to make a small space for Natalie to slip through. His hand rested beneath the cash drawer.

The closer she got, the more her stomach began to turn. He was the source of the cigarette and beer stench, but she reached up and put her hand on his chest, feeling for the enticing thud of his heart. "So how are we going to do this?" She licked her lips. "I need you on your knees."

His hand reached out slowly, as though he was afraid she'd draw back. His fingers sank in her hair and cupped the back of her head. "How 'bout you be on your knees, *fille*?" he asked, his voice gruff.

His nearness set her own heart thudding, and despite her initial revulsion, desire curled deep inside her. "I'm sure we'll get there, Arno," she whispered. "But first, I need a little something."

She undid her robe and spread wide the edges to expose her breasts, all the while gauging when his lust overcame his common sense. "Do you want to touch them?" she asked, fingering a nipple.

"Damn!" His hand twitched at his side then lifted quickly to cup her breast as though afraid she'd change her mind.

His caress was surprisingly gentle and tentative. "Them's pretty titties," he said, licking his lips. "What about the rest?"

"Not until you're on your knees . . . baby," she added, surprising herself with how easily she joined the game. Two days ago she'd been a virgin, and here she was showing her "titties" to a complete stranger.

He pulled his hand from the slot beneath the cash drawer and knelt in front of her, his gaze never leaving her breasts.

She hiked her robe up to the tops of her thighs and straddled his lap, gasping when his hands reached beneath the hem to cup her naked buttocks. "In a hurry?"

"I wasn't expectin' anyt'ing like dis," he said, his voice tight, his erection already straining against her naked pussy.

This close he was younger than she originally supposed—maybe mid-forties, his eyes a cognac brown. Nice eyes. She couldn't help the little grind she gave him. His answering surge upward was just the sensual prod she needed for her fangs to slide down.

"These titties are dying to rub against your hard chest," she whispered.

"Hope dat's not all the rubbin' you plan to do."

She laughed and leaned close, nuzzling his neck for just a moment, finding the best spot . . . and sank her teeth into him.

His breath hissed between his teeth, and his grip on her ass tightened. He'd leave bruises, but she didn't care. Blood spurted into her mouth, and she groaned as it slid sinuously down her throat.

This time she had no problem controlling her blood lust. When her stomach was satisfied, his odor and the small groans that rumbled in his throat, robbed her of enjoyment. She couldn't wait to remove her fangs from his neck.

* * *

No amount of washing in the filthy little restroom at the back of the store could get the taste of him out of her mouth or the smell off her skin. However, her stomach was full and her cheeks pink.

At least she wouldn't be craving another bite of Rene anytime soon. She'd noticed how he'd shivered inside the car with the AC turned low. She'd taken too much blood from him.

On her way out of the restroom, she approached Chessa. "I need some things. Can I have your card? I promise to pay you back."

Chessa passed her the card without a question. "I'll take Rene's shirt out. You get what you need. Sign my name." A small, conspiratorial smile tugged at her lips. "He's not gonna ask you for ID."

Natalie was still blushing as she paid for her items while Arno rang up her purchases, smiling blissfully.

"Any time, you hear?"

He didn't even have a clue she'd drank from him. As she'd finished lapping at his neck to close the wounds, Chessa had spoken quietly to him. Somehow in her soft intonations, she convinced him they'd had sex. That the slight soreness on his neck was a hickey.

When she slid back inside the car with her package held tightly in her hands, she avoided Rene's gaze.

"I don't think we have to worry about daylight breakin' through," Rene said, staring at the angry, black clouds above. They'd hit the interstate and finally gotten a good look at the storm the canopy of trees had masked.

Natalie stirred in the seat behind him where she'd slept ever since she'd stopped for her bite. He ignored the sound, tamping down the fury he didn't want to feel. He'd stayed in the car rather than watch her take another man again.

Natalie had been drowsy as a kitten after drinking milk. Images of her clinging tightly to a stranger as she sucked his neck had him hard and aching, grumpy as hell.

Chessa's cheeks had held bright, hectic color as well. He wondered if she'd fed or was just excited by witnessing Natalie's carnal feeding. That got him wondering if she worked in the same fashion and had to adjust his cock for comfort. Both vampires kept him in a constant state of arousal.

"You gonna let me drive?" he asked Chessa, hoping like hell she hadn't picked up on his problem. He didn't want to encourage her, didn't want to hurt her any more than he had.

She cast him a sideways glance. "You look beat, Rene," she said softly. "You have shadows under your eyes. Why don't you try to sleep?"

"You droppin' me at my house?"

The length of time it took her to answer sharpened his attention.

"Rene," she said at last, "you should know that whoever was after Natalie will be coming after you, now. You can't stay there, at least for now. They might think they can get to her through you—and they won't stop with a polite question."

His stomach clenched. "Dammit, Cheech. I want this over."

"Help me find the killers. That's the only way you'll be free."

Rene gripped the armrest so hard it creaked then slowly relaxed. He'd known all along he wasn't escaping anything.

# CHAPTER 16

Rene dumped Natalie's suitcase on the bed in the hotel, refusing to meet her eyes. His body was tense and horny. He could have slammed a fist or his cock through a cement block.

Anger rushed through him like floodgates had been blasted all to hell. Only it was his home that had been trashed.

While Chessa had shouted to Natalie to grab clothing and start shoving it into pillowcases, he'd stormed through his home assessing every scar in his walls and furniture, every shredded curtain and pillow.

Chessa hadn't rearmed the security system when she'd snatched him from his home. He wondered if that oversight had been an accident, or if she was trying to prove a point.

He got it.

His house was no longer his sanctuary, and he was being hunted, too.

He'd never relied much on his intuition, but this time the stillness in his courtyard had been eerie, almost like a hundred pairs of eyes were watching, waiting. Even before the garage light failed to come on, he'd been reaching for the pistol he wasn't wearing, ready to storm inside.

Chessa had grabbed his arm and pressed a finger over her lips. She strode into his house, her steps crunching on broken glass in the distance. When she'd called him to come inside, he'd thought he was prepared for the worst—but his imaginings hadn't come close.

The fury behind the destruction had shaken him. Once his rage was tamped down, he'd started to walk through and assess it like a cop. It became clear the intruder had begun clearheaded, methodical. When he reached the bedroom, that's when all hell had broken loose.

By the way the bedding was wadded, Rene could imagine the monster pulling up the sheets to smell the scent of sex and a virgin's blood. That was the moment he'd come unglued.

Even now, well away from the house he'd called home when Elaine was still alive, he couldn't shake the anger or the bone-deep fear. If Natalie had been there when the monster had come . . .

Rene knew he wouldn't have been able to stop him.

"Are you staying here at the hotel?" Chessa asked, her voice raised, and he realized she must have repeated the question.

He shook his head. He wasn't feeling very civilized at the moment. He needed to get far away from Natalie.

"You want to grab some of your things and head to the office? Maybe you could rack out on a cot there."

He grabbed a duffel and headed for the door. When he reached for the knob, he said over his shoulder, "Stay the hell away from those French doors. Pull the curtains shut. Stay put until you hear from one of us."

Behind him, he heard Chessa clear her throat. "I'll drop Rene then go see Simon. I'll find out what he's willing to do to help."

At the last moment, he looked back at Natalie. Her blue eyes looked huge in the pale oval of her face. "I'll check in with you later. Keep your head down."

As Natalie watched him leave, she felt like her feet were planted in shifting sand. She moved sluggishly around the room, putting her things into the tiny drawers of the built-in dresser. When she finished, she sat in an armchair and listened to the silence, half expecting to hear a scraping to announce another chapter of her life—or the final epilogue.

The sight of the destruction inside Rene's home had left her shaken and ill. Her parents' deaths had been more vicious, but she'd had the benefit of time and distance to dull the horror. Now, it was back in her face.

Rene's reaction had added to the chill. He'd withdrawn, his face growing tighter as he'd strode from room to room, the muscles of his shoulders tensing, his hands closing into fists.

And she was the cause. The killer had come for her and taken out his frustration on Rene's home—the message clear. Rene was next.

All because he'd fucked her. Possibly impregnated her.

She stared at the small paper bag she'd clutched in her lap ever since she'd left the convenience store. There was only one way to find out for sure. Dragging herself to her feet, she grabbed the paper bag and went into the bathroom.

The instructions were simple, the picture unambiguous, but after she'd peed on the little white wand, she stared at it uncomprehending for the longest time.

She was pregnant.

Only two days had passed, but she held the proof in her hand.

Her stomach rumbled—a gentle roiling that only hinted at the urgency to come. She thought about ordering from room service, but feared she'd want a bite of the wait staff rather than a raw steak so decided to lie down and sleep until dark.

Chessa had promised she'd be back that evening to take her out. She still didn't trust Natalie to curb her appetites.

Natalie didn't blame her one bit.

She lay on top of the comforter and let the overhead fan wash over her, lulling her toward sleep, trying to shut the sounds of the storm shrieking past her window. She was tempted to peek outside, but knew the streets would be practically empty. Only fools and the few who didn't fear the fury of the wind would venture outside today.

A soft knock on the door brought her awake in an instant. She padded on bare feet to the door and opened it, cursing the fact she hadn't thought to look into the peephole first. Only it was just Rene.

Water ran in rivulets down his face. His white T-shirt was soaked to transparency. The look on his face arrested her—haunted, stark—and savage. She stood to the side as he entered and closed the door behind him. Before she could open her mouth to ask him why he was there, he pulled her into his arms and backed her against the wall.

Natalie's mouth opened beneath his, and his tongue thrust inside. She wound her arms around his neck and pressed her body close.

A hand lifted her thigh and dragged it over his hip and he shoved himself between her legs. His thick, hard cock rutted against her pussy, pushing her up the wall.

She couldn't breathe, couldn't think beyond the taste of him and the heat that built everywhere their bodies met—but especially between her legs.

As their tongues dueled, her heart beat heavy and hard against her chest, and the tingling started in the roof of her mouth.

She tore her mouth away and lifted her lips to show him her fangs. "You know what you have to do."

Rene rested his forehead against hers while his chest rose and fell with each harsh breath. He ground his cock into her one last time then stood back.

She opened her robe and pushed it off her shoulders, letting it pool at her feet. She was already shaking, whether from blood or sexual lust she wasn't sure. Probably both.

He picked up the robe and ripped an arm off the silken garment, then held out the sleeve. Natalie took it and turned away, putting it between her teeth and holding up the ends for him to knot.

When it pulled snug against her hair, she started to turn back to him, but Rene's hands landed on her shoulders, and he pushed her toward the bed, forcing her to lie over the edge.

Natalie grabbed handfuls of the coverlet and spread her legs wide, tilting up her hips to give him access to her sex. His hands glided from her shoulders, down her back and over the globes of her ass. There, he paused and squeezed them, then swept his thumbs into the crease.

She shivered, letting him decide how and where he wanted to take her. His continued silence unnerved yet excited her. He'd been driven beyond his control to come here.

His zipper rasped and fingers thrust roughly between her legs.

But she didn't care. Moisture melted from her inner walls, flooding her pussy. She clasped her muscles around his fingers as he swirled inside her. She rubbed her hardening nipples on the bed, moaning behind her gag.

When his cock probed between her legs, she trembled, her breath hitching.

Rene dipped in, finding her channel, then slammed inside, the force pushing her up the mattress stroke by stroke until he followed her onto the bed one knee at a time.

His strong arm reached beneath her belly and lifted her to her knees, but he never stopped the pounding that butted against her womb with every thrust.

Natalie keened and pressed her hot face into the cool coverlet, closing tight her eyes as her desire curled inside her like a spring. Sweat and her own juices smeared her thighs, and his belly slapped noisily against her flesh.

Rene's hands landed on the mattress beside hers and his strokes shortened, powering hard and quick as a jackhammer, until finally, he groaned and jerked against her. Hot fluid spurted deep inside her, bathing her core.

When his hips finally slowed, he dragged air into his lungs in harsh gasps. Her gag loosened. "Keep that on 'til I'm gone," he said, his voice harsh and sounding rusty.

She lay on the mattress, her legs splayed, and her body still shuddering as he rose and dressed out of her sight.

Not until the door clicked closed did she roll over and spit out the gag.

It had to mean something—his coming back for her. He hadn't turned to Chessa or some other woman to ease his lust.

As she fell asleep, the image of Rene's face, tight with pent-up anger, stayed with her. She would have liked tasting the edge of his violence.

Chessa lifted the brass knocker on Simon Jameson's door and waited. A steady drip plopped on the floor, and she remembered her slicker and unzipped it.

The door swung open and a woman with waist-length golden brown hair and dark eyes stood in the opening. She wore a cream brocade wrapper, something so elaborate it looked like it ought to be a museum piece. Her pink mouth appeared blurred from kisses.

Chessa stared for a long moment. "Hello, Kestrel."

The woman made a dainty moue. "I hate that name. I'm Madeleine," she said, her voice musical, yet precise, "and you're one of Inanna's get."

"I need to speak to Simon."

"He's in the shower. Come in and I'll tell him you're here."

Chessa shouldered past the door and the petite woman, feeling like a bull in a china shop. Everything about Simon's "pet" screamed femininity. It figured. If you were going to have an enchanted familiar, why not one you'd enjoy fucking, too?

As she removed her rain slicker and hung it on a coat rack, she looked around his apartment, taking in the smell of dusty books and incense, finding objects she knew anyone else would mistake for gothic kitsch, but she knew were a mage's toys.

She was peering into a copper-framed mirror that oddly reflected only the contents of the room, when Simon strode inside, wearing a T-shirt and loose trousers. The outfit was totally at odds with his true Templar face and brawny physique.

"Your mirror doesn't work," she said, lifting a brow.

"Only demons find it useless for combing their hair," he said, his reflection smirking in the glass.

Chessa rolled her eyes. "I met your bird."

"Lovely, isn't she?"

"Tell me," she said, narrowing her eyes. "Is she your willing captive or your slave?"

His smile thinned. "She's not up for discussion. You've come about Natalie."

"I have." Chessa plopped down on an overstuffed sofa and put her feet on the coffee table. She wasn't sure why, but annoying Simon was tops on her list of fun things to do today. "She's decided not to accept Inanna's invitation."

Simon seated himself opposite her on another well-padded sofa. "Did Inanna see her to the door?"

Chessa examined her fingernails and found a hangnail. She stuffed her finger in her mouth and bit it off. "Not exactly," she said, not meeting his gaze.

Simon laughed. "My Natalie has good instincts. But you still haven't said what you want from me."

"Are you in a rush to get rid of me?"

His sigh was long and exasperated. "Is this something that can wait until another day?"

"She needs sanctuary," she blurted.

Simon's expression shuttered, but not before she'd heard his breath draw deep. "Is she asking for it?"

"She doesn't even know it exists."

"Then you have to find another way to keep her safe. Send her back to Inanna's and make sure they don't let her out again."

"Simon, you and I both know she won't be happy there."

"Since when do you care about Natalie's happiness? I suppose you've become great friends."

"Simon, I can't keep her safe long. She's ravenous. She'll draw attention the first time she steps out to find a meal."

"Is she really pregnant?"

Chessa laid her head back on the cushion and looked at the molded ceiling. Nice place he had here. "Inanna seemed to think so," she murmured.

"What about her policeman?"

"His name is Rene."

"Will he go with her into sanctuary?"

"He's not willing to become her life mate."

"Must be one stubborn human to resist her. Or maybe he's found someone to deflect all that lust building in him," he said, his tone insinuating.

Chessa flushed. "I'll need you to explain it to her—and she might be resistant to the idea."

"I can't imagine why. Who wouldn't be willing to leave behind the world they know? Take a one-way trip into another time and place?"

Chessa straightened, bunching her fists on her knees. "Simon, what part of this aren't you understanding? She's not safe here."

"Oh, I understand. But I also know you have your sights on her boyfriend. The daddy to her child. Do you really think this is the best thing for her? Or is it the best thing for you?"

Chessa's back stiffened ramrod straight. "I mean her no harm, and I've given up any claim to Rene. You know why I'm doing this. I only want her and her child safe."

"Take a long look in a mirror, Chessa—not mine of course. If you still want me to send her to sanctuary, I'll talk to her about it. But you need to purge your demons first."

The metallic rattle drew their attention to a doorway. Madeleine carried a large tray with a teapot and cups. "I thought you might want something to fortify yourself before you face that storm again." She placed the tray on the coffee table and perched on the edge of the sofa next to Simon. When her gaze met his, her smile said it all. She was his willing captive.

Simon's head swiveled toward Chessa. "Don't come back until the new moon. Our girl still has more growing to do, and I'm going to be very, very busy."

Natalie awoke in the darkness to the sound of her stomach grumbling. She checked the time on the digital clock on the nightstand. Nightfall had come. Soon, Chessa would arrive to take her to dinner.

She rolled from the bed and pulled clothing out of her drawers then headed to the bathroom. Once inside, she showered and applied makeup to her face. The task was pointless really. She wasn't trying to impress anyone, and the storm outside would likely wash it all away as soon as she stepped outside. But she needed to do something to while away the time.

Her hands shook with her hunger as she lined her eyes, and the result was a little ghoulish, but appropriate to her mind. She dressed in a silver sleeveless top and blue jeans that were very loose at the waist and baggy in the rear. She dug for a belt to hold them up and stepped into silver, jewel-studded slides. The clothes were silly, the shoes ridiculous. She was going to troll for blood and would likely stain everything she wore. She wondered if vampires ever wore bibs and thought the innovation might catch on.

When she'd dried her hair, she sat on the edge of the bed and waited, counting the minutes.

This time when the knock came, she checked the peephole first. Chessa stood in the hallway.

Natalie opened the door and gave Chessa's attire a quick glance. She'd overdressed. Chessa wore blue jeans and a scruffy leather jacket.

Chessa intercepted her glance and held open her coat. Her holster fit snug against her waist. Then she slid a long dagger from an inner pocket. "I never travel without a little reinforcement." Her eyebrows waggled up and down.

Natalie grinned. "I'll have to remember that."

"Now, that scares me. Get some lessons first." Chessa glanced inside the room. "You ready?"

"Since I no longer have a purse or any cash to put into it—yeah. It's on you, right?"

"You have what you need to make payment. Let's go."

Rene sat at his desk, tired as hell. His eyes felt scratchy and his underwear stuck to his cock. He needed a bath and to brush his teeth, but he'd been in such a hurry to leave Natalie's room the first time, he'd forgotten the necessities.

Staring at the copy of the faxed report from the Memphis PD, his gaze blurred. He sat back and rubbed his eyes. Damn, he'd lost so much blood to Natalie, he knew it would be a while before his body restored the loss and his stamina was back—that or he'd have to go to Charity Hospital and ask for a transfusion. But how would he explain how he'd lost a few pints?

*There was this girl who happened to be born a vampire . . .* It sounded nuts, and that's what they'd think he was. If that was true, a great big pair of baby-blues was responsible for his lapse in sanity.

Rene swiveled in his chair, trying to decide whether to get the cot from the lounge or sack out on the moth-ridden couch when his gaze fell on Chessa's filing cabinet.

The one sitting in the corner behind her desk that contained the cold case files she'd kept for forty years—since before he'd been born.

He'd read most of them. The ones in the upper three drawers. The bottom drawer was the only one she kept locked. He'd often wondered why and supposed it might have something to do with her screwy family. But maybe, there was another reason.

He'd never know unless he looked. No stone would be left unturned in his search for the killer threatening Natalie. He might not be the right man for her, but he wanted to know she'd be safe. It was the least he owed her.

Rifling through the tools, pens, and flashlights he'd accumulated in his desk, he found a screwdriver. The lock was the built-in kind—easy to break for someone who'd jimmied his own cabinet every time he'd lost the key.

# CHAPTER

# 17

The raucous sound of a cheery accordion and electric guitars blared from the open doorway. Natalie kept her head down against the driving wind and rushed behind Chessa toward the bar she'd chosen for her "meal." The hooded rain slicker she wore ended at the knees, and her feet and the bottom of her jeans were soaked. But she could smell food ahead. Her stomach was already gnawing at her backbone she was so hungry.

Just inside the door a grinning man flashed a megawatt, white smile that looked like the disembodied grin of the Cheshire Cat against his dark face. "Welcome, welcome. Da hurricane party jus' started."

Chessa greeted him with a lift of her lips, showing him a bit of fang.

His smile grew impossibly wider, and his gaze swept them both with curiosity. "You be in luck. Da room's full."

Chessa paused to remove her slicker and held her hand out for Natalie's. She handed both to the man. "Make sure I get these back."

"I never say no to pretty ladies."

His laughter followed them through the noisy bar, past a crowded dance floor, and beyond to a dark, narrow hallway with three doors—two marked as restrooms, the last with a sign that said PRIVATE.

Chessa pounded a fist on the thick door, and it swung open to a cloud of smoke and the smell of booze and sex.

Natalie tamped down the urge to moan. While her mind was revolted, her body yearned toward the room. She crossed the threshold into a devil's lair.

Once the door shut, the Cajun-flavored music was gone and in its place a techno-beat thudded like a heartbeat. The lights were low, but with her improved sense she found couples dancing so close she had to do a double-take to realize they mated on the floor. Others sat or reclined in padded booths in various stages of undress, engaged in sexual acts, some of which Natalie could only wonder about.

Chessa grabbed her arm and pulled her close. "Don't stare like you've never seen anything like this before."

"I haven't."

"Pretend. You don't want anyone to know you're fresh meat." Then Chessa shocked Natalie to her toes by leaning close and kissing her full on the lips. She nuzzled her cheek and whispered in her ear, "Anything goes here. You can drink, fuck—just don't kill your host. We don't want the attention."

She led Natalie to the bar, and they both slid onto wooden stools. Natalie tried to keep her gaze from clinging to the other customers, but the mirror behind the bar only seemed to magnify the luridness. Bodies rose and fell in unison on the dance floor. Groans of sexual excitement and pending orgasms were only partially masked by the loud music.

"What can I get you two ladies?" The bartender greeted them with a knowing smile.

"Thanks, we don't need you to find our dates," Chessa said, then leaned toward Natalie. "Let your fangs down," she whispered, "or they'll think you're here to bleed."

Natalie stared at the bartender's neck and felt the downward slide of her teeth, letting them press past her upper lip to dig into the lower.

His eyes narrowed, and he lifted his chin toward the dance floor. "Go ahead and have a look around. There are still a few who aren't taken and several who wouldn't mind sharing, I'm sure."

Natalie felt like she'd dropped through a rabbit hole, only the Mad Hatter was hosting a blood orgy. She swiveled on her chair to have a look at the menu.

"Remember what I told you," Chessa said.

Like she would ever forget. In the car, Chessa had briefed her, priming her for her new adventure. She'd been told certain bars catered to vampires, and human "hosts" came willingly to be used. Some hoped for the ultimate hook-up—to be turned. Others wanted the intense sexual thrill a bite provided.

"Just go with the flow," Chessa had said. "Everybody knows the score."

"What if they want to be turned?" she'd asked.

"Then they're doomed to disappointment. That's never something we do lightly. If a vampire finds someone he wants as a life mate, then maybe. Be sure to stay away from the *Revenants.*"

"I didn't think it mattered whom I drank from."

"It doesn't. But you don't want them taking a reciprocal bite. If they've tasted Born before, they'll make you. Be sure you bite first. If he's undead, make an excuse and get away quick. You do remember the difference in the taste?"

"Pasqual's blood wasn't as rich."

"Exactly. I'm not sure of the physiology, but it has something to do with red corpuscles and the constant cycle of replenishment to keep their corpses animated."

"Lovely," Natalie murmured, shuddering at the description. "How will I know if he's Born or a *Revenant*?"

"Assume all males are *Revenants*. We don't bear male children."

"Ever?"

"Not since Inanna's time, at least."

Natalie wondered why only female children. She opened her mouth to ask why—

"Would you like to dance?" a voice came from behind her.

Natalie's eyes widened. For a moment, she'd forgotten where she was. Casting a wild glance at Chessa, who nodded her approval, she rose from her stool and turned to find a man who appeared to be her age. His hair was curly and blond. His eyes a muddy hazel. His smile was nice if his body was a little tense.

She leaned toward him and raised her voice loud enough for him to hear. "Your first time here?"

He nodded, a sheepish grin stretching his lips. "My friends know this place. Said they have the best parties." His glance dropped to her breasts and below.

Best sex he meant, Natalie thought wryly. "You said you wanted to dance. Was that just a euphemism?"

His puzzled stare told her he didn't understand.

"Never mind." She opened her mouth and touched her tongue to the tip of one fang. By the wideness of his eyes, she guessed he'd thought his friends were only joking.

With one last glare at Chessa who gave her a thumbs-up sign, she led him to the dance floor.

They stood apart for a moment, and Natalie reached out to put her hands on his shoulders. "It's all right. You can touch me."

His arms pulled her close and despite the energy of the music, they shuffled on the floor for a turn or two.

"What's your name?" she asked.

"Jason. Yours?"

"Lisa," she lied, not sure about who might be listening in. "You know, I need to be higher." Another blank stare, and Natalie sighed. "Pick me up. I'd like to kiss you."

"Oh! Sure." His eagerness made him a little awkward as he gripped her waist and hauled her up his body.

Natalie draped her arms around his shoulders and bent to whisper in his ear. "Closer. Let me wrap my legs around your waist."

His Adam's apple bobbed as he swallowed, but he brought her body closer. When her breasts brushed his chest, they both shivered.

She grinned, sharing a moment of communion with her

nervous meal. Slowly, she raised one leg at a time and gripped his hips. Now that her crotch pressed against the placket of his jeans, he got the idea.

His hands glided down her back and cupped her ass, giving her a squeeze and gentle roll of his hips, and they both finally caught the rhythm of the music.

They slid together, sinuous as snakes, rubbing chests, grinding their groins together, building a friction that melted Natalie's inner walls and had his cock straining hard against his jeans.

When his eyelids dropped to half-mast, she bent and kissed his mouth. His opened beneath hers. His tongue was cool and tasted like rum. She sucked it, earning a moan that gusted into her mouth.

Natalie trailed her mouth to his jaw and down his throat, tonguing his clean skin until she found the vein. She sucked the skin above it, lulling him for a moment, drawing out the excitement for her own gratification.

When her teeth pierced his flesh, he gasped and strained away, but only for a second when she continued to feed. Jason groaned deep in his throat and gripped her ass hard, pushing her up and down his clothed cock quicker than before.

As blood seeped around her fangs and into her mouth, she remembered to seal her lips tight over his skin and suction. No use letting any of his precious gift stain their clothes. Her bite was just deep enough to puncture the vein, not sever it as she had Gerard's.

She could sip him like a smoothie, drawing deep to pull blood quickly into her mouth, and resting in between to let them both savor a respite in the buildup.

She opened her eyes and watched the other couples around them, no longer shocked by what she saw. She was part of it. Neck deep in it. Their fervor only added to her own, and she knew places like this could become an addiction.

Her gaze swept the room until she found Chessa who'd pressed a huge, muscled behemoth onto his back on a bench. She straddled his hips and held his arm to her mouth as she drank, and he rutted helplessly upward.

Natalie smiled around her mouthful. She guessed Chessa liked being on top.

Her gaze continued to sweep the room as Jason shuddered, his cock jerking and rubbing frantically against her as he neared his release.

One particular man snagged her attention. He was beautiful—his skin a creamy chocolate, his hair jet black. His body, although slender, sported an impressively wide set of shoulders which a woman in a short, dark skirt gripped so hard her knuckles whitened. She'd hooked her thigh high over his hip, which raised her skirt, baring her bottom to everyone near enough to see. With her head flung back, she issued an invitation for him to nibble at her throat.

His hands clutched her generous buttocks and squeezed, easing her closer as he bit, absorbing her momentary jerk of shock by pumping against her.

Natalie realized his trousers were loose and his cock likely deep inside the woman's pussy. Her own pussy clenched and liquid pleasure seeped to wet her panties. She ground harder against Jason.

The dark man's eyes opened, and his gaze pinned hers. Sin-filled delight danced in his eyes. While he drank and fucked his host, he challenged Natalie, silently urging her toward her own release.

It was as though he'd slid inside her body. Each rough motion of Jason's hips felt like a fluid glide. And although Jason still gripped her ass, she felt more hands caressing her back, rubbing over her breasts, fingering her clit until she cried out, lifting her mouth from Jason's neck.

Jason's trembling brought her back to earth. His legs shook so hard she felt sure they'd both land on the floor in a heap.

Giving the dark man one last questioning glance, she licked away Jason's wounds. "You can put me down, now." Once her feet touched the ground, she was ready to be away.

"When can I see you again?" he asked, his arms still encircling her body.

Now that she'd had her fill, she found she had no interest in him. Her belly was full, the urgency quenched. "I'll see you around." She stepped away, forcing him to drop his arms.

When she turned toward where she'd last seen Chessa, she found the dark man planted in her path.

Instantly, her arousal reawakened. "How do you do that?"

"Do what?" he asked, his glance seeming to catalog every one of her features, one by one.

When his glance fell to her breasts, she fought a losing battle to keep her nipples from beading against the thin silver fabric of her blouse.

"May I?" he asked, his tone polite, but his raised hand indicated a more shocking intent—it hovered above her breast.

*Don't let a Revenant get a bite*, Chessa's voice intoned in her memory. But she'd never said anything about not enjoying a touch.

She breathed deeply, lifting her breast to his palm.

His hand didn't squeeze, just lay there, warming her flesh. "Now, we can get to know each other," he said. "I haven't seen you here before."

Natalie remembered to lie—just! She swallowed to moisten her suddenly dry mouth. "I was turned just last week."

"Was your lover Chessa?"

Natalie blinked at that question. He knew Chessa. Must know she was a Born. "Yes, she made me."

"You don't seem her type. She likes cock." His hand lifted from her breast, then trailed down her tummy to the waistband of her jeans. His fingers traced the edge of the rough fabric, rubbing back and forth, grazing her belly and making it tremble.

Natalie's breath caught at the intimacy of his touch. Why was she allowing him to do this? His aroma was delicious, heady—a combination of spice and citrus—and sex. They were close enough to scent each other. Close enough to share a moment of mutual arousal. His nostrils flared and his palm flattened against her stomach. His fingers slipped beneath her waistband to touch her curls. "My name is Fernando. Yours?"

With her breaths becoming ragged, she gasped, "Lisa."

"Really?"

"Uh-nnnnh," she moaned, as his long fingers reached the top of her sex and rubbed the hood protecting her clitoris.

"Dance with me," he commanded, pulling out his hand and turning her in his arms to fit her bottom against his rigid shaft.

Her waistband gave, loosening, and his fingers delved deeper, sliding between her lips, stroking into her cunt. Her head fell back against his chest, and she found their reflection in the mirror. His darkness was a shadow next to her pale, luminous skin.

His cock pressed against her in time to the beat of the music and she undulated, curving her belly to bring his hand deeper between her legs, urging him to stroke his fingers in and out.

"Sweet, so sweet," he whispered against her hair.

"Hey there, Fred." Chessa stepped in front of Natalie and placed her hand over Natalie's crotch, halting his movements. Anger tightened her features.

Natalie wanted to scream. She'd been so close. Chessa's interruption reminded her of rules she wanted to forget just long enough to let his fingers fuck her into orgasm.

"Chessa, do you want to join us?" Fernando asked smoothly. "Your lover is very, very near her release. Would you rob her of pleasure?"

Chessa's glance dropped to Natalie, and she leaned close and sniffed, all the while her glance held Natalie's immobile. She lifted a hand and cupped her breast. "She's a bit of a slut. You can see why I have to keep her on a short leash."

Natalie bit her lip. With Fernando's fingers stroking deep, and Chessa now pinching her nipple, she feared she'd shatter into a million pieces.

Chessa lifted her gaze to Fernando and tilted her chin. Holding his gaze, she lifted Natalie's shirt and unclipped her thin bra, exposing her to the room. She stepped closer, her thighs pressing Natalie's wider. Her hands cupped her breasts, plumping them, thumbing her nipples until they drew tighter, harder.

"She's my treat," Chessa murmured and bent to suckle one nipple, her tongue curling around it while her lips drew painfully hard.

Natalie gasped, and her head rolled on Fernando's chest. A wash of fresh cream bathed his fingers.

When Chessa's teeth bit the tender skin of her areola, Natalie jerked and cried out, unable to stop the rocking motion of her hips as she rode the fingers shoved deep inside her, and Chessa drank from her breast.

Her orgasm buckled her knees. If not for Fernando's hand anchoring her crotch, she'd have slid bonelessly to the floor.

Chessa laved her nipple, her ministrations quick, efficient. When she lifted her head, she wiped the back of her hand across her mouth to sweep away a trace of blood. "You may let her go, now."

Fernando pulled his hand from her clothing and tugged Natalie's head back by her hair. His mouth came down hard for a kiss that promised this wasn't the last time they'd meet.

"See you." Chessa grabbed her hand and dragged her from the room, back through the bar. Natalie tugged down her shirt, leaving her bra dangling inside. When they stood outside the bar, rain pelting their heads, Chessa leaned close. The anger on her face cleared, and she grinned. "Not bad."

"What did you mean by 'not bad'?" Natalie asked as she drew a fresh T-shirt over her head, feeling a little awkward at flashing skin at Chessa after what had happened between them.

Chessa bent at the waist to rub a towel over her dripping hair. "You think on your feet," she said, her voice muffled, until she threw down the towel. "You remembered not to give away your name or what you are. Even under Fred's considerable powers, you didn't betray yourself."

"Oh," Natalie said, feeling a little disappointed and not really wanting to know the reason why.

"And you tasted delicious."

Natalie blushed at Chessa's sultry tone while her nipples tightened. "Was that necessary?"

"Oh, yeah. Fred and I go way back. Knows me too well to believe I would turn you without a really good reason."

"I think he doubted you were my lover. He said you liked cock," she said, lifting an eyebrow, not believing she was having this conversation.

Chessa flashed a grin. "My first preference, sure. But you will find that we vampires aren't that fussy about how we get off. Don't get too wound up about it. You did good."

"Why do you call him Fred?"

"Because he hates it."

Natalie flopped on the mattress on her back and laughed. "That was the wildest thing I've ever done. Well, other than raping Rene."

Chessa's eyebrows shot up. "You had to rape him?"

She tried to fight a smile, but gave up and grinned. "He didn't hold out long."

Laughing, Chessa flopped down beside her. "That sounds like our Rene, all right. Stubborn to the end. He doesn't think he deserves happiness."

Natalie turned toward Chessa. "Why is that?"

Chessa's breath bled slowly out. Her lips pursed and she looked as though she fought herself whether to tell her or not.

"You can trust me, Chessa," she said softly. "I only want what's best for Rene. Whichever way this turns out."

Chessa rolled onto her side, and rose on her elbow. "You know he was married?"

She nodded.

"His wife died in a car crash, sitting right beside him," Chessa said slowly. "I think he won't forgive himself for not dying, too."

# CHAPTER 18

Chessa strode into the station, waving to the desk sergeant as she passed through the metal detectors. Her steps felt light, her mood brighter than she could remember in a long while. Her trip to the "blood bank" with Natalie had turned out very interesting indeed.

And dammit, she was really starting to like the younger woman.

Natalie had handled herself well. Had managed to drink unsupervised without incident, and even helped her thwart Fernando's plans to take a bite from her lovely throat. She might just make it on her own.

She rounded the corner of their cubicle and found Rene sitting forward in his chair, staring at a manila folder dangling between his fingertips—a grimy, worn, tear-stained manila folder.

She drew up short, and her gaze shot to her filing cabinet. The lock looked like it had been filed. The bottom drawer was pulled open.

Chessa stared, unable to raise her gaze to Rene's. She felt as though he'd plunged his fist into her chest and was squeezing the life out of her heart.

"You shoulda told me, Chessa, what this was really all about," he said, his voice sounding hoarse. "You shouldn't leave a partner, *a friend*, swingin' in the wind with only half the story. I been flyin' blind with this case."

"It's not your concern—where it all started," she said, forcing the words past frozen lips.

"Damn, if it's not. It started with you!" he shouted, slapping the folder on the desk. He lurched from his chair and gripped her upper arms. "It all started with you!" He shook her. "With your husband . . . *your child*!"

Chessa tried to shrug his hands off, but he wouldn't let go. Because she wasn't willing to hurt him to make him release her, she lifted her face and let him see the tears filling her eyes. "Yes, I was the first!" she shouted. "The first to be hunted! The first to lose everything! It's why I'm here. Why I'm a cop." She turned her head, and her gaze landed on the black and white photographs spilling from the edges of the folders.

"I lived in *Ardeal*," she whispered, "before the wall . . . in a little cottage. I came into my moon-cycle and found a man I wanted for mine." She stopped to breathe, realizing each indrawn breath hurt. "We had a child . . . I came home and found them both . . ."

Her eyes closed to shut out the picture of her baby girl's small broken body. She couldn't finish it. Couldn't get the words past the lump in the back of her throat. She stood suspended by his hands and cried the way she hadn't been able to forty years ago.

Rene cursed and pulled her against his chest. "Cheech, Jesus. I'm sorry." He rocked on the balls of his feet, hating himself for his anger and her for not telling him the truth.

If he'd known . . . if he'd been prepared . . . oh hell, he'd still have fallen for Natalie like a ton of rocks. The pictures of the little girl, Ana Tomas, could be his own.

"Shhhh . . ." He cupped the back of her head and pressed her face into the corner of his neck and held her while she cried. By the layer of dust he'd brushed from the file, she hadn't looked at the pictures in a long, long time. She'd hidden the hurt away, out of sight. Covered her heart with a thick layer of hedgehog spines and tough-talking insults.

Kinda like he'd done after Elaine had died in his arms. Until one pretty little blonde in a pink dress twitched her ass and made him want something more. Only this time, he'd attempted to refuse his fate. He didn't want to head down the same tragic path. But he'd already let Natalie down when she'd been abducted and compounded the blunder when he'd been taken as well. He'd been mad as hell at Chessa and not willing to forgive . . . himself.

"It's all right. Don't cry anymore." He kissed her hair and hugged her again.

Her sobs were softer and her arms lifted from where they'd hung limply at her sides to clutch his waist.

Rene hadn't forgotten how to soothe a woman's tears. His hands smoothed up and down her back and he stood still, letting her drench the front of his shirt. "You know I'm useless at drying tears. Look at me. My shirt's all wet."

Chessa's laugh sounded more like a sob, and she drew away to wipe her tears with the backs of her hands.

He bent over her and pulled away her hands, and then used his thumbs to gently sweep them away. "Your little girl was a pretty thing. Just like her mama."

Chessa's smile wobbled. "She'd just learned how to say 'Shit.' Her daddy taught her. He thought it was funny and I got mad."

"I bet he knew you didn't mean it."

Her grateful smile tore at his heart. "Inanna fostered all the children out after that. Built that big damn wall around the grounds. Turned humans in exchange for their service guarding the place. We weren't safe in this world anymore."

"Why didn't you stay there?" he asked, already knowing the answer.

"Because I didn't care if they got me. And I wanted to go after the bastards and tear them apart, limb by limb."

He wrinkled his nose. "Figuratively?"

A shaky smile stretched her lips. "Literally, actually."

"You're the woman to do it."

"Yes, I am." Her smile faded, and she leaned toward him. "Thanks." The kiss she placed on his lips was chaste.

The one he gave her back was not. "Chessa," he groaned as he tore his mouth away, "I thought if I put some distance between myself and Natalie—"

She placed a finger over his lips. “You can’t help this. It’s too late to even try to resist.”

He sat and pulled her onto his lap, kissing her like he loved her, his fingers clutching her hair as he desperately tried to still the desire clamoring to be fulfilled. And he did love her, in a way. “I don’t get how I can do this with you, when I’m crazy for Natalie.”

“It’s a curse,” she murmured in between wet glides of lips and tongue. “We love and fight like this. Our passions all intermixed.”

“But I’m not turned. Not a damn vampire. Why do I feel this way?”

“You’re linked to us now. She was a virgin when she bit you. It’s something mystical. Something you can’t really fight. The same way she will always come back to you, you will never be free of her or this lust. You will want others.” She slipped off his lap and took a step back.

Rene didn’t stop to think. He thumbed the button at the top of her trousers and skimmed them down her legs, pushing her soggy socks and shoes away.

When he sat back in his chair, she reached for his pants and opened them, helping him wrestle them just past his hips to free his cock.

“Do you think we’ll finish conversations like this often?” he asked, his voice rasping with need.

“Only if Natalie ever lets you out of her hotel room. Hurry!” she said, and slid a leg over his lap to straddle him. “You realize we’ve worked together four years and this is the first time we’ve ever fucked? How’d that happen?”

He centered his cock between her slick folds and groaned

as she wriggled to ease down his shaft. Moist heat surrounded his cock, robbing him of the ability to speak. "Stupid . . . stubborn . . ."

She rose with her toes barely touching the ground on either side of him and lowered herself again, dragging her pussy up and down his shaft.

He wanted more. More to taste, more to feel. He shoved her jacket off her shoulders and pushed her shirt up under her holster to free her breasts. He latched onto a small pink nipple and groaned, all the while sucking hard.

Chessa rose and fell, faster, harder. The metal chair rolled forward and back, creaking beneath their frantic movements.

He leaned back as far as the chair would allow and hammered upward to greet each downward stroke. They worked in opposition, blending naturally like they'd done this a thousands times before.

"Rene?" Her cry was feminine, small, uncertain.

"Yeah baby, I'm here, I'm holdin' you. Come for me. Come, now!" He planted his feet on the tile floor and jounced on the seat, trying to tunnel deeper, trying to break beyond the crest of the wave, until suddenly they were both thrust high.

When their breaths slowed, Chessa snuggled next to his chest. "We need to get back to the hotel room. Natalie . . ."

He should have felt guilty, but he didn't. What did that mean? "Yeah, she shouldn't be alone."

"Neither should you."

"I was just about to say the same thing to you."

Chessa lifted her head and gave him a lopsided smile. "I was thinking about the storm."

He lifted one dark eyebrow. "Do you think . . . ?"

"Let's play it by ear. Don't wanna scare her off just yet."

Natalie sat huddled in the chair watching the newscast. Earlier, delicious-smelling men with heavy tool belts had barreled into the room to latch and nail the window shutters closed. The storm had made landfall and was sweeping across the city, hammering New Orleans with rain and hundred-miles-per-hour winds. At least the weather would provide some kind of protection from anything stalking her on feet, paws or wings. At least for now.

She thought of Chessa and Rene working to find a way to make her life safer and ensure she had a future, and she wished she could help in some way. Unaccustomed to waiting for others to do for her, a deep agitation settled over her, a restlessness she knew she had to control.

For the restlessness only speeded her metabolism. She needed to be busy, moving, doing . . . something. Instead, she was warehoused here in a hotel room, more isolated than before.

The soft snick of a lock preceded the door swinging open. Chessa and Rene walked inside carrying rain-spotted bags.

"Fajitas?" Rene asked, holding up one for her.

"Meat! Yes!" she said, reaching eagerly for the bag, grateful for something to fill her belly until the craving for blood returned.

She set aside the wrapped tacos and dove into the thin strips of beef. "They overcooked it," she said, speaking around a mouthful of spicy, bloody meat.

"They barely seared the outside," he said, smiling as he

seated himself at the small desk. "And we were lucky to find any place open."

"Any cooking is too much, right Nat?" Chessa said, perching on the edge of the bed.

"I shouldn't gripe," Natalie said sitting cross-legged on the bed in her undies and long T-shirt. "I'm just a little testy after being holed up here all night."

Natalie noted a glance between Chessa and Rene. It registered they'd shared several since they entered the room. She set aside her Styrofoam box and inhaled slowly, trying not to make it too obvious she was scenting the air.

But it was there. The smell of sex. On both of them. Natalie ducked her head and busied herself putting away the remnants of her meal.

"Not hungry?" Rene asked.

She shrugged and gave him a weak smile. After all, she couldn't rail at him. She'd gotten off with a total stranger in a seedy bar. He'd only fucked his best friend.

Her indiscretion was so much worse. But his still hurt.

"I have to get a shower," Rene said, avoiding her glance. He grabbed his duffel and headed into the bathroom, leaving Natalie alone with Chessa.

The camaraderie she'd felt earlier at the blood bar was tainted now by her jealousy. She felt badly that this was happening, because really—what right did she have to feel possessive of Rene? She was planning on leaving anyway.

"You know you needn't worry I'm stealing him from you," Chessa said quietly, plucking at a loose thread on the coverlet.

Since she'd brought the subject up, Natalie pinned her with a quelling glance. "You two had sex."

Chessa's eyebrows rose. "Your nose is getting good. We did. But it was comfort, not love."

Natalie swallowed against the lump burning the back of her throat. "I guess I'm just trying to get used to the rules."

"When it comes to pleasure," Chessa said softly, "there are none for us."

No rules. What a heady thought. "Go with the flow," Natalie said, her tone wooden. "You said that before."

"That's right. We have to use humans to survive, and our lusts are too closely intertwined to get too fussy about crossing lines."

Natalie ducked her head, wanting to ask but feeling more than a little embarrassed. "When you did that to me . . . before at the bar . . . was that pleasurable for you?" She peeked up beneath her lashes to catch the policewoman's expression.

Chessa's smile was slow, and she lay back, resting on an elbow. "I was creaming in my panties for you, darlin'. When his hand disappeared into your jeans, I was feeling what he was doing to you."

"It was odd. I could feel his touch from across the room."

"Some of us have special gifts."

"Damn." Natalie shifted her legs, bringing them together.

"Remembering is enough for you right now, isn't it?" Chessa asked, her voice pitched low.

Natalie blushed. Yes, her panties dampening, too. "I guess I have no room for jealousy, do I?"

"No, you don't. But it's totally up to you what happens next."

"What do you mean?"

Chessa shrugged. "We've still got the rest of the night to

get through. We're going to hunker down while the worst of the storm passes. How we spend our time is your choice."

Natalie's eyes widened at the implications. Chessa and Rene . . . and her. Her whole body warmed, blood zinging to every one of her erogenous zones.

She was in charge of what happened tonight. Her pleasure was entirely her choice. Thoughts of the three of them locked inside this room together spun fantasies that until now, she hadn't ever considered.

She stood and gathered all the half-empty food containers and set them in the hallway for the staff to remove, and then turned back to stare at the other woman from across the room.

Chessa had moved to the armchair. Her legs were crossed, one scissoring up and down. Enough proof of her agitation for Natalie to know she was aroused as well. Her dark gaze was watchful, her body seemingly relaxed, but her musk and warming floral scent wafted with each slow turn of the fan's blades.

Natalie held her breath and gathered up the hem of her T-shirt. She pulled it over her head, and then stood with it dangling in her fingertips while she stared at Chessa.

Chessa rimmed her lips with her tongue, looking as though she already imagined sucking on a nipple.

Natalie slipped her fingers beneath the elastic of her panties and pushed them down her hips, enjoying the feel of cool air wafting between her legs. "Do you think he'll mind if we start without him?"

"I think he'll die when he sees us," Chessa drawled. "It's every man's fantasy, isn't it? I just never figured it would be one of mine, too."

Natalie understood what she meant. The thought of doing this with any other woman held no appeal. Chessa had been an integral part of her initiation. She'd set the scene, whether she'd realized it or not, leaving Natalie isolated in close quarters with Rene. She'd instigated Natalie's jealousy from the start—increasing her awareness of Rene. She'd been present every time she and Rene had made love, hovering at the edges of their consciousness.

Chessa's gaze glittered as she stared at Natalie's sex-slick pussy. "Are you uncomfortable with the idea . . . of us?"

Natalie shook her head. "It feels kind of natural—like we're already connected, we've been through so much."

"We're not going to think about any of that now. Let's just enjoy ourselves."

Natalie tilted her head toward the bathroom door. "Do you think he's up for it?"

Chessa grinned. "He's working under the influence of your allure. It's like a super-charged Viagra. He won't be able to resist."

"How do you want to start?"

She shrugged. "You're in charge. I'll let you lead."

Beneath Chessa's avid stare, the now familiar heat suffused Natalie's body as blood continued to rush south to plump the folds of her sex, and excitement tightened her nipples until they strained outward. Natalie lifted her hands to cup her breasts and closed her eyes as another wave of heat swept over her.

The thought of Rene finding them together didn't shock her, instead it spurred her excitement. She opened her eyes and sauntered slowly toward Chessa. She held out her hand. "I want to undress you."

Chessa's shuttered, watchful expression was supplanted by one of uncertainty. Natalie realized Chessa was entering new territory, too.

Still, Chessa slipped her hand inside Natalie's.

Natalie squeezed it gently and tugged Chessa to her feet. Then Natalie leaned close enough to rub her nipples over Chessa's clothed breasts, staring into the other woman's face as her mouth opened on a gasp.

"Never figured you for a tease," Chessa said, her breath catching.

"Never knew this would feel so good." And it did. Her nipples puckered tighter and her pussy pulsed and clasped as she rubbed against the tips rising to points beneath Chessa's shirt.

Natalie placed her hands on Chessa's upper chest and smoothed them under her jacket, pushing it off her shoulders to fall onto the chair behind her. She made quick work of the holster, letting her fingers slip beneath the straps to caress Chessa's soft skin, acquainting herself with the lean muscle beneath.

When she had the harness unbuckled, she dropped it on top of the jacket. Then she reached for the buttons at the front of the blouse and opened them one by one, skimming her fingers along her bare skin.

When she drew the edges apart, she stared at Chessa's bared breasts. Hers were similar to Natalie's yet very different in intriguing ways—smaller, firmer, higher. The points were a bit sharper and darker. The differences excited Natalie, and she gave into the urge to suckle, bending to pull one spiked tip between her lips.

Chessa's hands rose from her sides and grasped Natalie's head, cuddling her close to her chest while it lifted and fell rapidly, her breaths soft, but coming faster.

Natalie marveled at how velvety yet hard nipples could be and finally realized what Rene must experience each time he played with her breasts—comfort, arousal, and something primal and burning she couldn't name.

She drew hard then used her teeth to gently chew the rigid tip, which added a ragged edge to Chessa's soft gasps. Finally, she kissed the breast then moved to the other, latching onto the nipple like a rooting kitten and sucking so hard, Chessa's hips undulated as though pulled by an invisible cord connecting nipple to cunt.

While Natalie continued to suckle, she ran her hand down Chessa's belly to the top of her jeans and thumbed the button open. While her hands didn't tremble or falter even once, her mind wondered at the sureness of her actions. Having sex with a woman hadn't been on any short list of sensual accomplishments. But having sex with Chessa seemed natural, even inevitable. They were linked—through Rene and blood.

Chessa's hands eagerly shoved her jeans past her hips. Natalie wasn't about to let go of the nipple to help Chessa strip entirely. As soon as her clothing cleared her pussy, Natalie slipped her hand between Chessa's legs, sliding her fingers between her folds, spreading the moisture clinging to her dainty labia until the little knot at the top of Chessa's pussy hardened.

Chessa's movements deepened, her hips rolling urgently as though she fucked a cock.

Natalie rimmed the vagina over and over, and then thrust

one finger inside. Here, Chessa didn't feel so different, but her aroma was unique.

Natalie wondered whether her flavor would be as well. She released her nipple and sat on her haunches, staring up at Chessa. "I want us both naked. I want us both on the bed."

Chessa gasped and nodded, then placed her hands on Natalie's shoulders as she toed off her shoes. Natalie pushed her pants the rest of the way down her legs until they were both naked.

Again Natalie noted differences, letting her glance skim the other woman's body, satisfying her curiosity. Chessa's pubic hair was darker, sleek and shiny like a seal's pelt.

She started to lean forward to nuzzle between her folds, but Chessa held out a hand to her and helped her rise. Together, they stepped toward the bed.

"So, we gonna wrestle to see who's on top?" Chessa said, one corner of her mouth quirking upward.

A laugh caught Natalie by surprise. "I don't think I want to waste any time or energy rolling on the bed." She swallowed and stared at Chessa's soft lips. "All I know is I'm so hot I want to know what it feels like to press my breasts to you . . . and taste you."

"My blood?" Chessa whispered.

Natalie gave her one shake of her head. "Will I sound like a complete slut if I say I want to suck on your clit until you cream . . . and then I want to drink it?"

Chessa stepped closer, touching her nipples to Natalie's chest. "No more so than I when I say I wanna bite your cunt."

Natalie's breath caught and a tremor shook her shoulders. "Will I like it?"

"Oh, yeah," Chessa breathed.

Chessa stepped closer, pushing her with her body toward the edge of the bed. Natalie sat and crawled slowly backward while Chessa crawled over her, not breaking contact with their breasts. When she was fully on the bed, Chessa lay on her body, stretching to cover her from shoulder to toe. "How's that feel?" she whispered.

Natalie raised her lips and drew once on Chessa's mouth. "I liked it when you kissed me."

"Me, too." Chessa ground her pubic bone against hers. "There's more."

"How . . . how do you want to do this?" Natalie asked, lightly running her fingers down Chessa's back.

"As equals, face to face. I don't want to make love to you. I want us both exploring."

"We'll do it together?"

Chessa nodded and rolled away, coming to her knees.

As they knelt in front of each other, Natalie grew a little nervous, not knowing how to begin.

Chessa took a lock of Natalie's hair and rubbed it between her fingers. "Your hair's beautiful, soft."

Natalie liked that she'd paused to let her breathe, feeling like she was in sensual overdrive. She reached for strand of Chessa's. "So's yours." She leaned close and brushed the ends across her cheek. "Where should we start?"

Chessa bit her lip. "I want you to touch my breasts again."

"I want that, too." Natalie grinned, feeling a little like she was playing a very naughty game.

They both reached for each other's breasts, lifting them, circling the pads of their fingers around their areolas.

"Come closer," Chessa said. They moved closer until their knees met and the backs of their hands touched as they played with their soft flesh.

Chessa pressed closer to kiss her, sucking Natalie's lower lip between hers, biting softly. A shiver traveled down Natalie's back, and she thrust her tongue into Chessa's mouth.

While they kissed, their fingers went to work on each other's breasts, working in unison, tugging on their nipples until they were rigid and distended. Every tug, every caress shot heat straight to Natalie's core.

Chessa pinched one of Natalie's nipples hard, and Natalie gasped into Chessa's mouth, and pinched her back.

"Like a little pain?" Chessa asked, leaning slightly away and bringing Natalie's nipples to circle the tips of hers slowly.

"I like this," Natalie said, pressing her thighs together to quell the need building in her pussy. "But I want to be closer. I'm starting to ache."

Chessa's lips curved upward, and she drew away her hands from between their bodies.

Natalie followed her lead and pressed her body closer until their breasts were mashed together and their pubic bones rubbing. Their hands encircled their backs, stroking over their shoulders, following the bumps on their spine down then smoothing over the globes of their asses.

When Chessa's fingers slipped between, fluid excitement gushed from Natalie's channel, trickling down her thighs. "I'm wet," she said, her lips so close to Chessa's she breathed only the air Chessa's minty breaths provided.

Chessa's eyelids dipped and lips pouted. "What do you want to do about it?"

"Lie down again? I'm so hot my . . . I'm swelling there."

Chessa's smile was quick and strained. She pressed closer, forcing Natalie to her back, then settled her body between Natalie's legs.

Natalie curved her hips, pushing upward, dragging her mound over Chessa's while the other woman rocked side to side, spreading Natalie's lips to grind into her clit.

They undulated as though they had cocks, grinding together, sighing softly into each other's mouths.

Chessa's knee slipped between Natalie's legs and pressed her upper thigh into her cunt. "Ride it."

"God," Natalie moaned. Friction burned hot as she ground against her leg, but she soon grew frustrated, not able to edge past arousal into release. "Chessa . . ."

"You want more. I know." Chessa lifted off her and scooted lower on the bed. She grasped Natalie's knees and pushed them apart. "Open your legs wider."

Natalie followed her direction, too aroused to be modest as Chessa stared at her pussy.

"Lift your knees and tilt up your hips." After Natalie quickly complied, she leaned close and blew a hot breath over her moist, open sex.

Natalie's pussy pulsed, opening then tightening, issuing a succulent sound that only seemed to excite Chessa further. Her cheeks were pink, her lips blurred and swollen. Her nostrils flared as she scented the air. "You're so pink here. So damn pretty. No wonder Rene loves to eat you out." She leaned down and stuck out her tongue, laving the slit with a long, hot swipe of her tongue.

Natalie felt another rush of liquid seep from inside her and held her breath.

Chessa plied apart the lips with her thumbs and lapped the opening, licking away the juices like a dripping peach.

"You taste incredible," Chessa said, then rolled her chin and mouth around Natalie's pussy. When she lifted her head, Natalie's excitement coated her mouth. Her tongue swept out and circled her lips until all the whitish fluid was gone.

"I need something inside me," Natalie gasped, her body on the edge of exploding.

Chessa cupped the younger woman's pussy with her hand and placed her fingers at the opening, not dipping inside.

"God, Chess, fuck me." Natalie pumped her hips upward, trying to coax her into sliding inside. Needing more, she glided her hands up her belly and over her breasts and squeezed them hard while her vagina opened and closed like it was clasping around a cock.

"Wanna be fucked?" Chessa drawled.

Her jaws tight, Natalie bit out, "Yes. Stop teasing me."

Chessa slowly brought her fingers to her mouth and sucked two inside to wet them then brought them down to Natalie's pussy. Without any further teasing, she thrust them inside.

Natalie groaned, her body jerking, her hips lifting from the bed. "That's good," she groaned, "keep doing that."

"Do you want more?" Chessa asked, leaning over her as her fingers glided in and out. "And what do I get?"

She rolled her head toward Chessa. "I promise I'll give you the same."

Chessa's dark brow arched wickedly. "Wanna do each other at the same time?"

Natalie nodded quickly while her hips kept rocking up and down. "Show me."

Chessa's strokes halted as she turned and climbed over Natalie, settling her pussy above Natalie's mouth. "Get the idea?"

Natalie lifted her head and drew Chessa's dewy labia between her lips, sucking and licking her way all around the cunt.

Chessa's thighs trembled, and she gave a little strained laugh as she leaned down, her fingers pushing deep into Natalie's cunt and her mouth closed around the clitoris. She stroked and sucked, all the while pulsing her own pussy against Natalie's swirling tongue.

Soon, Natalie was dying with pleasure. Christ, she was hot! Chessa's hair brushed her thighs and her mouth drew hard on Natalie's clit. The first spasm of release clamped around Chessa's fingers.

Just when the arousal curled tight in the center of her belly started to unwind, the thought flitted across her mind that at any moment Rene would walk out of the bathroom and find them.

But please, not before she came.

Which was exactly what happened.

# CHAPTER 19

Rene opened the door. The light inside the bedroom was dim after the bright fluorescence in the bathroom, but the rustling sounds from the bed drew his gaze. His eyes widened at finding the two women completely naked, moaning and writhing against each other, Chessa's ass undulating over Natalie's head, her head buried between Natalie's thighs.

Feeling like a voyeur and liking it a lot, he stepped deeper into the room and quietly closed the door behind him, not wanting to interrupt the show.

He adjusted his cock beneath the towel he'd wrapped around his waist and shoved Chessa's jacket and holster to the floor, taking a seat to watch, the noises he made masked by their sighs and groans.

*Merde!* He hadn't really gotten his hopes up after his conversation with Chessa, hadn't any idea how amazing it would be just to look at the two of them going at it.

Chessa's head raised, and she gave him a sultry smile. The quirk of her eyebrow said, *Any time you want to join us . . .*

He shook his head. *Soon.*

Virgin-girl was full of delicious surprises, and Chessa's gleaming body, so well toned, all muscles flexing as she covered Natalie, had his cock jerking.

He unwound the towel around his waist and glided his hand along his cock, stroking himself. Still steamy and moist from his shower, his hand pumped smoothly up and down his shaft while he watched Natalie's fingers disappear into Chessa's cunt and Chessa's head circle over Natalie's pussy.

He encircled the base of his cock and squeezed hard to stop the building release tightening his balls. He didn't want to spend his cum on the carpet when he had two women he could fuck.

Chessa lifted her head, and Natalie groaned her disapproval which was cut short when Chessa began to spank her pussy in short, wet slaps that landed directly on her clit.

Natalie gasped and her hips jerked. Her legs splayed wider, inviting more sensual torture.

The slapping continued until Natalie halted work on Chessa and reached outward to grab fistfuls of bedding while her hips pumped frantically up and down.

He'd never considered swatting a woman there. He guessed watching two girls do each other, showing each other what pleasured them most, was pretty damn satisfying all by itself.

"You gonna fuck her?" Chessa asked, not looking up. "She's primed."

Rene didn't need a second invitation. He hauled himself up from the chair and crawled up the bed between Natalie's legs as Chessa sat up with her pussy still hovering above Natalie's mouth.

Natalie's moans were thin, high-pitched.

Chessa pinched one of her nipples. "You okay with this Nat?"

Natalie's answer was to open wide her jaws and suck Chessa's labia between her lips.

Chessa's head fell back for a moment and her mouth gaped.

Rene hooked his arms beneath Natalie's legs and lifted her ass off the bed. "Chessa, put my cock inside her," he commanded, his voice tight as his balls.

Chessa blinked and bent to wrap her fingers around him, stroking over him from root to end. With a challenge narrowing her gaze, she tugged him hard, bringing him closer until he pointed straight at Natalie's pussy. Then she rubbed him around her entrance, circling until the crown was glistening. Only then did she spread Natalie's lips with her fingers and place his cock at her entrance.

He flexed his ass and slammed home.

Natalie's cry was muffled against Chessa's pussy.

"She's biting! Ahh—" Chessa's moan cut off as her eyes rolled back, and her head lolled as she held herself still.

Rene couldn't hold back a second longer. Natalie's cunt was soaking wet, burning hot, and already caressing his cock. Convulsing around him like a moist, tight fist.

Chessa gasped, and her eyes opened. She cupped his face and brought his head down for a kiss.

As he thrust inside Natalie, their tongues mated ferociously. He found it hard to keep track of whose pleasure he should see to when his own filled his mind. He slammed his hips forward, backed out and slammed again, faster now, harder.

His thrusts shook the bed. Chessa gripped his shoulders hard when her orgasm struck her. Her mouth opened beneath his, her head flung back, and a keening wail tore from her throat.

That was all it took to shove him right over the edge. With Natalie's thighs straining to lift inside his elbows, he hammered his cock into her cunt, stroking deep, until his orgasm ripped through him and cum jetted deep into her body.

He came back to himself, the sound of his own harsh grunts rousing him as he pistoned his hips in shallow thrusts. He was loathe to stop. The top of his head had felt as though it exploded, and he'd flown outside himself at the last moment.

He halted and flung back his head to drag air into his burning lungs.

Chessa slowly climbed off Natalie and lay down on the bed beside her, curving her body around Natalie's, her own body still quivering in the aftermath.

Natalie's blurred lips pressed together, and she opened her eyes. She slowly licked her lips, then sucked the upper one between her teeth, her gaze was shadowed by uncertainty. "Were you surprised?"

Were you pleased, was what she really asked. Rene pulled out of her and lowered her hips to the bed then lay over her, cupping her face between his palms. He didn't want to say what was on the tip of his tongue. Didn't want to tarnish what, to him, had been one of the most exciting and decadent experiences of his life with a careless word.

Instead, he bent and captured her lips, tasting Chessa's essence on her tongue as he stroked inside Natalie's mouth. They tasted like they belonged together. At least for tonight.

"My back itches," Natalie muttered sleepily, rubbing her shoulder against Chessa's chest.

Chessa awoke instantly. "Want me to scratch?"

"Please, it's making me miserable."

"Want me to take your mind off it?" Rene's deep bass rumbled from the other side of Natalie.

Chessa grinned. The best part of coming into a vampire's season was the limitless stamina she engendered in everyone around her.

They'd fucked like rabbits, only stopping long enough to switch positions and partners. Although she healed fast as any vampire, Chessa's thighs and pussy were sore.

She could only imagine how raw Rene was becoming with all the attention they'd paid his dick.

"Sit up," she said to Natalie, pressing a kiss to her shoulder.

"You can sit on this," Rene said in his sexy Cajun drawl.

Natalie giggled and rolled over Rene, yawning even as she slid down his cock. "Nice," she moaned.

"Should be better than nice," he said, his hands coming up to cup her breasts.

"Don't mind me," Chessa murmured, hoping Rene would keep Natalie occupied for a few moments while she checked something out.

She leaned over the edge of the bed and flicked on the lamp.

"The better to see you with," Rene growled.

Again, Natalie giggled then sighed as she rose up his long shaft and came back down.

Chessa smiled at how easily they played together now, all modesty gone. She moved behind Natalie and swept aside her hair. "Where does it itch?"

"Hmmm," Natalie moaned, her itch forgotten for the moment as she undulated, dragging her pussy forward and back on his cock.

"The itch? Is it bothering you still?"

Natalie reached lazily behind her, not breaking stride, and scratched a trail from the inside of one shoulder blade to her waist.

Chessa followed the path with the tips of her fingers, finding the problem immediately and silently cursing. Natalie, once again, was way ahead of herself. She followed a white seam of skin, feeling for any slight indentation.

"Don't be afraid to really dig your nails in," Natalie moaned. "That's tickling me."

"I'll dig in all right," Chessa muttered. She glanced over Natalie's shoulder and gave Rene a hard look.

His eyebrows rose. Then a frown furrowed his forehead as he realized something was up beside his dick. "Chessa?"

"Hold her still."

Natalie slowed her rocking motions and glanced back, "Is something wrong?"

"No, Nat, but this is gonna hurt." That was all the warning she gave as she dug her fingernails into the seam and split apart her skin.

Natalie's breath hissed between her teeth and her back arched away.

"What the fuck are you doing?" Rene said, his hands gripping Natalie's hips tight as she struggled away from Chessa.

Her skin parted like opening gills on a fish, and Chessa reached inside to tuck her fingers under the long ridged cartilage within the slit to pull it free.

As Natalie's wing sprang from her back, it opened and unfurled with a snap like a sheet in a brisk wind.

"The other, get the other," Natalie said, reaching back to claw at the seam on the opposite side.

Chessa scarcely had time to pry open the slim pouch when the second wing extended.

When she was finished, she ducked beneath Natalie's wings and lay on her back beside Rene whose mouth was still agape.

"Natalie, you look like a fish," Chessa said, reaching up to tip her jaw closed.

"Now that's not somethin' you see everyday," Rene said, his voice awed.

Chessa turned and caught his fierce frown. "So, what do you think about our girl. She's all grown up."

"That's the difference, isn't it?" he said. "Between you and the poor bastards you turn."

"It's the most . . . noticeable."

He was silent for a long moment, his gaze following the long, graceful length of Natalie's wings. Finally, he drew a breath. "They gonna pop out like that every time we have sex?"

Chessa laughed, relieved he seemed to be taking the transformation in stride. "Natalie can repress that urge, same as she has her need to feed while she fucks you."

Their gazes slid back to Natalie, who stared transfixed at the mirror above the dresser. The glass reflected light onto the wings that spread far beyond the width of the bed. The same pale color of her skin, they shone with the sheen of soft, short velvet that covered the thin membrane stretched between the cartilages forming the boning of her wings.

Rene ran his hand over the bottom edge of one of them. "I've stopped bein' surprised, I guess. Day before yesterday, I think I'd have had a lot more to say." His head swiveled back to Chessa. "Can she fly?"

Chessa snorted. "What do you think?"

His forehead furrowed deeper. "Damn, Chessa. What the hell you need to ride in squad car for?"

Chessa grinned and lifted her eyebrows. "Can you put them away by yourself?" Chessa directed the question to Natalie who still stared at herself in the mirror.

Finally, the younger woman turned, her expression still wide-eyed with shock. "Can I?"

"Give it a try."

Natalie closed her eyes and frowned as she concentrated. Her wings folded fluidly and withdrew into their pouches, the seams appearing to melt away.

"Guess that answers that," Rene said.

The whine of the wind against the shutters and the hum of the air conditioner were the only sounds in the room for several seconds.

Then Natalie rose . . . and fell, and came up again. Her jaw firmed and her lips thinned. Triumph, power fueled her movements as she took Rene, her chest rising and falling with her steady breaths and movements.

Chessa's breath caught as she watched Natalie and realized the scared young woman who'd cowered from a flock of birds was gone. She'd been reborn, finding herself and the answers to most of her questions within the cycle set by a rising moon and a curse that controlled the appetites and fates of all the Born.

While the couple continued to ebb and flow against each other, Chessa shoved off the bed and headed toward the shower.

In Natalie's face, she'd seen a glimpse of her own past and felt closer to the child she'd lost so many years ago. She quietly shut the door behind her, sat on the closed toilet seat and wept.

When the bathroom door opened, Natalie glanced up at Chessa and noted her features appeared drawn.

Worried, she opened her mouth to speak, but Chessa shook her head and raised a finger to her lips.

Natalie looked back at the bed. Rene was asleep and not likely to wake any time soon—the dark purple smudges beneath his eyes indicative of his exhaustion.

She followed Chessa's silent lead, dressing swiftly in jeans and long-sleeved shirt. She hadn't thought the rumblings in her belly were so loud they'd given away her hunger, but perhaps Chessa was hungry too.

They let themselves out the door and headed toward the elevator.

"Are we going back to the bar?" Natalie asked, trying to resist the itching at the roof of her mouth that urged her to let down her teeth. The thought of a meal already had her salivating.

"No way we can get anywhere in a car—the road's swamped. Rene and I barely made it here. But there's a bar in the hotel." Chessa flashed her a smile. "You game?"

"Find a dark corner to feed?"

"One of us play look-out?"

Grinning, Natalie's steps were light as she headed to the elevator. She liked the sense of connection she felt with Chessa. Finishing each other's thoughts. They'd even worked Rene like a tag team until he'd cried "uncle" from too much use and slept.

The patter of some small creature trailed behind them, and Natalie glanced over her shoulder. A rat sat on its haunches in a door well, its nose quivering as it sniffed the air.

She grimaced. "Yuck! Rats!"

"Probably driven off the streets by the storm. Filthy bastards," Chessa said, reaching for the down button.

The doors slid open, and Natalie stepped inside beside Chessa, turning to face the entrance. As the doors closed, she saw three rats in a line heading their way.

She shivered as the doors cut off the view.

Chessa's eyebrows drew into a frown. "We'll talk to the desk clerk after we feed. They should set some traps."

The bar was dark and packed. It seemed every guest in the hotel, except Rene, had decided to ride out the storm in the lounge. Pictures of men leaning into the driving rain played on CNN while glasses clinked and laughter rang out. Music played from an old-fashioned jukebox in the corner, and a couple circled on the small square, parquet dance floor.

"Pick one," Chessa said, "I'll find us a dark booth."

Natalie drew a deep breath and peered around the crowd at the bar for a target. Someone young. Someone stupid. And clean. The Arno's of the world were only meant as last resorts.

She trailed behind the men, scenting each, recoiling at heavy cologne or cigarette smoke.

One man caught her looking his way. "Can I buy you a drink?"

Not bad. Mid thirties, blond hair cut short and trimmed neatly around his ears. He wore a yellow polo shirt and blue jeans. Nice laugh lines crinkled around his eyes as his smile deepened at her perusal.

If he only knew what she really wanted.

"I'm with a friend," she said, leaning close to speak softly into his neatly turned ears.

"Shall I join you?"

It was so easy. She led him away from the lighted bar, into the corner booth where Chessa waited. He slid around the seat, appearing happy to be sandwiched between the two of them.

His interested gaze took in Chessa's intense expression and his chest rose.

He probably thought this was his lucky night. But it was theirs. He lifted his hand to snag a waitress's attention and ordered a round of drinks.

Natalie looked around the bar. No one paid them any attention. Laughter burst again from across the room. Everyone was in high spirits. Snug and dry while the storm swirled around them. She let the warmth of the man's thigh pressed against hers and the heated aroma of his skin seduce her teeth into lengthening.

Chessa gave her a little nod, and they both leaned into him.

His breath snagged. "Sure we want to keep the party here?" he asked.

"No one's watching," Natalie said, gliding her fingers up his thigh while Chessa distracted him with a little innocent nibble at his ear lobe.

Suddenly, Chessa jerked away and unsnapped her cell phone case which hung on her belt. "Back in a minute," she said. "I have to take this." As she walked away with the receiver to her ear, shouts erupted at the bar, drawing Natalie's attention.

Some patrons lifted their feet from the floor. Drinks spilled on the counter top as others lurched away.

"What the hell's happening over there?" the man seated next to her exclaimed.

That's when she heard it. Squeaks. The patter of feet. Tiny rodents' feet. Dozens of them. All heading her way.

Natalie brought her legs up onto the bench seat and then crawled onto the table. The blond man crawled over the back of the seat, escaping the first creatures that jumped to where she'd been seated.

Natalie stared, transfixed. Their eyes glowed red and the acrid smell of rotten eggs and rat shit filled the space around her, sucking the air from her lungs.

When the first one leaped to the table beside her, a feeling of inevitability, surrender, filled her limbs with leaden weight. They crowded around her, climbed onto her lap. The first little bite roused her, causing her to cry out, and she backhanded the creature, sending it slamming against the wall.

But just as quickly as they swarmed her, they moved on, like a wave lapping at her knees, crowding her with their little furry bodies, and then ebbing away.

It was over—so fast she didn't really have a chance to wonder what it all meant. An exit door had been pried open and the rats filled the doorway as they raced outside.

Natalie trembled as raucous shouts continued, mostly directed at the establishment. Behind her she heard footsteps. A hand clamped around her wrist.

When she raised her head, she was staring into Fernando's dark face.

# CHAPTER 20

"Let me help you," he said, extending his hand, palm up.

She didn't want to touch him. From his intent stare, she knew his presence here wasn't a coincidence. She decided to brazen it out and gave him her hand.

After she clambered off the table, she tried to pull away her hand, but his grip tightened. He tugged her closer, drawing her in like a fish on a reel, turning her until her back was flush with his belly and chest. Although lean, she could feel the tensile strength of every muscle pressed close to her.

She swallowed and glanced wildly around for Chessa, but didn't see her in the agitated crowd.

"You can still catch your friends," she said, glaring at him over her shoulder. "They just went out the door."

His smile was slow, amused. But it didn't quite reach his eyes. "I hoped you weren't the one we sought." His hand crept up to cup her breast and thumbed her nipple through her shirt. He pressed his cheek to hers and whispered, "I'd so much rather make love to you."

Natalie bit back a moan. Not of desire. Her heart raced, her skin broke out in cold sweat. She'd arrived at her moment of reckoning.

She closed her eyes and breathed deeply, trying to slow her breaths and recapture her calm. "Are you the one who's been stalking me?"

His cheek rubbed hers. "The one? No, love. We are many."

Revulsion rose up and she tried to strain away from him. "I don't understand why."

"I'd love to take the time to explain it to you, but in the end it really doesn't matter, does it?" His thumb toggled back and forth, flicking the tip of her breast.

It ruched beneath his teasing, puckering because she was so very afraid. Goose bumps rose on her arms, and the fine hairs on the back of her neck lifted. "Well, what the fuck are you waiting for?" she gritted out. She jerked against him again and slammed her heel against his instep, but he quickly shifted behind her, deflecting her kick so it glanced off the top of his boot.

"Easy," he crooned. "I didn't come here alone. We're leaving through the kitchen as soon as my men clear our way."

"I'm not going anywhere with you."

"Sure you will. You aren't at full strength yet. I can easily overcome you. And why fight? You're only upsetting yourself."

He forced her forward, butting his knees against the back of hers so they collapsed beneath her, only to scoot her forward toward the bar. The crowd parted, forming a corridor. How the hell could she escape when there were so many?

"I don't understand," she said. "Why are you doing this?"

"Not because I want to, I assure you. I'd much prefer sliding my cock inside you than taking off your head. But this is necessary."

*Taking off her head?* Her panic increased a hundredfold, and she bucked against him. To no avail.

The bartender looked up, and just as quickly turned away. There'd be no help there. No help from anyone in the bar, she realized as so many of them flashed the tips of their fangs while they passed.

"But why?"

"This is a revolution. We're fighting a war. You're just a pawn, love. You and the nit growing in your belly."

"But you're a vampire," she gasped, digging in her heels. "So am I. I don't know what war you're talking about." She knew she was babbling, but she wanted to stall him long enough to figure a way out. He shoved her along, her puny efforts not impeding his momentum one bit.

Where the hell was Chessa?

Rather than struggle, which wasn't affecting him at all, she hung limply in his arms and dragged her feet along the floor, forcing him to carry more of her weight. Slowing him down.

"I don't expect your cooperation," he said, grunting softly

as he hoisted her onto his hip, carrying her as easily as a sack of potatoes.

She reached up to claw at his face and managed to punch his jaw, but the blow held no real force due to the awkward angle.

"Quit fighting me," he said, giving her a hard jounce on his hip. "I promise to make this quick. I'll find no joy in killing you."

"Then why do it?"

Fernando brought her behind the bar and pushed open the swinging door, which led into a small kitchen. Then he dragged her through the kitchen down a narrow, low-ceiling hallway, until they were in a small back room with boxes stacked in every corner and a door to the outside.

He flung her into one corner and loomed over her where she lay crumpled on the floor. He bent and placed his hands on his knees. "We're all vampires," he said drawing a deep breath and leveling a cold, hard stare. "But those of us who were born human first, are treated like minions by your kind. We're good enough to fuck. Good enough to fill your ranks of workers and protectors, but we have no voice on the council. We're going to change that."

Natalie scrambled to put her feet beneath her, crouching in front of him. "I don't know anything about the council. I'm not your enemy."

His gaze narrowed, and his upper lip lifted in a snarl. "Every Born is our enemy."

"H-how did you know that . . . I was Born," she asked, her breaths growing choppy with her rising panic. Her teeth began to chatter, so she clamped shut her jaw.

"I suspected last night at the bar. Chessa watched over you

like you were her chick and she the mother hen. But the rats only confirmed it."

"Figures they work for you."

Fernando's low laughter, so cold and laced with a dirty edge, made her quiver. "As if we had that kind of power. Don't you know you have enemies all around you?"

"I don't know anything," she said, hating the tears welling in her eyes. If she was going to die, she didn't want to give him the satisfaction.

"Let's get this over with." He straightened and unbuttoned his cuffs and the front of his shirt. "Don't want blood stains, do I?" When he let it slide off his shoulder, she bolted up and past him, running for the outside door.

Her hand turned the knob, but he slammed into her back, trapping her against the door. His hot, naked skin burned her through her blouse as he anchored her there, pressing so hard she couldn't expand her lungs. His breath stirred her hair next to her ear, and she squeezed her eyes shut.

The hard ridge of his cock dug into her buttocks. "See what you do to me? You shouldn't have fought me."

"What? You're going to fuck me, first?" she asked, gasping for air.

"Would you like that? One last time to get lost in it? I could kill you at your climax. You'd never know."

Tears leaked from her eyes. For once her hormones weren't firing on all cylinders. His offer left her feeling only sick to her stomach.

"Back away from her, Fred."

Natalie sobbed her relief at the hard-edged and deadly sound of Chessa's voice.

"Now, what would be the advantage for me," Fernando murmured.

"You'll get a chance to fight."

"I think I'd be better off with the girl. I don't really think you'd risk harming her." He twisted around, bringing Natalie in front of him and stepped deeper into the room. Toward Chessa.

Chessa stood with a gun in one hand and a two-by-four that had been split so one end was pointed. She hefted it above her shoulder, her gaze narrowing on him, never straying to Natalie, who strained against the arm he'd slung around her throat.

He kept moving forward until Chessa was forced to move aside. "You can't go through the bar, Fred," she said. "You won't make it out alive. We've got your guys contained. Even as we speak, they're dusting them off, one by one."

Fernando's arm tightened, choking Natalie, cutting off her air. He halted in the center of the room.

Suddenly, the door slammed open and rain swept inside, carried on a wind that almost lifted them off their feet.

It howled around them, slapping Fernando's long hair into her face. Natalie stared at Chessa whose gaze had lifted beyond them.

A cry like a wild animal's howl rose above the wind and something large and heavy barreled into Fernando's back, pitching them both forward. But when Natalie's knees hit the concrete, Fernando's body didn't follow. Instead, his blue jeans flapped around her ankles, empty, sodden. She untangled them and lunged away, not understanding what was happening behind her but knowing she needed to flee.

When arms closed around her back, she rolled and fought, clawing with her hands at the face above hers, until she saw that Rene held her.

She drew back her fingers and stared in horror at the rivulets of blood she'd scratched along his cheeks. "I'm sorry."

He captured her hand and pressed a kiss into her palm. "Don't worry about it. I've had worse."

She let her head rest on the concrete and waited for her heart to slow its frantic beating. "Where did Fred go?"

"You don't wanna know." He cupped her face with one large hand, and she leaned into his warmth. "You all right?"

She nodded and blinked to clear the tears gathering in her eyes. "It was close."

Rene rose and helped her to her feet. "Let's get you back to our room. Simon's there. It's why I came lookin' for you."

"Simon?" Oh, yeah. He was going to help her leave. She didn't even have the rest of the night to spend with Rene.

Forcing back an inner wail, she let him take her hand and lead her out of the room with the wind still howling from the open doorway and water pooling on the floor.

Chessa preceded them, both weapons held at the ready, but the black-uniformed security team from *Ardeal* had pretty much cleaned the place out.

Clothing lay in little hillocks around the room as though the bodies that had filled them simply melted away. Rene was right—she didn't want to know where they went.

Chessa lifted her chin to Nicolas, whose gaze swept Rene and Natalie. As though satisfied they were unharmed, he turned away and shouted. "I want two men to follow them. Post outside their door while they pack until we can bring the van around."

The van? No! Natalie started to pull away, to make another dash for freedom, but Chessa gave a sharp shake of her head. Something in her eyes reassured her everything would be all right.

The trip to their room was made in total silence. Chessa stood aside as they entered, then closed the door, leaving the guards posted outside.

As soon as they were alone, Chessa tossed her weapons to the bed. "Simon, you can come out now."

Simon strode out of the bathroom, his sodden T-shirt clinging to his lean chest. He gave a half-hearted smile to Natalie, and then turned to Chessa. "How much time do we have?"

"About five minutes."

When his gaze returned to Natalie, he reached out both hands to grasp hers. "You have two choices, Nat. You can accept the protection you'll find at *Ardeal* until you deliver, or I can send you someplace they can't ever touch you or your child. The problem is, you won't be able to return."

Neither choice held any appeal. At *Ardeal*, she'd have to give up her child, perhaps forever. If she took Simon's offer, she'd never see Rene again.

There really was no choice. She sighed. "How do you propose getting me past those guards?"

His smile held a hint of regret. "I'm going to miss you."

Natalie forced a smile. "Thanks for everything. Thanks for being my friend."

His gaze searched hers then he nodded. "You're going to be okay, you know. Say your good-byes quickly."

Natalie stepped toward Chessa whose expression was shuttered, her lips a grim line. Only her eyes betrayed what she was thinking. They glittered with tears.

"Chessa, I'll miss you." She cupped her cheek and leaned in to kiss her mouth. Chessa's clung to hers for a moment before she backed away. Natalie cleared her throat. "I'm curious though. That phone call—"

"That was Nic, telling me he was on his way. The birds, those rats—he found some in a crypt his men patrol. The creature that dwells inside—well, it sent the animals."

"The rats left me alone this time—just as quickly as they surrounded me. Why?"

"You don't have to worry about creature attacks anymore. You're already pregnant."

Natalie shook her head, knowing she didn't have time for her to fully explain what she meant. "Then I won't worry anymore."

She drew in a slow breath, preparing herself for her final farewell. Rene stood with his fists clenched at his sides, his face all harsh angles, his jaw flexing. His dark gaze scanned her face as though committing it to memory. Like she was doing now.

"I'm going to be okay," she said. "Trust Simon on that."

He didn't move. Didn't respond to her words in any way.

Not wanting to make a scene or let him see how badly she hurt, she reached up and kissed his cheek. "Good-bye," she whispered and turned back to Simon.

Only Simon didn't stand behind her. In his place stood a rugged, handsome, much older man with brown hair and a beard. Only the crooked smile he wore told her it was him.

"I'm starting to think the whole world's crazy," she said. "Is nothing what it seems?"

"Not in your life, my dear. Ready?"

"What do I do?"

"Nothing, yet. I'm going to open a portal. When I tell you, you'll step through it and you'll be somewhere else. No turning back. There will be a trail in the forest. Follow it to a church. Say my name to the priest who opens the door. You won't be able to communicate with him, but trust him. He'll lead you to sanctuary."

"I'll never see you—any of you, again—will I?"

"Perhaps. If you live long enough."

Natalie stood still, feeling hot and cold at the same time, light-headed, and near to tears. So much she didn't understand, but she couldn't really think and didn't know what other questions to ask.

"Take this," he said and handed her a leather pouch that she nearly dropped due to its surprising weight. "It's gold. You'll need it to start your new life."

Then Simon held out his hands and made a motion for all of them to move back. He turned and reached for a bag on the bed and emptied its contents onto the mattress. Round, colored stones, like polished crystal balls, rolled out. He picked up a yellow and a pale blue stone and spread out his arms with one crystal orb resting on each of his open palms.

Natalie gave Chessa a questioning glance. Chessa smiled and lifted her chin. "Watch," she mouthed.

For a long pregnant moment, nothing happened. Then a flicker sparked inside the yellow stone—a small, wisp of flame that brightened then nearly winked out. But it flared again, this time brighter, and it burst to cast a golden light into every corner of the room. While they watched, the blue stone erupted, its radiance more brilliant than the first and seeming to draw the yellow rays into its aura.

Simon began an intonation, his deepening bass murmuring words in a language she'd never heard that sounded soft and liquid, like water burbling in a stream.

As he chanted, the stones brightened into the intensity of two tiny suns, the rays they cast bending and curving, yellow and blue, interweaving until they seemed to melt together in a brilliant green braid, forming a circle. Looking through the center of the circle, the bed seemed to stretch and curve until it swirled into a vortex, leaving only a smooth, glinting surface, like that of a pond in sunlight.

Simon's incantation faded, but the shimmering, vertical pool remained.

"Now, Natalie," he said softly. "Step through the portal, love."

Natalie looked back one last time at each of them, her gaze resting finally on Rene. *I love you.* She couldn't say the words aloud, didn't want to leave him with a burden. Turning back to the portal, she took a deep breath and straightened her shoulders.

"Oh, hell no," Rene muttered behind her.

Natalie glanced back to see him striding toward her, and her heart stopped as she read the determination in his squared jaw as he pinned her with a glare.

"What are you doing?" she asked.

"I'm not letting you go alone to wherever the hell he's sendin' you."

"You don't have to," Natalie said, although gladness already had her heart thudding against her chest. "I'm going to be safe."

Rene's fingers tipped her chin up and his mouth slammed down on top of hers, taking her breath away. When he lifted his head, he said, "You're not going anywhere without me, *chère*."

"How's your French?" Simon asked, standing at his elbow.

Rene's head swiveled to aim a glare at the man who now shared a similar size and ruggedness. "I'm Cajun. It's shit."

Simon grinned. "It's about to get a whole lot better. And you'll need to learn to ride a horse."

"Where are we going?" Rene asked, wrapping an arm around Natalie's shoulder as though afraid she'd disappear if he didn't hold her tight.

"What? And spoil the adventure?" Simon said, with a waggle of his eyebrows. As his gaze came back to Natalie, his smile faded. "You'll be among friends. They'll teach you. Help you assimilate. You'll be safe for a time."

Rene let go of Natalie and glanced back at Chessa. Tears welled in her eyes. "Come here," he said, his voice gruff.

Chessa stepped toward them. When she stood in front of Rene, her face crumpled and she reached out.

Rene's arms enfolded her, pressing her head to his chest. He kissed her hair. "I guess you're gonna be lookin' for a new partner," he said, his voice roughening with emotion.

"You just watch your ass." Chessa's words were muffled against his chest. "I won't be there to cover it."

Rene grabbed a fistful of her hair and pulled her head back and planted a hard kiss on her lips. When they drew away, tears spilled down Chessa's cheeks.

"You know, you're going to have to turn," Chessa said. "The only way we'll ever meet again is if you live a long, long time."

Rene nodded, and took Natalie's hand. "Ready to roll?"

Together, they stepped toward the shimmering portal.

Natalie reached out to touch the surface and watched it ripple outward as though a stone had dropped in its center. When she drew back her finger, no moisture clung to her skin. A light, cool breeze wafted from the other side, along with the inviting fragrance of lush vegetation.

"Why are you doing this, Rene?" she asked, keeping her gaze straight ahead.

"Why do you think?"

"I don't want you with me if it's only because you feel you have to."

Rene sighed beside her, and pulled her to face him.

Reluctantly, she raised her gaze.

"Oh, I have to, all right," he said, wrapping his arms around her waist and pulling her hips flush with his. "If I let you leave, I'll never see you again. Never touch you. I won't get to see that baby they say you have growing in your belly." His forehead furrowed with a fierce frown. "And I won't get to love you."

"There's a lot of ways a girl could interpret that last little bit," Natalie murmured, her body warming with arousal.

"Want me to make it clearer?" he said, his voice a low, tender rumble. "I'm saying I don't want to be here, in this world, if you aren't in it."

"Sounds good enough to me," Chessa said softly.

It did to Natalie, too.

"Time's a wasting, you two. This spell won't hold much longer."

Rene kissed her, brushing his lips lightly over hers. A promise in the blessing. "I'll die for you, *chère*," he whispered.

Natalie slipped her arm around his waist, and together they stepped through the portal.

The portal flickered then winked out. The hotel room was as it had been before, except the bed was no longer there.

Chessa wiped away her tears with the back of her hand before turning to face Simon. She aimed a scowl at the mage. "Don't start thinking you and me are gonna be buddies."

Simon sniffed. "As if. Don't darken my doorway too soon." With a grin curving his lips, he turned to gather the stones into his bag.

A knock sounded at the door, and Chessa went to answer it.

Nicolas leaned indolently against the door frame, the guards no where in sight. He looked beyond Chessa to Simon and tilted his head to the corridor. "Coast is clear. You can leave, now."

After Simon strode out of the room, Chessa's gaze fell beneath Nicolas's.

"Got him out of your system?"

The deep rasp of his voice made her shiver with awareness they were alone. She shrugged, pretending she wasn't affected. "Doesn't matter now."

"We've got an hour until daybreak," he drawled.

Chessa raised her chin. "I still have the scent of him on my skin. Want me to shower?"

His nostrils flared. His gaze darkened. "We haven't time, if I'm to punish you properly."

Chessa's body flooded with heat. "Got one little problem. No bed."

Nicolas snagged her wrist and pulled her hard against his chest, his mouth hovering just above hers. "You're going to have one nasty rug burn."